THE
CONTRAPTION

The Contraption

Copyright 2023 Barton Allen Stewart

First Printing

Release Date March 25, 2024

Great Whale Books

info@GreatWhaleBooks.com

ISBN 978-0-9785817-2-5

Part One

"And the people bowed and prayed to the neon god they made."

Paul Simon

A n aura, like the presence of an intruding force, hung over the off-white cargo van parked at the split-level home. The lady across the street felt it, standing with a garden hose overwatering a spot while she monitored the motionless van. A dog in a neighboring yard got it too, sitting at the chain link fence in rapt attention to the van.

The dinginess of the vehicle was magnified by the countless micro-cracks in its aging paint. Some old peel-and-press letters remained from a long-gone business. An unreadable graffito sprawled across one fender. Gray dust covered it throughout. Its banal ugliness transcended ugly somehow, and moved on to the objectionable, approaching menace.

It had appeared here yesterday too, and the day before. The neighbor with the garden hose had been around for its arrival on the first morning, and had watched a handful of people dressed in medical white disembark and hurriedly enter the home of her nominal friend, elderly Alyson Crane. On that day the neighbor had time to take notice of the blank-faced teenager who remained in the driver's seat, waiting, hour after hour, and now day after day. His gaze seemed always to be fixed straight ahead to the vanishing point of the street in front of him.

It was a fine, sun-splashed Carolina spring day, but the only sound of birds singing was so far away as to be nearly inaudible. At this address – no birdsong.

Silence was broken by the piercing voice of Alyson Crane, muffled by double-paned windows. The anguish in it could be seen in the reaction of the neighbor's dog, whirling to lock his attention on the bay window of the house.

The neighbor shut off her hose, dragged it over to its rack and hurriedly coiled it up. She had been unable to make out what Alyson yelled. It was likely the name of the adult daughter who was living with her. No good listening to what goes on behind closed doors. No point becoming entangled. She withdrew into her own, similar-looking brick house.

On the other side of the red lacquer-painted front door of the Crane home their living room was stuffy from not being aired out all winter. Light was muted, streaming in only from the kitchen. The bay window was hidden behind heavy blue curtains. Gaunt, white-haired Alyson paced back and forth with her cane in a confused manner, barefoot and clad only in a pink bathrobe. Tentatively she approached a closed bedroom door in the hallway. Monotone male mumbling emanated from inside.

"Audrey!" she cried against the door, "I wish you would take a break and fix your friends and me some lunch!"

The muttering voice continued unabated. Ms. Crane said, "... I never got my breakfast, Audrey. Only some strawberries ..."

In an odd rhythmic cadence, the man's voice jabbered on in rising intensity. With sudden force he spoke an unintelligible phrase, in three sets of three. Then, all quiet from the bedroom.

"Audrey, please," said her mother. She raised her bony hand to tap on the door, but lowered it, and made her way with her cane back to the living room.

She was approaching her recliner when the sound came of the bedroom door flying open. Two young women in plain white uniform dresses came drifting out, one behind the other, staring straight ahead. Third in the procession was Audrey Crane in her white terry cloth bathrobe. Her normally wavy, flowing dark brunette hair was gone. Her head was clean-shaven, completely bald.

Alyson gasped, and cried out, "Audrey!"

Only then did she seem to take notice of her mother. A look of disgust flashed onto her face. She took two steps toward her, and roared out, "My name is Prindibin!"

Gasping again, Alyson found she could not release her breath. She staggered backward, caught the corner of a coffee table, and down across it she went.

Sunlight flooded in, illuminating dust motes. Prindibin moved at a measured pace toward the front door, now held open for her by the first two women. Another lady in white followed behind her, mumbling to herself in a rhythmic way. Last in line was a slender, middle-aged man, resplendent in bright white formal attire. His craggy face bore the expression of one well sated, departing the all-you-can-eat buffet. His attention only briefly shifted to Ms. Crane, as she slipped off the coffee table to the floor.

The sound of the van door rolling open filled the room. As he stepped out into sunshine the last to leave paused, then reached back and eased the red door closed behind him.

The procession filed into the open side of the van as the driver stood nervously gripping the door handle. With everyone seated he raked the door shut and dashed around to his seat, as the neighbor's mongrel alternated whines with barks of alarm.

A rough, sluggish engine came to life, and the cargo van crept forward, pulling away from the Crane home for the final time.

In the opposite direction of the van, many miles distant, stood a place that could not have been more different from the pleasant residential neighborhood of the Cranes. It was entirely institutional here. Spartan. Military. In fact, it was the largest military base in the United States.

Well within its confines stood a plain block structure with a camo-pattern paint job and an antique cannon out front. Inside, at the end of a freshly buffed hallway, a coffee break room was closed and in darkness. Only a shaft of fluorescent light seeped in under the door. But numerous people were crowded inside in the dark, chuckling and whispering among themselves; they went silent at the sound of Army boots plodding up the hall. Shadows of a man's feet appeared to them at the bottom of the door.

He rattled the door open, stepped in and felt around for the light switch.

"Surprise!" yelled the crowd.

The soldier recoiled as one of them hurled a handful of confetti in his face.

"Farewell Matthias!"

The noise and confetti sent him into a crouch, with a fist drawn back and ready. Now he uncoiled, amidst applause and whistles, and stood up straight. He saw the layer cake, blobbed up with icing, and so wide it covered the little rolling table on which it sat.

"Ahh God," said Matthias.

He stepped forward and managed a smile for them, which got bigger and more natural as he surveyed the great cake.

"What have you people done? You spent money on this."

"Just taxpayer dollars, Matt! That's Army cake!"

"... Army cake," he said, "So it better be good. Or else."

Back pats and shoulder slaps came from all around, and a camera flashed in his face as he shook his head and surveyed the red cursive icing – "Godspeed Matthias!"

"Fourteen years!"

The shield insignias of Fort Bragg and the military police unit stood side by side in sugar and food coloring. Three tiny words in blue block letters at the bottom got him laughing.

"It's Been Pleasant."

The fourteen years became the focus of his attention, though, and soon he raised a hand to his eyes. He felt compelled to say, "You threw that confetti right in my eyes, Dalton." But he knew they could tell he was choked up over the cake, or what it meant.

"Gettin' out of the Army, Dalton," he said, sounding as if he only just now realized it.

Dalton checked his watch and said, "Almost. Not quite. Pretty soon."

He took another camera flash to the face, this one they said for the base newspaper, and one more with him cutting the cake, then they all wanted to talk to him at once. No doubt most of them needed to get back to work, he thought.

"Now, you're all invited to the wedding!" he called out, "She's gonna mail out the invitations pretty soon, but that's June 20th, so plan on it. We're not spending much on the wedding. The money's going into the honeymoon."

The crowd approved of that, though Matt could see a few faces that weren't so happy for him. Were they envious of his situation, or just reflecting their own private pain? He was leaving the tough life. They weren't.

He confirmed for one of the officers that he and his bride would be honeymooning on a cruise around the world. Yes, it cost a fortune, but he had been frugal throughout his Army years. Living at the barracks. Driving a cheap car. Meals at the chow hall. No restaurants. No gambling. No frills. Now his first three months of married life would be in finery, at tropical ports of call.

The Lieutenant raised his coffee cup and said it couldn't happen to a better guy.

"Oh ... I don't know," came the response, "I could think of a few guys off the top of my head." He didn't have to elaborate. Afghanistan mindset was well understood here. He moved the conversation along, "So, I believe you met Audrey at the Christmas bash last year, sir."

Matthias hauled out the photo of her. She was smiling radiantly, with dark wavy hair suspended in the wind, the Charlotte skyline rising behind her.

"Wow," said the lieutenant, "Terrific shot. Yeah, I remember her now. She makes an impression."

"Like nobody else," said Matthias, "Well, for one thing, she's totally brilliant. She can hold a conversation on any subject. She could have been rich. But she has always had this great interest in – child psychology! She has written her own thesis on preschool education. She has this entirely original theory on child psychology. I've been reading up on it, too. Promoting it may be one of the businesses we start. Anyway, she says that's the future. Little kids. That's what's important. Little kids."

Looking down at the name stenciled on his uniform, the lieutenant asked, "Is she going to take your name? Sometimes women don't these days."

"Would you believe we never talked about that!" Matthias laughed, "Hell, I might take her name! It hasn't been easy being an MP named Pleasant. Try hauling some drunk AWOL commando out of a dive bar when the first thing he sees of you is the word Pleasant."

Everyone laughed, except for Dalton and one other who had been with him for just such an operation.

"Makes for some memories," said Pleasant.

The giant cake began shrinking away as chunks were wrapped up in paper towels to go home to spouses and kids. He gave a military journalist the thumbnail sketch of his Army career as it entered its final minutes, interrupted by the hugs and handshakes of well-wishers as they went back to their jobs.

Started out in Motor Pool right out of boot camp, but in six months got bored and tried out for military police. No, it had nothing to do with his initials.

"And I hate to say how long it was before I made that connection!"

He was tempted for a moment to give her a real picture of life in the military police. But there wasn't time. Instead he gave the pared-down overview of his two tours of Afghanistan.

A little piece of shrapnel had zipped through his left armpit one day, he said, and then another time he was standing a little close when a guy blew himself up in a marketplace. He got a Purple Heart for the first incident but not the other one. And that had been the one that took longer to get over. But it hadn't been life threatening. Just nerve damage and temporary hearing loss and vertigo. He was shuttled around to easier outposts after that. Germany, Korea, eventually he got his request for Fort Bragg, not far from where he grew up.

The buzz of an incoming call at the office across the hall interrupted his thoughts, and he wasn't sure why it should, as common as that sound was around here. He had probably already said enough to this reporter for the small blurb that would run on the Hail and Farewell page. It struck him how inadequate it was to cover the experiences of these fourteen years. Not even bare bones.

He started to say how much he wished he had time to give a more fitting testimony.

A voice from the hallway called out, "Sargent Pleasant, phone call for you. They say personal and urgent."

"A prank call from the night shift," said Dalton.

He didn't think so, and felt unease turn into trepidation as he walked nearer the phone.

He answered, "Sargent Matthias Pleasant."

Several seconds passed before he jammed a fingertip against his ear and cried out, "*When!?*" Over a minute passed, and he said, "Well ... where did she say she was going?"

Looking across the hall he could see what would be his own expression mirrored in the party-goers. One after another alarmed, troubled face made eye contact with him.

"I can be there in forty-five minutes," he said, "Do not leave. Give me forty-five."

Pleasant drove his aging Volkswagen Jetta at top speed to the Fayetteville neighborhood where the love of his life resided. In front of the Crane home a dark stain of transmission fluid on the street was big enough to catch his attention. That wasn't there last time. As he jogged to the front door he had no idea what sort of scene he was about to walk in on, but he imagined chaos, with plenty of weeping and wailing.

He was thrown a bit to find silence, and only the two grim-faced, stunned and stupefied sisters of Audrey. He had spent more time with the younger of them, Yvonne, who looked a little like Audrey. Della, he assumed was much older, and was not someone with whom he had much rapport. He had only met her a few times and got the feeling she didn't like him. He also wondered if she had a different father than Audrey, though he never got into that with them.

Della spoke in her low, melodramatic voice before he had a chance to say anything, "There's nothing I can tell you that I didn't say over the phone. She's gone. We have no idea where she went. My mother is in the hospital."

"Yes, well umm, how is Ms. Crane?"

"Two broken ribs, a hairline fracture of the pelvis, and a possible concussion. She is way, way too old to be going through anything like that."

"I know, I need to go see her. But look, did she say anything at all that you haven't told me?"

"Audrey only said that one ... thing. And then she left, Matt. You are welcome to see how she left her bedroom if you want. That's an interesting sight. We don't have anything else to tell you."

Yvonne spoke up, "Mama said she had been meeting with some of those people for a couple of weeks. She wasn't sure exactly how long. Said they told her they were doing Scripture studies. Then for the past few days it was every day, all day. One of the ladies was even sleeping on a cot in Audrey's room. The lady never said much to Mama."

Della said, "Show Matthias Audrey's room."

He knew where it was, having been there with Audrey many times. But he let her lead him down the hall. Entering the room struck him speechless for some time. The sisters, too. Looking like nothing so much as a snow cave, every square inch was covered in bright white bed sheets. White sheets, sagging from pins in the ceiling, the walls, and covering the desk, bed, cot, and floor. Not a spot was left uncovered.

He stood mute, taking it in. It was like being in a giant tent worm nest. The glow of a streetlight came in through a sheet over a window. He stepped toward the center of the room where a clear glass punch bowl sat on the floor. It was filled with clear liquid, and the only thing in the room with any color sat settled at the bottom.

"That's mineral water in the bowl, I think. And ... that would be her hair," Yvonne said. A long pair of shears lay next to the bowl, spray painted white. White plastic shavers lay scattered around the bowl.

Della said, "If you look close, you'll see that even the thumb tacks holding the sheets are white." Through the fog of his battered nerves he saw that white-headed thumb tacks had been used to hold up the sheets.

"They were meeting in here for three days. All day, every day, for three days. Three women, a dude, and Audrey," said Della, "She told Mama they were studying Scripture. You ever known Audrey to be particularly religious?"

"Religious? No," said Matt, "She could be idealistic. Used to talk about the future a lot. The next generation. You know, how we have to look out for little kids, because they were going to see the future, or be the future, or something ... Neither of us wanted kids of our own, but Audrey was always so interested in the welfare of kids that already existed. She told me once that was her spirituality. I told her I thought it was great."

He fell into contemplation, and found himself muttering, "... I came to embrace it. It was a part of our relationship. I told her how in Afghanistan we would do operations sometimes where we set up schools. Especially for the girls, because you know they are forbidden to get an education. And we would try to keep the women and kids out of the Taliban's clutches ... Audrey loved that."

The state of the room had a way of stifling conversation. Matt stood struggling to conceive of what must have happened in this space, and in the days leading up to whatever this was. The sagging bed sheets had the effect of making it seem smaller in here. He felt a pang of something like guilt, thinking back to the times he and

Audrey had made love on that bed, now all covered over as if in cob webs.

"Smells musty in here," he said.

"It's lint in the air from all the sheets," said Yvonne.

The three of them turned as one to move out of the oppressive atmosphere. With weighted-down movements they made their way down the short distance to settle in numbly at the kitchen table.

Surrounded by old lady bric a brac and crocheted wall hangings, Matt listened as the forceful Della made a point.

"You asked me if there was anything I could think of to explain this. I am going to hand that one right back to you. You spent a hell of a lot more time with her this year than either of us. Mother is not real communicative right now. So, how 'bout it? What did she do or say recently that was out of the ordinary? Because this afternoon was out of the ordinary!"

"I have been trying to come up with something, Della. Believe me. There just isn't anything."

"Well think!" she snapped, "There had to be some tip-off in the past month that this was coming!"

He shifted his voice to the flat, firm, conflict-resolution tone he used on the hot heads where he worked. But instead of, "Sir, you are required to display a Fort Bragg sticker or temporary card on any vehicle you operate on base," he said, "Della, there was nothing unusual. We were both gearing up for the wedding, and the cruise. We were winding up our work situations. I was spending a lot of time training new people at work ..."

It struck him then that Audrey had spoken some weeks ago about a Scripture study group, but never mentioned it again. She was always in some book club or lecture series. He hadn't thought much about it at the time, and did not mention it now to Yvonne and Della.

"It's just odd that someone who was with her so much would have zero clue about this," Della said.

As if to rescue the disintegrating civility at the table Yvonne spoke up, "There is something else, Matthias. Are you familiar with her jewelry?"

He was. Her late father had been a moderately successful retail jeweler. She had once shown him her collection, her "box of rocks" as she called it.

He said, "The box of rocks."

"That's right," said Yvonne, "All three of us have one. Daddy would add to them at birthdays and Christmas and so on. One of the nice things about being a jeweler's daughter."

"Yvonne and I still have ours," Della interjected, "Audrey's was in a floor safe in her closet, as I understood it. Today that safe is open. And empty."

Matt's eyes slid closed. He raised a hand to his forehead. He recalled several nice stones in the brief memory he had of the time Audrey showed them to him. She had described the set as having a value of around a hundred thousand dollars. Mentioning it to the sisters now brought up disagreements.

"She was being a little conservative, I think ..."

"If it was anything like the one I have you could tack on another fifty grand. Not any vast fortune, but a nice nest egg."

"That's how she spoke of it," said Matt, "Just a nest egg for her retirement years."

Della drew herself up and unloaded her view, "Unless she was keeping it somewhere else, it's gone. And if you ask me, so is Audrey. Every hour that goes by without a call from her it is less likely we ever hear from her again."

"Way too early to be saying that!" Matthias cried, "No way. She'll call me if she gets the chance."

The women didn't argue, but they didn't have to. Matt felt the rationale behind Della's words. It looked bad, in extremis. Yvonne's face was all anguish and dismay. Della's was simmering fury.

He spoke up, "I think it's pretty clear that these people drugged her and abducted her. They found out somehow that she had jewelry and they got in here and doped her up and marched her out of here. Okay, so we'll work with the cops and we'll find her. We'll get her back."

"The cops. They've already been here, Matt. I told you that on the phone."

"Okay, but I want to talk to them myself, see? Did the lead investigator leave a card?"

"We got a card. Yeah," Della said, "Got it right here." She lifted it from between the salt and pepper shakers and flung it on the table.

He picked it up, "… Patrolman?"

"They didn't dispatch the Chief of Police, Matt. We told them what happened and they wrote a report. It will go in their files. They stayed until the paramedics loaded Mother into the ambulance, and they took off."

"I'll talk to the officer in charge in the morning," Matt said, "Kidnapping is FBI jurisdiction anyway."

"Takes a ransom demand for a kidnapping," Della muttered.

"Abduction then! Audrey has been abducted, Della!"

She hesitated very little before saying, "Audrey … walked out."

He slumped back in his chair. She went on, "The cops say she walked out. Unusual circumstances. Highly unusual. But she was a grown woman and she left of her own accord. She took jewelry that belonged to her and she split."

Della stood and took up her bag, slinging the strap over her shoulder. "As far as I'm concerned, after what she did to my mother, she can keep going."

Matt looked to see a tear moving on Yvonne's face, as Della intoned, "Mother could have lain on that floor until she died. Nobody would have been here for days. The only reason she's alive is because whoever was the last to leave didn't pull the front door all the way shut. The lady across the street noticed it was standing ajar for hours. My mother will never be the same again. She has lost years off of her life. Audrey is to blame. If you ever see her again tell her that's what I said."

He took to his feet as she was walking out, but only followed to the kitchen doorway, saying "She was forced to go! She was abducted!"

Della had no trouble getting the front door closed all the way. Matt plodded back to lean against the kitchen sink, bracing one arm atop the refrigerator. But this only confronted him with photos of Audrey, magnetically held on the door.

Audrey, with her sisters and a glass of wine at Thanksgiving. Audrey, with her knowing, insightful eyes and a fabulous smile for an old studio-posed shot. Audrey, at the beach with her bare-chested boyfriend Matthias, who rippled with the muscles of a swimmer's build, while her own physique was rounder, something less than athletic. They had made love hours before, and their faces strongly hinted at it. Audrey, in a silken cowl and white-face make-up – a ghost for Halloween.

Her younger sister sat weeping at the kitchen table. Her fiancé mumbled on and on, "... She was forced to go ... She was abducted ... She was abducted ..."

O   O   O

Prindibin stood in the limbo of a backstage area, on the back side of a weighted curtain, and heard a crowd go into euphoric pandemonium. A lanky man in a white business suit was striding out onto the stage of what she thought resembled a high school auditorium. The crowd wasn't as big as those of TV game shows, but that's what they sounded like. As with the TV shows, there was a "handler" who stood before them thrusting his arms up and down for more noise. Numbering around a hundred, they sounded like more than they were.

The gangly guy stood for some minutes receiving their acclaim, wireless microphone in hand. Behind him, a 12-foot video screen was filled with the face of another man of craggy features, this one with a lank gray mustache, beard, and piercing gray eyes. He was in an outdoor setting, in natural sunlight. Every few moments a shift in a cloud or sunbeam would reveal that this was not a still photograph, but rather video of the stationary, staring man.

The curtain was open wide enough that the little cluster of women backstage could glimpse part of the audience, which was diverse in age and race, but segregated by gender.

Prindibin and her new sisters huddled together, sometimes hopping up and down in an almost psychedelic ecstasy. A joyous song was being sung by the audience, followed by the silence of a brief prayer of stony solemnity. Then it was back to rejoicing and rejoicing.

In this present moment she had a return to the undiluted joy of early childhood. Shrieking in delight at the water park, in a cluster with other girls, their little toes overlapping and wiggling together in the fountain of the splash pool. Their rapturous exultation fed off of one another, building ever greater. This was their day, their moment. The time of their lives.

Now as then she was barefoot, like the other women around her. Hugs were frequent, coming in waves, with much high-spirited patting of bald heads. "I can't wait 'til I get fuzz on my head like a baby!" one of them cried out; it triggered a round of squealing laughter.

Thunderous music, like 1980s anthem rock, blasted all around them, heavy on electric guitar and droning male chorus. A baritone voice boomed from stadium speakers at times, the words so garbled in echo as to be largely unintelligible to the huddled women, but always drawing cheers from the crowd. A group of men stood separately backstage, all with freshly shaved heads and wearing identical white dress shirts and white slacks. They, too, were barefoot.

At the podium center stage, the slender man gave a brief spiel about how new blood was the life's breath of the church, then pointed backstage to summon the first of the new male recruits. This youthful fellow came bounding out, to receive his roaring introduction.

"... Entagmua! ... Entagmua! ..."

The audience screamed as he jumped up, pumping fists in the air. He was electrified.

"Entagmua!!!"

Prindibin was having some trouble exhaling. Waves of tiny spheres in rows and columns filled her mind like organized champagne bubbles. The presence of conscious entities of indescribable profundity surrounded her, intangible, invisible, but radiating and imbuing her heart with their love-beyond-love. Time was flowing differently now. It was like a slow-motion, high-definition movie, with every nanosecond imprinting distinctly on her consciousness. She felt she would be able to clearly grasp this moment in her memory from now on. Every moment of her life from now on would be in the new, crisp, bright, fine, ascendant mind. She was reborn, in a fully superior state.

After the last of the men went on, Prindibin was introduced to the crowd. Stepping out from the curtain, the exultation she had been feeling up until that moment became mere prelude, and was now blown away. A volcano of approval blasted her from the frantic throng.

"Prindibin!!! ... PRINDIBIN!!!"

She had barely enough presence of mind in this love hurricane to shout out a reaffirmation of the pledge she had made earlier in her bedroom, "... My name is Prindibin! Descended of Earnest Seamark! Ascendant in his will! I give myself to God! I give myself to our Shebbevunseh! ... I give myself to Earnest Seamark!"

"PRINDIBIN!!!"

Tears rolled on her face as a sparkling whirlpool of spherules rotated and rotated around her. The throbbing baritone voice of God filled her mind with words of His own language.

The next woman was introduced, and Prindibin shuffled over to one side. Life had begun.

When the last of the new recruits had been brought forth and feted, the elder called for silence, which he instantaneously received. A monotone prayer was mumbled.

When it ended, the newbies were led away to a solemn group study of Ascendant Scripture. Prindibin could not begin to follow any of it. Soaked in sweat and adrenalin, her breathing not normal, the dichotomy of experiences was like two or three people taking turns pulling or shoving her in different directions. She was spinning. But the importance of all this was undeniable, and she wondered why she could not have discovered the Church years ago. The waste of time she had been living through until now was appalling.

After an hour, or two hours, or six hours, a silent woman walked up and guided Prindibin and her two compatriots out of the room. They were split up, and she found herself in an office with someone she knew as one of her new superiors, along with an unknown man in a business suit. Smiling even as sleeplessness began weighing on her, a mind-numbing round of signing papers and documents commenced. All of it important, they cheerfully agreed.

Sign and date here. And here. Initials here. Waiver. Non-Disclosure Agreement. Waiver. Initials here. Sign here. Power of Attorney. Last Will and Testament. Free Will Declaration of Religious Commitment. Petition for Change of Name. Payment On-Account Agreement. Social Security Transfer Agreement. Waiver.

Waiver.

Waiver.

O   O   O

Matthias had drifted in his lane. He was jolted by the up-close air-horn of an on-coming 18-Wheeler. He didn't need more evidence that his mind was shattered, but he got some anyway, and began looking for a place to pull over.

As he rolled to a stop on a flat patch of land, he knew his mental fog, or forest fire, had gotten worse since last night in the Crane home. He had just visited the Fayetteville Police for an infuriating hour and fifteen minutes of wasted time.

They didn't want to hear about it. A legal adult had walked out, of her own accord, in the company of people she had known for multiple weeks. The report of the responding officer was held up as the final word. Held up to his face, in fact, with the relevant phrases highlighted in yellow. He could have his own copy if he wanted.

The legal adult in question had changed her residence of her own accord.

A paunchy old cop cheerfully offered, "Ya got dumped, bud."

It was doubly rankling to him because he could not imagine being so dismissive if any soldier had come to him with such a situation. Another cop had been a little more compassionate, but what he said still boiled down to – "What am I supposed to do about it?"

That was the question, and one so very prominent in his own head at the moment. All he had achieved in these crucial first hours had been to get politely elbowed out of a police station, and make some crude MISSING posters on his parents' old obsolete computer.

He had a bit of trouble getting the dot-matrix printer to function, and ended up punching a hole in the drywall of their home office. A note he stuck above it said, "I will repair this."

He shifted his Jetta into park and left the engine running as he lowered his head to the steering wheel. If this had only happened forty-eight hours earlier, he might have possibly had Army resources at his disposal. At least the efforts of his fellow troops. As things stood, a phone call to his old Lieutenant had driven home the point that when you're in the Army you're in, and when you're out you are well and truly out. The guy had offered to put up three of his Missing posters on base, not the half-inch stack Matt had imagined being all over the installation.

The load that was bearing down on him was just enough that he checked in on his internal fortress. Not to enter it, just to sense it, and make sure it was there. He never called it a fortress; he never called it anything. It was like a fortress for him because his mind or soul, or whatever he was, could go into that place and attain total safety. His body was stuck outside, of course, but his consciousness had an impregnable position in which he could compose himself, and make a decent plan.

The internal zone was as real to him as any place he had ever been. He saw it in his mind's eye. Not a building or vault, it was more like the chamber of a bodily organ. It was rounded, and lozenge-shaped. Being of the mind, not physical, its size was undefined. Its existence was entirely his private affair. Never had he told another living soul about his internal refuge. Sitting up straight now, focusing straight ahead, he checked in on it.

It was there.

Then, as he began looking at his surroundings, he saw a scene so familiar to him from early years of his boyhood. It would have been just down there somewhere, he thought. Down a grassy slope there sprawled a maze of paved and unpaved streets and narrow half-hidden passages. They laced around modest brick homes, miniscule businesses, and single-wide trailers. Where the streets have no names. It would never be a postcard photo for Fayetteville, but it was on long runs through places like this, and probably this very neighborhood, that he had first emerged from childhood. Here was where the internal fortress first took shape.

Somehow, instead of climbing into a pile of comic books, or a screen, or something worse, Matthias had escaped into running as a kid. The inception of it may have been a literal running away from the rants and rages of his father's on-again-off-again alcohol problem. The man had good years and bad years.

Distance running and swimming had started up instinctually with him around the age of seven, no coaching involved. Well before his teens, Matt had settled into a life of graceful efficient movement, runner's high, and a richly oxygenated bloodstream. The longer he gazed down the hill at the humble network of backroads, the more certain he was that he ran here.

This area likely was not one where he had his worst incidents. That was, being chased down by local kids, usually just to harass, but sometimes to attack him. Once or twice full-grown men, drunks, had come screaming after him. He never tried to outrun anyone, always stood his ground, always gave as good as he got. Usually they would leave off, after doing some verbal abuse and chest-beating threat displays.

If he drove forward a few miles on this road he would come to a city park. Mazarick Park. It was there he had first met one Audrey Crane. It had been too cinematic for an actual movie. This had been real world, all the way.

For some now-forgotten reason he had taken a day of leave. He was in a surly, dismal mood. Why was lost to memory. But he remembered the park, and being there with half of his uniform on, something he would have written up another soldier for. Dungarees and a ragged T-shirt. Unshaven. He looked like shit and didn't care. He had planned to run at the park but instead went wandering around in it, lost in thought.

He was walking in a grouping of bushes that had been trimmed to have rounded, mushroom shapes. There were several of them, and as he was marveling at the fact the city had paid some gardener to shape them, he caught sight of a tiny little kid. No more than a toddler, really, she came wobbling around one of the bushes into a clearing in front of him.

He was so struck by the sight of her. She was angelic, and far too young to be walking around on her own. He immediately sat down, cross-legged on the ground, so as to try to limit the scariness of his visage. The last thing he wanted was for her to start crying. When she took notice of him, he smiled, and gently said, "Hi."

The child stood there some distance in front of him, making for a dreamlike image amongst the shaped shrubs and soft light filtering through trees.

It went from dreamlike to the fully numinous as a woman of striking presence appeared noiselessly, and gently lifted the child into her arms. The two stood regarding Matthias. Audrey's face conveyed almost as much sensitivity as the baby's. Being more startled than either of them, he drew himself up from a sitting to standing position, lifting himself up on one powerful leg in a smooth motion. Almost coming to attention on the soft, blue-green grass, he stood facing her, his feet shoulder distance apart.

He was hyper-aware of how disgustingly slovenly he looked, and quietly lambasted himself for going out in public like this. The moment of silence that ensued then and there would take its place in his memories, for life. It was only broken up when the little tot pointed her chubby hand at him and softly mumbled something to Audrey.

Audrey began to laugh. Soon she was laughing fairly hard, and it became embarrassing. She blurted out, "She says you look like a

Kewpie Doll!" Matt raised his hand to the one, lone lock of hair on top of his head, as he came to understand.

"I guess she has a point," he said, smiling. He laughed himself. Then he had an idea, and asked the little kid, "Do you have names for your Kewpie Dolls?"

She started to nod yes, but with a sudden reticence at talking to a strange man, she forcefully shook her head no.

Matt rolled right along, "Well, this one has a name! Sargent Matthias Pleasant, US Army, at your service!"

When the woman only smiled vaguely, and with bemusement, he added, "I'm not in full uniform today because I have the day off." She acknowledged it with a nod, not making eye contact with him anymore.

Presently she said, "This is Rosie, and I'm Audrey." He could not believe the door was ajar a little bit.

"Why, she couldn't be more than three!" he exclaimed, happy that he had thought of something to say. They both smiled as the child held up three fingers. Matt went on, "She gets around pretty well! She was off to explore the whole park, I bet."

"She is a little mobile unit," Audrey said, "Rosie, let's show Sargent Matthias where you win your Kewpie Dolls."

She turned and started walking away, back the way she had come. Somewhat astounded at the turn this day had taken, he stepped right along. Soon he saw that she didn't mind bringing him over because she wasn't close to being alone. A softball field had five other women, three guys, and about thirty rambunctious kids, most not much older than Rosie. A little obstacle course had been set up and they were tearing through it.

A lovely afternoon unfolded, with the kind of puffy white clouds and bright yellow sun one might expect in a child's artwork. The kids were infectious in their joyfulness, and he was grateful for the delighted mood it afforded him as he got acquainted with Audrey.

"Are you a teacher, then?" he asked.

"No. Not yet. I'm studying it. These children are all from the foster system, Sgt. Pleasant. This is a big day out for them before they start pre-school."

"Volunteering?"

She nodded.

He chimed right in, "I do volunteer work at the Boy's and Girl's Club! I coach kids in basketball and judo." Never had he been gladder of it, either. Any trace of awkwardness in the conversation vanished. She spoke a little about herself, how she had lived most of her life in Fayetteville but had somehow never visited Fort Bragg. That can be remedied, he thought.

Later, their conversation still somehow rambling along, she told him of her interest in child psychology – "The most important subject in the world." Human personalities form early. She wasn't sure of the exact age in which our identities lock into place for life, but these little ones were at a crucial juncture. Without the least self-consciousness she told him she knew how lucky she was to have had a loving, nurturing home in her first years. She felt a sense of obligation to those who weren't so fortunate. Beyond that, what could change the world more than bringing in a generation of people who had healthy, happy formative years? What religious or political theory could top that?

She was so straightforward and up front about it. Well spoken, even at a casual encounter like this. Not pretentious, and she really knew her stuff.

When the other adults showed signs of needing her help, he decided to move on and not wear out his welcome. But he wanted that phone number, if one was to be forthcoming.

When he asked, she said something about needing to "hold on" to her cell phone number at present. She was so chipper about it she made it seem almost as if it was some kind of big win for both of them that she wasn't coming across with it.

Then she seemed to have an idea, "I volunteer at Carolina Cattery on weekends. You could call me there sometime. It's not exactly intense work. We don't get very busy."

He couldn't say that about his work. He nodded, and with a warm smile said, "Nice meeting you, Audrey." He took his leave, drilling the words *Carolina Cattery on weekends* into his memory bank. He had no idea what it was, but found out on his phone when he got back to his car. A rescue shelter for cats, it was on his way back to the base. He slowed as he passed it, and saw a sign that said, "The Kitties Need the Following ..."

Saturday afternoon he was there, in his dress uniform, with a thirty-pound bag of kitty litter under each arm. Their dating began shortly thereafter. Over not much time, they fell in love.

He shifted the Jetta's gears and rolled forward. He may have slept two hours overnight. It would not have been more than three. His eyes in the rear-view mirror were bloodshot and dry. He was headed to his parent's place where he was originally supposed to have stayed until the wedding, and the cruise around the world. The right-hand fork in the road up ahead would let him go by his old high school. He kept it well to the left.

After he graduated out of that place he was offered a couple of athletic scholarships, but he came from an Army family. His grandfather, that is, had a distinguished Army career. His Dad had served one hitch of no consequence and strutted around like General Patton thereafter.

Matthias thought the Army might accommodate his athleticism and the feverishly high energy level he had at the time. He also enjoyed working on cars, so he planned to spend four years in the Motor Pool before leaving to become a certified mechanic. After a year he was bored, and on a dare he took the Military Police entrance exam, and aced it. He remained for the next thirteen and a half years in that specialty, or situation, as he called it.

The officer had been right who talked to him about the job when he was first looking into it. It would mean being in an Army within the Army. You won't have a range of friends like most soldiers. Everybody will think you are looking to trip them up or write them up, or something. Many of them will consider you as the bad guy, at least until they need you. The Command will use you for whatever they need. "Multi-Purpose" is what MP means, he said. Your chances of being deployed to Iraq or Afghanistan are 100%.

At the age of nineteen he was in stellar physical condition, was possessed of a particularly sharp focus of mind, had a remarkably high pain threshold, and was gifted with a capacity to maintain inner calm that some people found scary. So, away he went.

Wounded twice. It left him declared as fit only for softer duty stations. Which meant Germany at first, then Korea, and finally Fort Bragg not far from his parents' place. Fourteen months ago in Mazarick Park he met Audrey Crane.

He slowly drove around Fayetteville in a daze. In a span of hours life had gone from the superbly ordered into – shambolic chaos. Somehow he thought this morning was going to be the resolution. Surely she was going to call him, or barring that, somebody was going to give him some help with this.

Instead all he had was a box of MISSING posters. He pulled over at the Boys and Girls Club where he volunteered. A group of pre-teens were playing basketball, and for a moment he sat watching through the chain-link fence. Some of them were in the Judo class he taught. He sounded his horn and yelled out "DeJuan!" He waved him over, and about twenty of them came running.

"Look, guys," he began, when they were clustered around his car, "It may be longer than I thought before I can do the Judo workshops again. Something has kind of landed on me." His voice was cracking. That was unexpected, and he found it mystifying and embarrassing. His eyes were tearing up here.

He pulled out a big stack of the posters. "Look ... I would like for you all to tape these up around town. Ask your folks to put some up." He asked DeJuan to give some to his relatives that worked for an airline. Crackling with energy, the boys divvied up the posters and scrutinized them. One of the younger kids went, "Whoa! Missing Person!"

They declared to him that the posters would be distributed far and wide, and they wished him all the best. They were good kids, and he pulled away regretting there would probably be no further coaching from him.

Matthias left the central city area and finally turned in at the mailbox he had painted "PLEASANT." His mother was heading out for a drive as he came in, and he pulled over in the yard and walked over to lean his arm on the roof of her minivan for a talk. He spotted his father and two younger brothers on the picnic table in the distance, but didn't acknowledge them.

"What I said last night wasn't true," he said to his Mama.

"What was that?" she asked.

"When I said we would know more today. My increase in knowledge is zero."

He described the cops stiff-arming him, the order for a thousand posters he put in at a print shop, and his inability to find takers for more than a few of the 200 posters he printed off of her home computer.

Ms. Pleasant lifted the cigarette from her mouth as if it was heavy, and placed it in the car's ash tray. She said, "I see you had a little trouble with my printer last night. Or my wall."

"Yeah. Well, you know I'm good for the repair of the drywall, Mama. And I finally did get the printer to work. Here, find homes for some of these ..." He plucked a couple of dozen sheets from the box and handed them to her.

"It's not the hole in the drywall that I'm worried about. It's your fist. What if you had hit the stud? And I'm not as concerned about your fist as I am about the rest of you."

He was unused to having such lapses in demeanor, much less having it pointed out to him by someone he couldn't tell to bugger off. It was just one more aftershock from the main quake. He figured it had to show in his face.

She looked down at his poster, with the two prominent smiling portraits of Audrey, then looked back up to him, and said, "Matt, what are you going to do?"

He shook his head, heavy in dismay. "First I am going to get on the phone and see how much money I can get back on these cruise tickets."

But his mother wasn't having any evasions, not with her engine idling. "What are you going to do?" she asked again.

"What I am going to do ...," he said, every word straining, "... is, I am going to find her." He added that finding out what happened to her was bare minimum, but then he was going to try to find her.

"Okay," said his mother, "What then?"

"I just want to talk to her," he said.

She didn't look like she was buying it, or maybe she was just harried by her own problems and needed to go.

If there was any way possible, Matt said, he was going to convince her to come home, and work things out. Whatever kinds of things these were.

Mama had to go, but this was a conversation that would be taken up again soon. She said, "Deidra and Blaine are here. They drove all the way from Raleigh to see you."

He thanked her, said he loved her, and got off of her car so she could leave.

The red-hot need to be doing something *right now* to find Audrey had been in him since the start of this. Wrangling with friends and relatives was not going to help with that, but he needed a base of operations and more of a plan than he had put together so far. And maybe talking to one of them would lead to ideas.

Making his way to the front door, he gave a quick wave to his gray-whiskered Daddy, who made an embarrassed nod in return. He would not be able to begin to deal with this situation. But who could? His father was the only one sitting at that picnic table that he had any semblance of a relationship with. His delinquent kid brothers, "you and you," were a long-time source of trouble in the home. They did not look at him at all, and he said nothing to them.

The Pleasant residence had been a double-wide mobile home, but now was augmented by additions, built single-handedly by Matthias in his teens. A brick wall of five feet stretched around three sides of the home. At the end of construction he had declared the trailer tornado-proof, but it had never been tested.

Entering through a front door sturdier than that of any other mobile home, Matt was confronted with the enlarged framed photograph of himself from the day he was inducted into the Military Police. Enlarged nearly to life-size, he was standing by a furled flag in his dress uniform. His eyes were wide open and looked confused, as he didn't know when they were going to snap the photo. He never liked the picture for that reason, but it was the one his father insisted on having for the living room.

"That's the picture we have to use! It's your official picture! That expression is fine! When you're arresting somebody for drunk and disorderly, that's how you look to them!"

Drawn by the sound of a conversation, he drifted toward the kitchen and had a seat on a stool by the island.

He sat shamelessly listening in on the voices of the young couple in the next room, not getting many words, but picking up on the chemistry that existed between them these days.

Back when his sister Deidra was first getting serious about this guy, she had Matt and Audrey to go on some double dates with them. Not knowing him, on one occasion he made the mistake of asking Blaine to tell him a little about himself. This triggered a wide-ranging ramble, during which Blaine said that he had been raised on pop culture, and later the fine arts, and included the statement – "If you look closely, if you try, you see the inter-connectedness of things. Even if you start with an old comic-book. It all connects!" He tried to explain, and Matt remembered it only for how it had baffled him, until Blaine tied it in with one of Audrey's favorite sayings:

"... The universe is always bigger! That's what she likes to say, right?"

She did, and it was.

Between his sister and him only Deidra had been inside of a college. Their other two siblings aspired toward staying out of jail.

DeeDee would sometimes talk about living out her life as a professional student. He figured she was just being dramatic, as so often she was. Today, as he listened, her voice sounded like she was stoked about something. All wound up. But that was often the case with her. He thought of his sister's personality as being so upbeat, witty, funny and alive. Somebody in the family needed to be, he thought.

She must have moved closer to the door. Her trilling voice carried clearly, "And here's the new addition to the wall ..."

"Crikey," said Blaine, "You could set a grapefruit in there."

"... It's a good thing I didn't hit the stud," Matt called out. No response from the office, and he said, "... Think of the structural damage that would have caused."

The two of them emerged hand in hand, their expressions sheepish as they regarded him. His sister broke away to stand by him; she hugged his shoulders and patted the little lock of hair atop his head.

"All the way from Raleigh to console me?"

"That's right," said Deidra, whose resemblance to their mother was striking, though thankfully without the cigs. "And there is something else, too," she said.

"Don't you two have classes?"

Blaine retrieved a beer from the fridge and said, "We're only skipping one day, Matthias. No classes on the weekends."

Dee said, "When you called Mama last night she called me, and then I told Blaine. We started doing some digging around online." She was building up to something, but he didn't imagine it could be much.

Matt said, "Yeah, I dug around online last night, too. There is very little on any search engine for 'Room draped in bedsheets.' In fact, nothing."

Deidra was actually excited. Psyched. She had news. He could remember her like this when she was six.

She said, "Blaine found something."

Blaine stood there, his hair a mass of cowlicks going all directions despite having length enough to weigh them down. He was regarding Matt with the same wary, nervous expression he had back in the days when it was first becoming obvious he was sleeping with his kid sister. Yes, something was up, but Matt was not in the mood for exploring it. Blaine's face was not that of someone stoked, and looked closer to reticent if not regretful. It could not be clearer that he had been made to drive out here and give his big news to Matt. He looked down at the kid's T-shirt. Emerson Lake and Palmer. A band that broke up before Blaine was born.

He said, "I found something, or somebody, online. But I wasn't ready to come to you with it yet. I wanted to check it out a little more on my own. See, right now, I can't vouch for this lead at all. It could be a prank, or something worse."

"But it *is* a lead!" Deidra said, "There was no way we were going to keep it away from you. If it doesn't pan out, okay. But we think you should hear it and decide."

She had moved around to stand by Blaine in the cramped kitchen, which needed a paint job. They both focused intently on him, and Matt perceived a hint of something like daylight in this situation, his first in 24 hours. He sat up a little straighter.

Blaine took a deep breath and a gulp of beer and said, "Okay. I typed out a rough description of the circumstances you described to your mother. I started pasting it into these message boards I know of. Basically, I was asking, does anyone know of anything like this? Before I went to bed my computer chirped and it was somebody on the Skeptic.com board, saying I should post it to this board with a fifteen-letter name that I can't recall exactly, but I have the link. Not that any of these posts are on it anymore. So, I posted there, and went to sleep, and early this morning I get a chirp. It's a reply, with only a phone number that turned out to be a voice mailbox telling me to leave my number ..."

Matt, who had been planning to take a nap clicked into sharp wakefulness as the guy's hesitant narrative went on.

"The recording only gave the name 'Craig.' I left him my number! I said if you think you can help us, give me a call!"

Deidra broke in, "How about this guy? Is he afraid to get involved? This is what I've been telling you about, Matt." She slung an arm around his neck.

Blaine muttered, "The Craig person called me then, as I'm eating breakfast. I talked to him briefly, and he's overly-polite, which gave me a bad feeling. He said he figured I was in-state

31

because of the NC State Wolfpack icon on my post. I gave him the town I was calling from, but he wouldn't return the favor. He was cheerful but *very vague*. He said, based on what I said in my post, he might have some information that would help me. When he found out I was calling for a friend, that sort of ended it. He didn't want to talk to me anymore ... He only wanted to talk to the friend."

"Okay," said Matt, "Give me the number."

"Umm, he says he wants it to be in person. See, I told you this was a half-baked situation! That's why I wanted to work on him some more myself before I got you involved!" He shot a look at Dee, and said, "I left him another message, but never heard back from him. Might have blown it, I don't know. My main worry is that he's not for real, and I have wasted your time."

"Why does it have to be in person?" Matt wanted to know.

"He had a string of reasons. He was holding all the cards! I was worried he might hang up, so I went along with whatever he asked. He said for you to call him, and I guess that's who he wants to hear from."

"Did he say where he proposed having this meeting?"

"That's another problem. He's way out in the country, Matt. He will give us the GPS when we set up the meeting, but it's halfway across the state. Closest town is Ferrous, he said."

"Never heard of it."

"It's not close."

Matt thought for a few seconds, and said, "Punch in the number and give me the phone."

Deidra said, "Ferrous is two hours. Craig said anytime this weekend would work for him."

"I'm going to see if we can do it today," Matt said.

He took the phone and heard a recorded answer, with the strangely breezy, chipper voice of a mature male asking that messages be left for Craig at the tone. He spoke carefully for the recording, "This is Matthias Pleasant. Friend of Blaine Wheeler. I am calling for Craig. I would very much like to talk to you, Craig. At your earliest convenience." He left his own phone number, and kept the call short.

"Probably we never hear from him," Blaine said, "But if we do, I want you to understand something. I am not happy about this individual. He was nothing but evasive with me, and would only give up a lot of vagueness about how he 'might have something for me,' but wanted all kinds of information from me. Based on that, you're supposed to travel two hundred miles to meet somebody with one name at a GPS point in the sticks. Really not happy about it."

With furrowed brow, Matt thought it over.

Blaine piped up, "It's half-baked!"

Matt took out his phone and checked the weather.

Deidra gave Blaine a forceful defense for making the trip, "Matt did hostage rescues and all kinds of combat missions in Afghanistan, and dealt with every kind of shady freak as an MP. He's not afraid of whatever this is. He's not getting any help from the police, so I don't doubt he wants to track down every lead."

Matt said, "You loved Audrey." She nodded.

Blaine said, "All right, but there is one more thing. On the message board where I found him, he apparently opened his account just to respond to my post. So, literally, a lurker. After we spoke on the phone, I went back to the message board. His account had been deleted."

As Matt processed this, Blaine went on, "You know I'm a skeptic by nature, but this Craig inspires nothing else. I mean, there is criminality involved here, right? You said Audrey was drugged and abducted. Who's to say this Craig isn't in on it?"

"Blaine, the way I am feeling right now, if this dude isn't on the up and up, he has more to worry about from me than vice versa. I say we make the trip. You and me. If you're up for it. But I am going. I would rather not go it alone, but I'm going." He headed off Deidra as she took a breath to speak, "I want you to stay by the phone, and be here when Mama gets home. Blaine is only just going to drive and be another pair of eyes and ears. If he will make the trip. I will understand completely if you don't, Blaine. But I do have to ask it of you."

The phone chimed. It was the number. Matt said, "I'm going to ask him to meet us today. As soon as we can drive out there. Decide if you're going."

He answered, "This is Matthias ... Yes, Craig. I want to meet up as soon as we can do it. Well, we would be coming from Fayetteville." He looked at Blaine, who nodded his head, "Why don't we say two hours? I'll need your GPS." He jotted it down, "... Parking lot of Incarnation Church, Old Pine Top Road? No street number? ... Nothing else around! Okay. We'll find you, or we'll call back if we don't. Good enough. Two hours. G'bye for now."

He took his sister in arms for a hug, then headed for the door with her boyfriend tagging along.

As they stepped out into the yard Matt said, "Drive your car and I'll gas it. Mine needs an oil change," then, taking notice of something, he said, "... Hold up a minute."

He broke away and headed for the picnic table, which now held only his two younger brothers. You-and-you. They saw him coming, and seemed to flinch and grimace.

He got within speaking distance, and said, "I'm sorry I was on your backs so much, for so long. There won't be any more of that. I'm sorry. I apologize." They said nothing and he made his way back to the car.

"Let's get something out of the Jetta first," he said, "Come here."

He followed him over to the trunk of the car. Matt popped it and reached in alongside the spare tire. His hand came up with an eye-catching sight – a cobalt blue handgun.

"Ever fired one of these?"

"Not lately, and I'd rather not now," said Blaine.

"Good. I'd rather you not, too," said Matt, "And you won't have to. It's for – just in case. On the off chance that things go very sour out there, you will have a noise-maker."

They departed in Blaine and DeeDee's Ford Focus sedan, with Matt saying, "Making noise is probably all you'd ever need to do. Just a warning shot. And that is in a highly unlikely worst-case scenario. If a warning doesn't work, if they are total psychos, you point it at them, and verbally threaten them. If they are full-on suicidal and it's you or them, you fire at their legs. At that point it's self-defense. Don't worry. It will never come to any of that. We'll stop at a drive-thru and get a bag of hamburgers for you to hide this in. Keep it on the seat beside you for easy access. We'll have a code word that means I'm in trouble and in need of the warning shot. But don't worry, it's all just precaution, for safety's sake."

In short order they had rolled out of Fayetteville environs, with a bag of heavily armed hamburgers on the floor between Matt's feet, and the kind of music Blaine liked wafting out of the speakers. To Matt it was different, mostly instrumental. Something like jazz. It sounded African. Anyway, it wasn't jarring, and he found it helped him to think.

The two kept talk to a minimum and Matt's mind dispensed with worries and agonies, and stole some time for peace in this situation. Over time they entered the Carolina hill country, and the beginnings of the Blue Ridge Mountain chain. Being some of the oldest mountains on earth they were eroded down over the eons into great wooded, rounded knobs. He had forgotten their unique aura, having not been here since childhood.

GPS being a wonderful thing, in less than two hours the guys were turning in at the empty gravel parking lot next to a prominent sign for Incarnation Church. Topped with a simple white-painted steeple, the building was positioned well back from the road. Up front, all alone in vacant space, stood the unknown factor.

He was revealed as a paunchy, grinning, middle-aged chap in a sky-blue polyester business suit, his sandy hair cut into straight bangs. Blaine brought the Focus to a stop at an angle that presented the man in clear view to Matt in the passenger seat. They scoped each other out for a moment. Some of Blaine's nervousness had passed into him on seeing the stranger in the flesh. There was also the matter of a pickup truck, parked up by the church house, which seemed to have two men watching them.

The stranger's smile seemed like that of someone in another world. Stoned? Empty-headed? Or merely in love with the sunlight and being on his feet and alive. Apart from the distant pickup truck, he was standing all on his own. A surreal touch was added by the Technicolor blue sky that was his backdrop, replete with tiny, phony-looking, bright white popcorn clouds.

"Craig" exuded amiable charm as he introduced himself, but then at the outset he said he would like a reference, just so he knows he is dealing with the right party. Matt was outraged, and blurted out, "A reference?"

He came within a hairsbreadth of asking him for a reference of his own, then decided that might lead to things going downhill, which he wasn't ready for just yet. He rattled off the phone number of the Fayetteville Boys and Girls Club, which happened to be an easy one to remember. "I coach kids there," Matt said. The gentleman called and verified it. He then introduced himself as Reverend Craig Moultrie, of this very church.

Matt snarled, "The sign has a different name for the minister."

Moultrie said, "... Youth pastor! I'm the youth pastor. I work with kids too!"

36

Craig sort of took charge then, hopping into the backseat of the four-door sedan and telling Blaine to drive down the road. He said they can't meet at his office at the church, for reasons he would explain later. They were going to a nearby farm where they can talk freely.

"Not far at all!" he said in his upbeat way.

It was far enough, as it turned out, and Matt noticed that they were being watched from the farm house as they pulled in and parked some distance from it. Craig said he now wanted Matt to take a walk with him down to a pond. Still feeling a load of suspicion, Matt told Blaine to stay put, and not eat all the hamburgers.

As they walked toward an expansive pond, Craig asked Matt to elaborate on the circumstances of Audrey's departure. He responded that it was the most outrageous, inexplicable turn of events of his life. Apparently, she was drugged and abducted, but the cops didn't seem to allow for that. Craig cryptically said, "No cops are going to help you."

Matt gave him the details of the bed sheets pinned up all over the room. Moultrie nodded, and interjected, "Snow white sheets only. No flower prints. No little sailboats." Surprised, Matt acknowledged it, and mentioned the white scissors and shavers on the floor, and the glass bowl containing Audrey's sheared-off hair. They discussed the scene in her bedroom until they arrived at the pond, and stood, arms folded, looking out across it.

Craig asked, "... Have you ever heard of something called Mountain of Radiance?"

Matt thought about it and said no, but something in the tone of the man's voice, and even the words themselves, pierced him.

"Church of the Mountain of Transfiguring Radiance? How about Heart's Lighthouse Fellowship of Triumph? Clock Tower Executive Management Advisors? God's Army of Eternal Honor?" He said it was okay, they have numerous front groups. "It is a kind of an organization. Based on what I have heard from you and Blaine, I'm thinking Audrey is with them now."

"So, what are they about?" Matt demanded.

"Well, they call themselves a church!" said the reverend, which seemed to rankle him, "It's a bad situation," he added. He recommended prayer.

Matt insisted on knowing more.

Moultrie asked, "Was Audrey in any religious study group or philosophy group? How about a paranormal studies group? Ghosts 'n UFOs?"

Matt told him about the ladies she had been meeting for scripture studies, adding, "She never mentioned much about it to me. Told me about starting with it, then nothing more."

"Sometimes they call it scripture. 'Ascendant Scripture.' It's not Biblical Scripture, or text of any other religion. It's their own thing. Don't feel bad that she kept it to herself. They would insist on strict secrecy until she has progressed in the knowledge far enough to speak properly about it. That would be hugely important to them. Just another isolating strategy, of course."

Matt said, "Okay, what makes you so sure Audrey is involved with these people?"

Moultrie said the shaved head was the clincher, "But the first tip-off was the white sheets, white clothing, white everything. They claim that their initiations are witnessed by interdimensional entities. Angels, space aliens, deceased ancestors, unborn descendants, and so on. They say the nearest you can get to a total white-out makes it easier for these ... ahhh, beings, to tune in. The ceremony is as much for their benefit as anyone's. So they say. The ascended entities bond with the new Adherent at that time."

Matt stood thunderstruck almost to the point of nausea listening to this insanity, delivered in such a cheerful cadence.

"There are a few things that don't fit," the man said, "The main thing that's different is it's usually done at their compound, in a special white-painted room. And the full process from introduction to affirmation usually takes more like months, not weeks. I don't know why they did the ceremony at her home like that. It's like she got a rush job."

The new name also fit, and sounds like one they would have come up with. "Everybody gets a gibberish name when they enter," he said, "So, yeah, this is MOR, or a splinter group."

They are quite active in this state, which he knew from personal experience. Before he went into all that, Craig wanted to know more about the situation leading up to the disappearance. Matt described how they were to be married soon after he was discharged from the Army, and Moultrie said that might have added the urgency for them to do a rush job. He said, "Tell me, did Audrey have any kind of liquid financial assets?"

Matt gritted his teeth as he acknowledged it, "There was a box of jewelry."

"Okay. That's gone now," said the reverend. He thought it over, looking out across the pond. He said, "For you, I have some bad news and some good news."

"Give me the good news first!"

"She could call you today. She could call any minute," he said, "Or just show up at her home. Her involvement with them could be that brief."

"The bad news would be what?"

Craig said, "I think that you should prepare yourself for the very real likelihood that you will never hear from this woman again."

Silence crashed down. Matt looked over the rippling water surface, and felt his eyes begin to well up, rippling in tears.

As if his tears had imparted some kind of connection between them, Moultrie announced that he would now tell a little of his own experience.

"... A few years ago, three young men appeared at my office saying they wanted to explore having an interfaith event between their church and ours. A softball game, or fish fry. It was something we had done on occasion with the Catholics and Jews in the area, so we scheduled something. One thing leads to another and they were having guest speakers show up. We sent speakers to their place, too, supposedly to present our spiritual beliefs. I was one of them. The pastor of our church went, too."

Moultrie went on to tell of standing before an all-male assembly of Mountain of Radiance Adherents. They grinned at him as he spoke, somewhat relentlessly. It became disturbing, like a new prison inmate being ogled by lifers. It turned out that they did have a kind of rape on their minds. Not sexual, but that might have been no less damaging than what transpired.

"The interfaith encounters had been entirely a Trojan Horse operation to access to our congregation for recruitment purposes. They pinpointed the most promising people, or bank accounts. From there, the hard sell was on.

"I personally endured one of the most intense, grueling recruitment encounters I ever dreamed could exist. They wanted me, buddy.

"It was around this time that some of the younger women of our congregation began researching MOR online. They came forward with some pretty horrifying articles. These ladies had been put off by what they called the 'medieval' sexism of MOR. Then they uncovered just how bad things were."

Matt fought against the dizziness he was feeling from the man's words. How could the woman he knew be absorbed into this? Whatever this was. He still couldn't imagine. Not really. At this moment was she even safe?

"We broke off relations with them, to which they reacted with a kind of theatrical acrimony," Craig said, "But the damage was done. We lost five congregants. That's a real blow to a small independent church like ours. And, well ... things have never been the same. We're still here, but something has happened to the people; they lost something. They lost the pastor, for one thing. He didn't go to MOR, but sometime afterwards, he stepped down. He moved away. I am in touch with him, but he is a changed man. His confidence and personality aren't the same."

Moultrie said he was not an expert in all this himself, and never meant to imply it. But he knew of some people who were. One guy in particular, lived "driving distance" from here.

"It would be better if you could meet with him sometime," he said, "I could introduce you."

Matt thought it over. Craig seemed legit, but he still knew next to nothing about him. And now, if they went off to see this other person, it would mean there would be no link at all between himself and those at home if anything were to happen. Deidra had the GPS location of Incarnation Church, for all that was worth. But now he and Blaine were to be off on some unknown, untraceable tangent to a second location. It was breaking a basic operational rule.

He decided to go. Not next week. Now. Can it be arranged? Moultrie hauled out his phone, and in a few minutes a meeting was set – with someone.

When they made their way back to Blaine, he was standing outside the Focus. He pulled Matt aside to talk.

"The look on your face is troubling me," Blaine said, "Nothing has happened so far that has me feeling any better about this. The whole time you were gone I have been monitored by faces in that farmhouse window. I didn't think you were ever coming back. Some screen door kept slamming somewhere and I had my hand in the burger bag."

41

"Blaine, we have to go a little further."

"Further to what?" he asked.

Matt said, "Craig isn't the main guy we need to talk to. It's ... somebody else."

Blaine seemed pretty steamed by that, and he wondered how much more loyalty was in him. It was his car, and he could easily announce he was heading back to Fayetteville. Matt braced himself for that statement.

Blaine shook his head, and seemed to be searching for the right words.

Matt clapped a hand on his shoulder, and said, "I can't order you to make this drive, Blaine. But you know what? I am ordering you to make this drive. I *need* you to do this, Blaine! The other party – a Charles Bienville – has agreed to meet with me. I don't want to have to reschedule it and find the place again."

"Yeah, well, *finding* the place is something that's on my mind, Matt. But not as much as finding our way *home* afterwards. These roads remind me of a video game I didn't like."

"Reverend Moultrie is going to direct us out there," he said. Then he called out, "The door's unlocked, Craig! Have a seat! We'll be right there!"

Blaine, his fists on his hips, spoke in a tone that was a little firmer than what he had ever heard from him before, "So exactly how much longer on these back roads with the mystery man, to find the other mystery man?"

Matt answered him honestly, "I do not know."

Blaine said, "Do you know that it's going to start getting dark in a couple of hours?"

O   O   O

Two hundred and seventy miles away, Prindibin was back on the stage at her Home Base, the Mountain of Radiance Service Center outside of Macon, Georgia. The weariness had to be showing in her movements, she thought, as she was stepping out a dance routine with eight other women and nine men. Genders separate. A canned vocal track played. The video of the gaunt, haggard face of the bearded man gazed out again from the screen.

The rehearsal was not going well, although she was beaming smiles without a let up. She was doing her part. Not her fault if there were problems.

"I don't know how long it has been since I have *moved* this much! Not like this anyway!" she called out, to no one in particular. The choreography felt endless, the whirling, bowing, and gesturing with up-thrust hands. It took on some complexity when the rows of men and women marched through each other in a crisscrossing diagonal promenade.

"Gettin' dizzy here!" she cried out, laughing. It was wonderful, though, to express her newfound commitment with her entire body.

Two men stood front and center of the empty auditorium watching the dry run. About every third minute they stopped the dancing to bawl somebody out: "You must have the phoniest-looking smile I've ever seen in my life! Are you sick?"

Dancing resumed, and was stopped again to castigate another person for lethargic, stumbling, stupid-looking moves. At times a dancer would be pulled out of formation altogether and put in conference with a third man offstage. Prindibin felt almost euphoric, super-charged by the idea that her own performance was from the heart. Also, she was so woozy from lack of sleep that the dancing seemed a surreal experience, and ludicrous to the point that she couldn't restrain herself from silly laughter.

"Stop! Cut!" bellowed a deep male voice from the side of the stage. She saw he had raised his powerful hand, his index finger jabbed in her direction. "You!" he yelled, and whipped his hand about in irate summoning. She broke away and ran to him.

"Do you know how important this performance is? We have until tomorrow night at five to get this down! Down cold! Without screw-ups! This presentation goes out on closed circuit, Monday morning, nine AM, to every church we own!"

She was about to say that it wasn't her fault if not enough time had been allotted for rehearsal, but throttled the statement within her. Something had just happened here. He was not loving, and not happy, as everyone else had been. The eyes, screaming from his sagging face, assaulted her with internal strife unlike any she had ever seen in any person. She didn't know this man at all, and felt it was probably best not to antagonize him at such a stressful time for him. But then he snapped, "*This* is how you say thank you to everybody? You're looking like shit out there, lady."

It was beyond jolting, and left her with a sudden feeling like that of being unmoored. Unconnected, and somehow hollowed out. He followed up with, "I had hoped you might be chosen for Singing Bell. But if you are no more committed than this, I'd say that's out."

Prindibin didn't defend herself very well, didn't know what Singing Bell was, and said she couldn't understand what she was doing wrong. She then made the mistake of saying she was in need of sleep.

Adherency means commitment, that was the general theme of the extended earful he delivered to her. She knew the others on the stage were hearing and seeing it. She had not fully left the giddy, trippy state she had been in moments ago, and now struggled to come to terms with the harshness of this brother, whose name she didn't even know, who was snapping and gnashing at her in a truly unkind way. The incongruity of the experience was nearly unique in her life. She found herself staring at him, vacantly, and with fear.

He said he wasn't sure that her faith was strong enough yet to allow God to give her the strength to do the work required of her. It was stunning, the speed at which things had taken a turn. He was an imposing figure, and he glared at her with such hatred.

Ultimately a short nap, dosed with guilt, was allowed her. He barked out three names, and she found herself being guided down a corridor of glazed brick walls by a trio of young women who spoke so sweetly and lovingly to her. One held her hand.

They were so reassuring and nice, and they confirmed for her that the brother who spoken so brusquely to her was just under pressure to get the show together. They warmly and cheerily confirmed everything she said. They led her to a dim room of bunk beds, and she crawled into one, which smelled of perspiration. It struck her that people slept in shifts here.

Prindibin lay still, and in darkness found that her mind began spontaneously recalling her introduction to the church. In her bunk, immensely exhausted, she was still wide awake. She very much *wanted* to remember it. It had all moved so fast! What happened?

On an average day at the cat shelter, three women had approached her. Their eyes locked onto her as soon as the door opened and the bell jingled. They made their way directly toward her, engaged her in conversation straight away, and were soon complimenting her on her work with the animals and disadvantaged children, which they saw as "spiritually triumphant." One of them intoned the word "Ascendant."

They spoke of having sensed transcendent spiritual energy in her when they saw her earlier in the week, when they were there adopting a cat. Audrey dimly remembered them and the cat they adopted, did *not* remember telling them about her work with children, and said she was pleased they had rescued the animal. She chatted with them a while, which was hard to avoid the way they stood around her. She recalled being intrigued by the insights they claimed to have into her spiritual life. Of all things to say!

These three returned the next day with boxed lunches, imploring her to join them at the picnic table out back. Audrey did, and the talk was all about "paranormal" stuff. Ghosts? Well, that's one word for them. Yes, they are all around us. Space aliens? There are thousands of races which visit planet Earth, both physically and "interstitially." This visible, conventional life around you is like the outer layer of dead skin cells coating the body. One of them said, "You can do without it!"

They told Audrey she had a "glow of radiance" about her which they immediately recognized. These three were eccentric, and following their own drummer, but at times she found them nothing short of fascinating.

"Have you ever contemplated your true place in the universe?" one of them asked her.

Audrey seized on the opportunity to get a word in edgewise, and began telling them she was developing her own theory on child psychology, part of which would emphasize children working with animals. This wouldn't be the standard classroom hamster, but children working together to care for various animals. The hands-on process will teach empathy and cooperative interaction, as well as physiology. The living animal would also have a way of interrupting the distractions of the digital world in which they were soon to be submerged. It would stimulate their intellectual development. It may not be entirely original, but her wording and approach to it would be. She told them she had most of it well developed, and now she just has to spell it out in academic terms for peer review.

The ladies were "so glad to hear it," but all three of them felt that a higher level of importance was awaiting Audrey. They made some dismissive, almost anti-intellectual remarks about the peer-review process, and what a biased, unfair joke it is.

"Don't let them stomp on your dream," said one.

"What do they know?" asked another.

She mentioned that she was getting married in a couple of months, and kicking it off with a cruise around the world.

"Marriage is a big step," said the most outspoken of the women.

Another chimed in, "I thought I was going to get married once, but then I considered how much of a boat anchor it would be on my spiritual progress. Didn't take long to see that it would be."

In subsequent meetings, because they kept showing up, it seemed they knew an awful lot about her, which Audrey was sometimes amazed to hear. Her father had been a jeweler! Had she ever mentioned that? She couldn't remember. Casually, they would rattle off all kinds of odds and ends. She found one factoid especially arresting – her supposed love for Belgian waffles. Odd, because they were a part of her life only during a fling with an old boyfriend years ago who owned a big Belgian waffle iron that they would use most mornings.

Then, completely mesmerizing, was their offhand mention of the time she was nearly killed when a speeding van appeared around a curve on a road near Asheville, heading straight for her in her lane. That had happened, just the way they described. Audrey's reflexes had been barely good enough to save her life, and that of the man in the passenger seat. She briefly wondered if there was any significance in the fact that the man who was by her side for the near-collision had been the same old lover with whom she shared all those waffles. But they made so many "direct hits" about her life, off-handedly, those were just two out of many. She waited to hear what they knew about Matt, and her upcoming marriage to him. But that was one subject they never touched on.

For some reason she found herself agreeing with whatever the strangers said about her, all of which was true, after all, and flattering. They closed their eyes and held the palms of their hands toward her, sensing the greatness of her spirit, which they said was destined for magnificence.

47

"We know a few things about you, only because your personal angel talks with someone we know."

Another of the three ladies cut off this eye-popping statement, "Have you ever wondered about your protecting angel? Or montralaveo, as they are properly called? He is here with you now, and so *beautiful*..." she shot a glance at the empty space by Audrey's side, "... and I think not very happy about some of the people who are impeding your advancement."

The woman who seemed to be third in the pecking order chirped up, saying, "Can you imagine actually having a conversation with the mind of an advanced entity of that level? You know, life is not about marking time. It's about ascension." They invited her for a study of "Ascendant Scripture" with a brilliant teacher who would soon be visiting one of their homes. That time, and on another occasion, Audrey had politely turned them down cold. But they kept contacting her, always cloying in their flattery about – something.

"It's not a bunch of hocus pocus. It is all scientifically validated. Confirmed. You really, really need to go with us to the seminar at the Marriott. Here are some web sites to check out, too."

Audrey joined her new friends one morning at a park in Fayetteville, for a special event that they insisted she would never forget. It was in the overcast gray morning light of that day that she first heard about "the gateway to everything that is wonderful beyond this dead life."

The Spherules.

"Sometimes we call them the BBs, because that's what they look like: an infinite and eternal field of tiny spheres, all together in perfect rows and columns. They are everywhere, suffusing everything, throughout space time. *They* are the true universe, or at least the entry point. It's certainly not this excrement you always have around you. A single Spherule can be your contact point with wonder worlds beyond imagining. You only have to connect – to align with the field."

"Have you ever wondered what was special about all the great geniuses and special people of history? Was it genetics? No. They were simply able to align their minds with the great field of Spherules, and transition off into eternities of infinite radiance! Only with the emergence of the Beneficence, Earnest Seamark, fifty years ago, was there a real hope for the average person to align, and ascend. Why do you think we even have a consciousness, anyway?"

As unexpected and unreal as this shpiel was, there was something about the women themselves, especially the one who seemed to be in the lead. She believed it. The others did, too. And Audrey had not ever seen anything like their belief. Nor had she ever felt the warmth and depth of love these strangers had for her. So, what was the reality that drove their belief?

Standing alone with them in the empty park in muted morning light, a moment of the surreal took shape. It felt and looked like a scene from an old black-and-white arthouse movie.

Did Audrey want to try to align her mind with the boundless sea of the spheres?

Audrey did.

Sheer curiosity, as much as anything, launched her into what became multiple hours of subtle head movements. Mostly it was with eyes closed, sometimes facing the sun, other times face down. Alignment could be a matter of microns. The pineal gland behind the forehead and the medulla at the base of the brain stem had to form an equilateral triangle with one single Spherule in the array. Feel your way. The conjunction had to hold long enough that her consciousness recognized what was happening.

The tiny spheres could vary in size or spacing depending on location, and some other conditions, but on that morning, at that place, things were said to be especially promising. One of the ladies quickly aligned, and cooed and sang about the loveliness of it. Two of them eventually were in, but the third was dedicated to helping Audrey.

It was fatiguing beyond words, the precise positioning of her head. At more than one point she was sure she would fall over, or scream out – What in hell was this all about?! They kept talking to her, trying to help her find "it."

She thought she saw a fuzzy, indistinct blob or ball in her mind's eye.

"I think ... I see something," she said.

"Is it perfectly spherical?!" the leading lady wanted to know.

"It was. I don't really see it anymore," Audrey said.

"You were almost there," she informed her.

The memory of whatever she had seen became the subject of an intense conversation as they sat on the weedy grass. Did the sphere appear to have layers? Was there a visible central core? Could she tell if it appeared to be vibrating or holding motionless in space? Audrey's memory of it was indistinct at first. It seemed to become clearer only as they discussed it.

On that day she came no closer to experiencing the phenomenon. But they were so insistent that she "capture the moment," and come to full realization, they all but demanded she return to the park the next morning and start fresh. She could still remember sunrise on that day, lying in her bed, watching the glow of dawn increasing on the venetian blinds. She debated in her mind, with some ferocity both ways, on whether or not to get up and drive over there.

She went. And there stood the three of them, as she pulled in to park.

She was in her most comfortable free-flowing sun dress and soft shoes, as they recommended. They walked together to the spot she had been the day before. And by the time the sun was directly above her head, Audrey Crane was striding gracefully through an orderly array of tiny, perfect, little bubbles. The rows and columns had a perceptible bend or wave, as a vast cloud might have in the ocean, or in outer space.

The tiny BBs were best viewed in her mind's eye, with her eyes closed, but there was no mistaking them. Her sensation of them registered in a perceptive area of her mind which had newly awoken, for the first time in her life, for the specific purpose of perceiving the Great Field of Spherules. Immediately she could see that, as they said, it was the starting point. This was the launching pad for magnificence unimaginable.

One of her new sisters said, "It will get easier over time. Soon you will be able to plug in on your own, any time. Personally, these days, I am never unplugged." Special headgear, although expensive, can help a person align, and link up. And plug in.

Their discussions were always so high-minded and cosmic, but at one point during those days, she remembered telling these women again of the fact that she was going to be getting married soon, and moving to another city. Thinking of that moment made her brow furrow, as she lay in the smelly bedding of the bunk.

They had told her she would easily be able to deal with her various responsibilities while she studied Ascendant Scripture. They spoke of how she and Matthias should get married at a Mountain of Radiance center. But for now, she had to keep it all entirely quiet. She was so new to the understanding of MOR that she was not authorized to speak about it to others just yet. There could be some legal issues involved with doing so, too. Intellectual property and copyright considerations, they said. She didn't understand what that could be. But anyway, just for the time being, they said, it was imperative to keep all of this to yourself.

She recalled having every intention of continuing on with her past affiliations. All of them. The marriage was still on. It had been a few days since she had spoken to Matt. But she had to get things all straightened out regarding the new paradigm of reality that had hit her like a floodlight in the face. After she came to a proper place to pause in her scriptural studies, she had planned on picking right back up with everyone. She had to have things together in her head so that she had something cogent, or at least coherent, to say to Matt and the family.

That had been the plan. But after myriad on-line study modules, all-day seminars at a hotel, the Spherule alignments, the group outreach sessions to higher-order sentient forms, and the three-day formal Adherency Inception ceremony in her white-draped bedroom, her previous life was finished. All of that was dead. True life, life in the light, began in a very big way.

She fell into dreamless sleep only to be shaken out of it by her immediate over-seer, an older woman, Esocush, who proudly supervised nine groups of three women. The two church sisters who comprised her Three were here, too. They all took turns hugging the groggy Prindibin.

Time to rise and shine!

O   O   O

Nearly an hour's worth of country lanes passed by before the Focus turned in at an old-timey farm house with gingerbread latticework above a wraparound porch. With Craig Moultrie and Blaine Wheeler in tow, Matt strode up the steps of the secluded home of one Charles Bienville.

A stout Korean woman, holding a strangely lumpy bag of knitting yarn and needles, greeted him in silence. Her face was impassive. She held the door open for them. No other introduction.

He guessed her to be Korean from his time in service there, and was going to greet her in the language. But he wouldn't be able to speak it for long, and right now he was in more of a listening mode. Something heavier than yarn was weighing down the bottom of that bag, and he couldn't help thinking of what Blaine had in his sack of hamburgers.

He had been building up the unknown man in his mind on the drive over, to the point he was expecting James Bond 007, or one of the villains. So, he was taken aback, on being shown into his study, to see an obese geriatric with a white wooly beard, shaky hands, and gray bags under cloudy eyes. He sat at an oaken conference table, bookcases all around him.

To Matt, the full beard and grimacing expression triggered images of ranting Taliban clerics from Army intelligence videos, raising the hair on back of his neck. The old guy remained silent and seated, his eyes locked into Matt's.

Had he been more smiling and hospitable – it still would not have helped. Moultrie had been entirely sunny, and it had not elevated Matt's mood, which remained about as stricken and anguished as when he stepped into Audrey's shrouded bedroom.

Bienville startled him by suddenly leaning toward him, and thrusting out his chubby hand for a shake. He apologizing for not standing, "Having some trouble with that just now. I got the sugar. Circulation is bad. And … it hurts. But my activities continue with the help of my wife, Jin Kyong," he gestured to the joyless woman, who also drilled into Matt with her eyes, "and Reverend Moultrie, and others."

Matt took a seat at the polished wooden table, only just then taking in the shocking frailty of the elderly fellow. But he spoke in a distinguished, eloquent manner, like an old-time radio announcer.

"For decades my life's work has been the study of groups like the one Ms. Crane is with," Bienville said. His use of her name threw Matt for just a second. "I was able to help my wife and two of her relatives out of a similar organization in Korea," he said, "These days I don't get around as well, but the work continues."

Matt said, "Anything you can tell me, go for it. Anything at all. Right now, I could not be more in the dark."

53

"I spoke only briefly to Craig about your situation. I bet he described me as an expert. I call myself a researcher. I say there can only be just so much expertise on the human mind. Anyway, I am not a trained psychiatrist or psychologist. I can tell you that Ms. Crane will be needing a specialist like that when she gets out."

That was hard to hear, but Matt gave a nod and continued with the listening. The old dude went right along, "First off, you need to know that she was not 'drugged and abducted.' Not exactly! It is more accurate to say she has been deceived, and taken in by a con game. Highly sophisticated, but that's the root of it. Charlatanism. The organization is pyramidal, with the people at the bottom being generally decent, but deceived and deluded, and the higher up you go the more insidious it gets."

With a bit more emphasis he drove home his point, "She has been drawn into a complex deception, and her entire life is now side-tracked. The only question is for how long."

"Groups like these, they come in a spectrum of severity," he said, "Some are worse than others, okay? At the benign end they're merely a waste of time. Though benign can always turn malignant. At the other end of the dial, it can mean the total destruction of a person. Psychologically. Physically. Financially."

In a sudden sadness he looked down into the wood grain of the table, sighed, and shook his bearded head, "... Mountain of Radiance ... That's one of the bad ones."

"So, what's it all about?" Matthias exclaimed, "What do they do?"

"They grow!" said Charles, "They metastasize and expand! They extract money and free labor from their followers and feed them a head trip in return. And then the new followers recruit and recruit and recruit. They have to keep bringing in new followers, because they burn up the existing ones. Look ... understand ... it's a top-down totalitarian society living parasitically in a democracy. Worldwide, they have about a hundred thousand active Adherents.

They claim twenty million." Matt was rocked by the size of this group that he had never heard of, and figured was no bigger than the ragtag bunch that had carried Audrey out of his life.

"They are a little hard to categorize. Religious, for sure. Sort of mystical New Age, though they always claim to be scientifically verified. They co-opt bits and pieces from other groups and traditions. They have holy texts and a messianic father figure and layers of high lamas beneath him, down to the local level. They are entirely male dominant, and fascistic. There is a significant para-military wing. They control around a billion dollars' worth of real estate and businesses. Tax free. They have tentacles in government, business, academia, pop culture, anything lucrative or powerful.

"They've been around for forty years! They claim fifty. Only in the last twenty have they emerged as the powerhouse they are. They've gone through several stages of evolution. I'll give you more on their history some other time ... Uhhhmmm ... about fifteen years ago, they came up with a new doctrinal commandment, involving the fertility of the group. They wanted bigger families amongst the Adherency. Artificial insemination with sperm of Ascendant Masters, and their Grand Poohbah, Earnest Seamark, became a big thing." His voice weakened as he went further into their fertility and family-building fixation. He then hunched over a bit, and looking into wood grain again, brought himself to say, "Women are basically baby factories in this cult."

Matthias recoiled internally, just noticeably to those assembled. From a chair in the corner Blaine glanced grimly at him, and respectfully looked away. The Reverend Moultrie stood, arms folded with a foot braced against a radiator, observing and appraising his reactions. Jin Kyong was evaluating the visitor as well, in stoic silence, clearly grasping all the English and all of the ramifications of the scene before her.

Matthias was roiling inside, thinking, "What are they doing to her, *right now?*"

Charles said, "They won't immediately pair her off with a husband until higher authorities determine who that should be. And anyway, she has to prove herself first. There is a period of solidifying her Adherency. They live in communal dorms with other new members, gender segregated, until it is decided she can be married and live out in society. She would be required to live in celibacy from the time of her initiation ceremony until ... such time as that."

The room went miserably quiet for a minute or two. Charles then said that the recruitment process involved something he called spherules.

"So, the infinite Eternal Field of Spherules, and guardian angels, space aliens and ..."

Matt cried out, "Now, hold up! Audrey has an intellect like nobody I know! No shortage of willpower, either. There is *no way* she would ever fall for hokum like this! She was *drugged!*"

"You were an MP, I believe," Charles calmly said, "Are you at all familiar with judo?" Taken aback yet again, Matt affirmed it. He continued, "Then you know that with the right training and practice, a ten-year old kid can throw you across the room. Right? Okay. This is psychological judo. Audrey's strengths have been identified and used against her. Virtually anyone is susceptible. It just has to be the right time, the right approach, and the right cult. There's a definite luck factor, too. Mind control doesn't always *take*, and it doesn't always last for long when it does. It's not perfect, like in *The Manchurian Candidate.*

"That's why they recruit nonstop. Their burn-out rate is over the moon. But sure, Audrey was a potential recruit. Anybody is. So don't blame her for what happened. There is a mind control cult for every demographic. Thousands of them."

Bienville apparently felt it was a moment to pause and allow that to be digested. Matt could feel sweat droplets on his forehead.

His muscles were tremulous. At least he wasn't sobbing like a toddler, which he really wanted to do, but not in front of these guys.

After a long moment, Charles said, "Can you imagine having your identity supplanted by that of another? I don't mean having a mentor. This is psychological parasitism. It is like a foreign object, or machine, inserted into the consciousness. A man-made thing, faulty and buggy, but an *intrusive system* placed into the normal workings of the mind. In my book, I call mind control the Contraption."

His book sat on the table in view of Matthias. *The Manufacture of Mental Illness.*

Charles said it doesn't matter how intelligent Audrey is. Do cults sound crazy? Cults have to sound crazy. They would not offer an alternative to reality otherwise. They cannot be grounded in the real world. They are selling an all-new paradigm. A new worldview. People leave reality for one thing or another every day. Not every such move is as disastrous as escaping into MOR.

In a clear voice that carried, Matthias stated, "Audrey had nothing to escape from."

Charles said she may have been convinced otherwise, "Operations like this are dishonesty incarnate. They justify the lies by saying it is for the overall good of downfallen people who can't yet handle truth. Milk before meat, they say."

Craig Moultrie spoke up to say that maybe the deception was not about how bad her current life was, but rather the superhuman wonder world that awaited her in MOR. That was how they worked on the people he knew. He said Matt should understand that he didn't lose Audrey to another man. He lost her to an almighty god. Or what was sold to her as one.

Matt said he hadn't lost her at all. He insisted that he still needed a better idea of how she got pulled in to begin with, for the sake of his own mental health. There was no hint this was coming. It was like getting hit by a car.

Old Bienville drew and released a deep breath, and launched into it. The initial approach typically involves flattery, and a feigned interest in something she was passionate about.

"In this case it looks like a special effort was made to recruit her, likely because of that jewelry box," he said, "Somehow, they found out about that.

"The typical MOR recruit has their first introduction online, or through some unctuous ego stroking from recruiters working the street. Then would come spacey talk about your place in the universe, leading up to the Spherule shuffle, which I will tell you about. Finally, you get the hard-sell at live seminars. Anybody who balked at going further would be told that having Spherule connections without follow-up training would bring about a ruinous pivot in their life."

"Bringing one's mind into conjunction with the Spherules is really the beginning of MOR Adherency. It's all just self-hypnosis, and guided imagery."

Once you have learned how to "adhere to the field," you can proceed on to the many wonders of the MOR universe, including radical life extension, curse removal, addiction cures, and gay conversion therapy, to "pray away the gay!" At higher levels they are communing with arch-angels, UFO pilots, inter-dimensional "elementals," even Earnest Seamark in person.

"If you're really hip and cool you get to glimpse the celestial mountain at the center of the universe that is the goal of it all. Not that there is a center to the universe, according to astronomy," Charles said, "Anyway, if you pour enough money or new recruits into the church, you get to learn the meaning of life, the universe, and everything. Want me to go ahead and tell you what it is? Ready? It's a war.

"The whole point of everything is to wage this big gruesome war, so God can secure the magical mountain from the unspeakable 'nameless one.' MOR has a devil figure, but they don't name it. They make silent facial expressions, like shuddering horror, and that means they are referring to the unmentionable one."

"They can get pretty theatrical!" Moultrie interjected, "They have their own language, or a pretense of a language. People at the higher levels pretend to speak it. They just toss out words of gibberish they make up on the fly. It's supposed to be the language God speaks to angels, or something. There was a study done at a university language lab, and they couldn't identify any structure or syntax, or more than thirty repeating words in the Ascendant Language. But everybody gets a new name in this language when they go in, as in Prindibin."

Charles said, "They have some stock phrases in English, too. 'Believe Only' is a greeting if it is said once, and a kind of a prayer or outreach to higher powers if chanted in sets of three."

MOR is monotheistic, in that they teach of a single omnipotent God, but He is represented by trillions of angels and saints and space creatures and high lamas and super-heroes. A big part of the hold they maintain on their members comes from the endless studies that must be performed on the 900-page holy text – the Umyashuntopudda, which they say Earnest Seamark wrote by hand in three days.

"Nobody understands it. It is unfathomable word salad loaded with hundreds of little charts of numbers and symbols. But the idea is to keep *trying* to understand it, see? If an adherent will follow the lead of superiors, make a pretense of understanding, and do as they're told, that shows they're making enough effort."

Later, with iced grape sodas all round, Matt had composed himself a bit, and listened to the researcher telling of how the word cult had become controversial, "It's more controversial than is justified. It's not a nice sounding term, but it is not a very nice reality. It describes a definite psychological pattern, the understanding of which has advanced so much in the years since the Jonestown massacre. So, only use it if it fits, not just as a vague insult.

"I've always felt that cult operators are going on instinct. They have their framework of tactics that they know can work, and which now we know about. Cults study each other. It has been evolving and getting more sophisticated since the 20th century communists and Nazis. Certainly, the Third Reich was nothing but a cult that was allowed to get out of hand. Now it's these Islamist groups. Al Qaeda. ISIS. Taliban. Same psychological pattern! Same Contraption!"

He mentioned other terms: undue influence, high-demand groups, and coercive persuasion. He said, "I use the term cult when I see that it fits. I'm not concerned about offending any cult leaders ... Or cult apologists. At times I have told some of them, why don't we just use the word 'scam?' That works for me!"

He said he was willing to help Matt as best he can. He had connections with former members, and knew some good private detectives.

The two of them agreed that time was of the essence, but also that a comprehensive plan was needed, which unfortunately would take time. Charles told him to get some sleep at one of the cabins on the property. They were once used by former cult members, newly exited, and trying to get back on their feet. They would get a fresh start in the morning, and come up with a working game plan.

Rev. Moultrie said he would guide Blaine back to the highway to Fayetteville. Tomorrow Matt could grab a Greyhound bus that stopped at a crossroads nearby and go to Charlotte, and from there back home.

Matt unzipped his money belt and handed Charles a hundred-dollar bill, saying "I didn't bring my checkbook. This is just to show that I want you to work with me. We can figure out the particulars in the morning."

Charles said he wouldn't charge for an initial consult. "Anything more will be based on what I can do for you. Again, so there are no misunderstandings, I am really just an interested, well-informed layman, with some connections that may be helpful for you."

He took up a four-footed cane, struggled to his feet, and set out to show Matt to the cabins.

As they ambled across grassy acreage, Charles said, "You know, after all these years, I still don't understand why there aren't a lot more people like me. Just concerned citizens! Awake to this problem! It's not like it's a small problem, or an obscure thing that rarely happens.

"It's only controversial because cult apologists have made it controversial ... And, also, I think because every demographic group has their own affiliated cult. If you have a certain defining part of your identity, and there is an extremist group claiming to be the champions of that, you may be resistant to having criticisms made of them. You might feel they over-do it a little, but you don't want anybody else objecting to them. That might be a slippery slope toward somebody objecting to you. Thus, the dangerous, extremist types are shielded. Anyway, most people's understanding of cults is caked in myths and sensationalism. Not that sensational things don't happen sometimes."

He pointed out a tiny shack by a pond, and said it had fresh sheets in the chest of drawers. They would put together a breakfast back at the conference room at 8 am. He said goodnight, and began toddling on his cane back to the ornate farm house.

Matt was left standing by the water's edge, and remained there as darkness set in and the arc of the Milky Way stood before him. It hit him that this spot was a place where any number of former cultists would have stood, looking out at the night sky, and trying to sort things out.

"You're not lost forever," he said aloud, "I will find you and bring you home."

O   O   O

About four hours south of Bienville's farm, Prindibin slipped away from the other two of her Three. It was impulsive, almost a hide-and-seek while returning from a group Spherule Alignment workshop. But in truth she had grown tired of always having to be with them. She fell behind as they were walking across the grounds of the compound, and ducked into one of the buildings as Vetunsill and Zintopell kept walking.

Alone, she glided along in a dancing, grooving way down glazed brick passages of the one-time private military academy that was now residence for new Adherents. When she was placed with a husband, she would live in an apartment, in a city. "With an *Ascendant* husband," she said to herself, and instantly stopped and wondered why she had to add that. Why was that necessary? And from whence was the sudden flush of indignation coming from that she felt rise inside of her? She must focus on the future. Fix the mind on ascendancy, on going forward, as so many counselors had told her. No looking back!

It was wonderful to have so many life decisions lifted off of her brow and placed in super-competent hands. She figured the sense of security she had now was unlike anything she had felt since her baby days.

She went exploring. It was a little dark in here. They kept the lighting to a minimum to save money, which was sensible, she thought.

A soft, shuffling sound stopped her. She turned to encounter a clearly troubled, distraught-looking young man. Making eye contact in the dim light, he beckoned to her from an alcove. He proceeded to speak in a Scottish accent, or maybe Irish, she couldn't tell. He had tears in his eyes, which startled Prindibin, as she felt they were standing in what would have to be one of the most delightful places on Earth.

"Please, I need you to help me," he said, "I must get out of here. This is not what I thought it was going to be."

Prindibin said, "... Are you struggling in your commitment, brother? I would not feel ashamed of that if I were you! We all do!"

"This is not what I was told it would be. Okay? I – I want to go home!"

Prindibin smiled, and clasped his hands, "Would you like to know something about yourself?" she asked. She brushed a tear off his cheek, "I have just met you, and already I know more about you than you know about yourself ... Know how?"

He looked at her with eyes like that of one being electrocuted, and said, "Please. Just take me to a telephone. That is all I ask. *Please* get me to a phone I can use."

She offered him her most soothing and caring voice, "Sometimes we lie to ourselves, but the Spherules never lie. They speak perfection only! They are telling me all about you right now, brother. There is nobody on the other end of any phone that is worth talking to. And you won't *need* a phone for those who are ... Your montralaveo. Your Shebbevunseh ..."

The hands she held were shaking as if freezing. He looked into her eyes in a searching manner, and then started shaking his head.

Prindibin said, "It's time to reclaim your heart. Time to reclaim it, so you may give it to God."

A sound of footfalls came to them. It doubled in loudness as two men in white dress shirts, red neckties, and black dress pants rounded a corner, and made straight for them.

He wrenched his hands to and fro, trying to break her grip. But Prindibin held on, saying, "Don't give up! Reclaim your life! Don't roll over and die!"

The men eased Prindibin aside, and one of them embraced the weeping foreigner in a bear hug that lifted him off his feet. Without a word they walked him back the way they had come. As they rounded the corner, he looked over his shoulder at Prindibin, who gave him what she meant as a look of love.

She strolled on, with a mood almost as buoyant as a couple of minutes before.

Posters appeared on the walls at regular intervals with young men and women beaming glorious smiles above lines of text, which included, "We do Battle in a War of Joy," and "I Love You for Letting Me Love You, Shebbevunseh." The only face on the posters that was not smiling to the limits of facial musculature was that of the Shebbevunseh himself.

Earnest Seamark, the man who regularly gazed into the eternal, unblinking eye of God, stared out from his posters implacably. No text accompanied his image.

This facility was a little bigger than she had imagined when she started gaily marching through. She had made some turns in look-alike hallways, and as she was starting to worry about where she was, voices came from up ahead. It was more like whining. Mumbling. Mewling. As it grew louder with her approach, it began to sound childlike, if not infantile.

A door stood open a few inches. She peeped inside, and entered, to find herself in a vast room that was dim, stuffy, warmish, and smelly, despite its great size. It was taken up with rows of bassinettes. Babies and toddlers lie in them, along with certain children surely too old to be there. These sat cross-legged, their sweaty little heads rising above the rails, staring vacantly at Prindibin as she passed through. There was no decoration or even signage in what was clearly the nursery for this MOR facility. It was a scene deeply puzzling to her.

She went toward a well-lit office, separated by frosted glass windows. Putting her head in the door brought a cool waft of air conditioning.

"Hi!" she said, with a sunny smile.

Two women sat within, one of them thumbing through a copy of "*How Now!*" the glossy magazine about celebrities who were Adherents of the church. Prindibin had a copy of that very issue on her bunk. The women, wearing what looked like meat packers' coveralls, regarded her blankly.

"I was passing by, and heard the children! I am fairly new to the faith, and to this place, but in my before-time I did a lot of work with children. The name's Prindibin! I was wondering if you needed a hand around here, because ... like I say ... I have some experience."

The woman with the magazine spoke in a flat tone, "You're proposing to do what?"

"Just basics. Nothing that would get in the way," she said, "Kids this age need to be held ..."

"Held?"

The nurse, or attendant, took up a phone and began rapidly poking on it.

"Yes sir!" she began, "We have some new Adherent in here, *alone,* who sure sounds like she is challenging your authority on child housing practice and policy!"

Prindibin said, "Oh, I never meant to do that. It's just that I have studied child psychology and child care, and ..."

The other woman in the room rose from her seat by the window-unit air conditioner, and began snapping pictures of her with a cell phone.

Prindibin withdrew her head from the doorway with a barely audible, "I'm so sorry."

Dashing away from the door she made for the passageway, but was stopped this time by what she saw, and smelled. They were limp in their cribs. Gurgling sounds reached her. In a petrified way her gaze shot from one to the next. Dozens of them. An unsteady child tried pulling up on the railing of its crib, and the two of them locked eyes together. A puffy, jaundiced face, its hair was matted in sweat. She was staggered, backing away two steps as they beheld each other. From deep within her, a three-word phrase that attended the worst moments of her life erupted, internally, in a voice sounding like her own as a panicked teenager:

"OH MY GOD!"

Whirling from one horrid sight to the next, she broke away and sprinted to the hall as the office door flew open to reveal the nurses. Prindibin barreled down to the next cross hall, where she turned, and turned again, quaking at the thought they may be pursuing her.

Later in the morning, when she was scheduled to be having breakfast, Prindibin found herself instead standing in the office of her Personal Directions Adviser, Granavulid, and her Ascendant Training Coach, a woman with an unpronounceable church name, whom she typically addressed as "Ma'am." To herself, she thought of her as "Bouffant Lady."

For some time now she had endured a "counseling session" with these two. It was, they said, "a last-ditch effort to salvage your Adherency from sinking into apathy and indecision."

First, they reviewed her intrusion into the nursery. She was informed that her studies of "child care and child psychology" were thoroughly *downfallen* studies of child care and child psychology.

Granavulid casually told her, "This whole 'psychology' thing that you speak of is, in particular, a pitfall of the Off Mountain. There's no scientific verification for any of it. Proper Ummyashuntopuddaic practice, which is cross-clarified through charting, is backed up through research and review processes. Your studies of that amounts to squat."

She stood spinning internally from the shock she had absorbed in the nursery, along with lack of sleep, stultifying hours of parsing holy text, and too much of the watery soup they called chowder. When she spoke to these supervisors, a mile a minute, about what she saw this morning, it was transformed into what she *thought* she saw, and is there any chance that the exalted Prindibin could possibly be *flat wrong* about something? The raking about her previous philosophy of child care began then.

Like someone who had swallowed food that was too hot, she struggled to suppress the inner agony that came from taking in all those years of material about human behavior in the formative years. As she saw only now, it was all garbage and downfallen. Purging it from her mind would require immense supernatural intercession, and great personal abasement. She had to rise above, somehow, and find a way to get beyond the dismal void that was her past.

Youthful Granavulid and the older one with the hair sat comfortably as he accused her of all kinds of things. Leading questions came in a flurry, and he would often supply the answers. He said he could tell she was lying by some sort of power that he had. Strangely, her boundless reverence for her new faith had never translated into any respect for this guy, or for many of her other immediate superiors. It was a source of terrible inner turmoil for her, but despite his position, she just didn't feel any particular deference toward him. Her adherence to Mountain of Radiance came *in spite* of the people at her level, and just above. Why would God have His church made up of the likes of this bunch? She was torn, miserably, about it.

He snapped, "What's up with that weird expression on your face?"

Prindibin apologized, and said only, "You seem so young."

Bouffant Lady spoke up, "I think you had better be listening to him."

He said her progress since arriving here was borderline, in fact a little below. "The others here at your Home Base are now officially carrying you, and that is not sustainable."

In what felt like somebody else rising up from inside of her, she heard her voice break out, "With all due respect, sir, I have only been here, what, two weeks, or however long it has been. How badly can I be failing? Also, I just gave you a hundred and fifty grand in jewelry."

"Prindibin, you haven't given me anything. Hearts Gifts are to Earnest Seamark and the church. You are expected to deliver something else to me, and to your Ascendant Training Coach, and that is ... *signs of life!* Do you know how much is riding on the mission of this church, Prindibin?!" He took a deep breath and bellowed, "Nap time is over, Prindibin!"

She knew she had taken some naps, and it was considered a selfish act. Apparently no one else had asked to take a nap. All right, that was bad. She went silent as he chewed her about it.

"All that matters at this stage of your spiritual development is – spirit. Attitude. And your attitude is on life-support, lady. I have been reviewing some of what you've said in the scriptural studies workshops. When people align with the field, they usually attain input from God and His allies! I believe you speak English, Prindibin. The others in the room were speaking it. You just weren't *getting it.*

And now I am to be expected to send the likes of you out in public to represent our church and teach people about the mission of Earnest Seamark? I have to answer to my superiors, too! Personally, I am not convinced that public presentations are happening in your case. And, you know, for you, there really isn't much else. Is there? I mean ... what else is there for you?"

Shock transformed into something else, a state she had never felt before.

Granavulid continued on, now in a detached, almost bored manner, "One of your Three has told me about certain comments you made during a morning meal. It doesn't matter which one of them it was, the point is what you said. I am not repeating it, because I don't want those words in the memory tracks of my brain tissue. But they are in yours. They originated in yours, and as such are plainly visible to Earnest Seamark and all advanced entities allied with him. Problem is, the snotty, sarcastic tenor of those words are hard to miss as being anything less than a kind of disloyalty to the Beneficence."

The only sound in the room at that point was a long, extended exhalation from Bouffant.

In the kaleidoscopic anguish and humiliation that filled her head, she somehow took note of the fact that one of the other two women of her Three had reported something about her to this man, or teen. This guy who was now her direct superior. And what had he said, about reviewing her comments in the scripture study sessions? So, those are all recorded, then.

He went on, "I have to tell you one thing, Prindibin, you are incredibly lucky. Or destined. As I said, I have superiors, and one of them wants Prindibin to have another chance. I was all set to downgrade you to Primary. He said no, you are to be given a chance to redeem yourself."

Her eyes flicked upward, off the linoleum.

"You are going to be given the chance to prove yourself on overseas mission," Granavulid said, "Most people are in for a year or more before they get this opportunity. You will be going on yours ... pretty soon, they say. So, Prindibin, *try* to keep your nose clean."

She was unsteady on her feet, which felt all but pulped from dance rehearsals and prolonged standing on concrete slabs reciting scripture. She met his eyes, and saw them twitch slightly. She managed a smile for him. She was trying to figure out what exactly this meant, and why it was such a wondrous breakthrough for her life, when he said, "Amazingly, in your case, it gets even better. They want your Three to try out for Singing Bell."

Bouffant Lady gasped, and brought her hand up to grip Prindibin by the shoulder.

"They are far more advanced in mentation then I will ever be, so there is no questioning them, even when it seems to run so contrary to what I would have done. Yes, you are going to Singing Bell, Prindibin. I implore you, from the depths of my being, do not squander this rare chance for a *life.*"

She only stammered, "Thank you, sir." She had not the remotest idea what any of it meant.

Delivering a further whipsaw move away from the bleakness of a moment ago, he cocked his head to one side and said he knew how important her guardian angel was to her.

"I know the love you have in your heart for him. Your montralaveo. I wanted you to know, he is standing with you now, in this very room." He looked briefly at an empty spot next to her before continuing on, "Actually, I know this one well. Do you know his name, Prindibin?"

She gently shook her head.

Granavulid seemed to stumble on it a bit, as he said, "It is ... Ishde ... gaden."

"Oh," Prindibin softly muttered, "Ishdegaden."

He rattled off more bland sophistries, but somewhere in Prindibin's mind a muted message popped up. Though indistinct, the crux of it was that he had pronounced the name of the angel in such a way that did not sound as if he was well acquainted with it, as he said he was. Indeed, the way he said it, so faltering, it was as if he was making it up on the spot. He said he wanted her to work with her coach on her tendency to cling to old, irrelevant memories. He can sense that she is "hung up" on thoughts of the past.

Turning his attention to a glowing tablet that had just chirped at him, Granavulid said, "You know, Prindibin, you are quite new in the faith. You are going to figure out that associations from the downfallen phase of life are of no worth anymore ..." He batted the screen with his fingertip, "They are like old bowel movements, from years past. All long flushed away. All gone now, Prindibin, and about as relevant as the fecal waste from a sandwich you ingested ten years ago. I want you to reflect on that as you go forward."

"Yes sir. I surely will, sir."

"You will be returning to Home Base Center with Training Coach, now ... And I am happy you think I have a youthful look, Prindibin," he said, drilling his eyes into hers, "I am over three thousand years old."

She stared back at him for several seconds, breathing only little sips of air through her mouth.

Bouffant Lady took her gently by the arm, and turned her toward the door, chatting to her in a chummy way now. She returned to her Three in the spare, bare cubby-hole down the hall that was their waiting room during individual counseling. She sat down as the woman beside her, Zintopell, was taken to Granavulid's office. Prindibin was silent, with a trace of a smile on her lips as she gazed at nothing in particular, and made a point of remembering and remembering again the slow stumble with the name of the angel.

o   o   o

The morning found Matthias well refreshed after a good nine hours sleep, and now re-convened with Charlie and the ever-serious Jin Kyong over pancakes and coffee back at the oak table. Jin actually said a few words to him today, but it was a spare communication, laden with the kind of gravity he knew from wartime.

His rotund, white-bearded host told him that Craig Moultrie would be stopping by later, having taken an interest in the case. Matt retrieved the paperback he had been given the day before and sat it by his plate. Author, Charles Bienville.

"Yesterday you said you needed more of an explanation on how your fiancée got into all this in the first place," Charlie said, "I thought I would wait until today to go into it. Figured we would have a more businesslike mood at the table."

Matt said he probably was a little frantic and panicky yesterday, "I'm sure I came off like a total ass. Now Blaine will go home and blab it to my sister who will blab it to my mother. Oh well, so be it. Yeah, I'm feeling better today."

Charlie said, "You asked how this could have happened to begin with. No two cases will be identical, but from what I know of Mountain of Radiance, I can give you a pretty good idea. The mechanics of mind control work at a very basic level in the head. So basic, even little kids or toddlers can experience it. In fact, it may be easiest to describe it to you with the example of a young child," he said.

"Kids know instinctively that there are threats around them. Falling. Fire. Bad people. So, a child's mind needs a base of security. To function and grow, they need to know there is access to a safety zone, which is the parent or adult nurturer. The child can return to the protection of the nurturer, then venture out again to explore the environment, feeling secure of a safe space nearby if needed. This is a basic, foundational part of any human mind! The child has a sense of security restored, and then sets out again. Explore, check in on the safety zone, explore again. Basic stuff, which we internalize, and never exactly discard as we grow older. In psychology it's called Attachment Theory.

"Now, if that safety zone is unreliable or missing, as in cases of child neglect and abandonment, the seeds of future mental health problems are planted. But it can get much worse. If the safe base is also sometimes a place of danger, as in the child *abuse* scenario, this can cause the greatest psychological peril. Disorganized Attachment, as the professionals call it. Which leads to Dissociation, as they call it.

"The meaning is right there in plain English – two parts of the brain no longer associate. In cases like this it is the rational and the emotional parts of the brain. The thinking and the feeling, they are unnaturally separated. The person is divided against himself, internally. Part of the therapy for a former cult member is to get him thinking about how he is feeling, and having feelings about his thoughts. Reintegrate the mind. Cults instinctively try to separate the two. All kinds of mental dysfunction springs from this. The cult works to keep it that way, all for the enrichment of a sociopathic leadership."

Matt brought some paper to jot notes on, but decided he understood it well enough so far. He was able to imagine how that must feel. It was, as the man said, basic.

"So, the example I gave you was child-rearing. But it's not limited to children. The same machinery can be put to work against strong, independent adults. Deception is used to achieve isolation. Isolation from all previous associations is essential. That's key! Isolation, and a confused, 'off kilter' state from prolonged exposure to cult propaganda will soften up the defenses, if any defenses were ever raised.

"Those pre-existing associations have to be cut off! From there, 'love bombing' is followed with fear indoctrination. The leader of the group becomes the source of all nurturing and security, as well as – *sheer terror*. The only course of action is to 'get with the program.' The encouragement of the group will be there. The hive mind will support you staying in the cult."

Matt thought it over, gazing down at the paperback, *The Manufacture of Mental Illness*. He understood what Charlie was saying, but never before had he considered anything like this. Not even in all his studies of the Taliban, which he now saw as being a perfect fit for this pattern. He said, "I can imagine how that could be the case. All right. No PhD required to grasp that one."

Bienville said, "There is no safety for the mind in this situation, you see. Safety and danger, love and terror, get mashed together in the same place. Long term, it can break a human mind.

"Cult ideology first presents the leadership as the only true safe haven. Secondly, all other relationships must be denounced as dangerous. Thirdly, it must drive home fear, threats, and other stress in the person's mind to bring about the disorganized attachment to the group, and set in place dissociation. They are *changing* a person's *brain*, in fact. It is a re-wiring."

As bad as all this sounded, it seemed as if Bienville was gearing up for even worse. He allowed himself a long pause, then said, "Ironically, many times, abuse results in greater dependency on the abuser. You were in law enforcement. Did you ever work any domestic violence cases?"

Matthias answered the old guy with a sidelong glance and a nod in the affirmative. "You could say so," he said.

Bienville said, "In children of violent alcoholics it is commonplace to see kids who will take a kind of pride in how much abuse they can withstand. They will belittle the sibling who cries or complains. They bond, ever tighter, to the abusive adult. Abuse is the fundamental reality of their lives, and they embrace it! They have nothing but contempt for the kid who can't take it, the whimpering 'weak one.' Such kids often grow up to be abusers themselves. Sure. They have come to fully accept it.

"Full-grown adults will bond to their abusive spouses. Blaming themselves. Taking part in their own mistreatment. Big segments of society encourage it, too, with a blame-the-victim stance. It's commonplace! Most people know about this. They don't want to talk about it, but they know examples of it, if they're not living it. Okay, how is that any better, or any different, from somebody getting bound up in the machinery of a totalitarian belief system?"

Bienville said as a young man he first noticed that the same psychological pattern he saw in abusive spouses he could also see in dictatorial governments. Domestic violence was the micro level of mind control, despotic dictatorship was the macro. Cults are operating the same game at a level somewhere in between. Realizing that was a profound moment for him, he said. It was for Matt, too, just now as he was seeing it for the first time.

Matt spoke, "I'm sure you could say we have never been to war with any power that didn't fit that pattern. Not to mention our own, domestic troubles."

The two men seemed to observe a moment of silence then, as if in memoriam for the millions killed or maimed in wars, and murdered or traumatized by domestic abusers, down through the ages. For Matt at least, that was what the moment meant, now compounded by realizing the depredations of thousands upon thousands of hardcore mind control cults.

Charles said, "I have more information on all this, as you can see." He gestured to the sprawling book cases along the walls. "What I just described for you is not the one-and-only way that cults recruit, but it is a very common scenario. It's a complex subject. Well, it's the mind. We can talk more about it sometime. Just understand that fear is the main motivator of mind control. Cults deal in fear. False fears, and the false sense of security they provide. It's like the mafia offering you protection for your pizza parlor."

While Bienville nursed a generic orange soda pop, Matt looked at book titles on the shelves. He asked, "What are your thoughts on a certain group known as United States Army?"

He looked up from the soda can, as if trying to read Matt's expression, for seriousness or humor, or whatever may be there. Matt wasn't giving him much to go on, and Charles ended up chuckling, and saying, "Well, it changes the personalities of its members. It is a high-discipline thought-reform environment. It is a kind of mind control. There are some essential differences between the military and ... what we're dealing with. Cults don't have a UCMJ. There's no constitution. No courts. Also, you sign up for a set time of service in the Army, not for life, or afterlives, or reincarnations. In countries that are democracies, the military is supposed to be answerable to the people through elected representatives. That's why it would be nice to strengthen democracy in the United States, and not let it erode away. Beyond that, with hostile powers in the world, we have a need for a military. Even if we could achieve a world without war, we would still need a highly disciplined professional service. But nobody needs totalitarian cults, except the leaders who profit from them."

He described a similar situation with churches, "In a mainstream church you have bylaws and governing documents. The Doctrinal Statement is the main one, then the bylaws. It's not just one guy being the lone dictator. A legit church will also have a financial report. You can ask to see it ... That's in a legit church."

After the orange drink and a whopping candy bar went down, Charles said, "I know you want to get down to the brass tacks of Audrey's case, but there are a few things that would be helpful for you to know, so you're not going in blind. You need to know what you're up against. I'll keep it concise ..."

Matt listened to a bit of the history of Mountain of Radiance. What might have been interesting content for a documentary now took on the feeling of something very personal, very relevant to his life. However utterly bonkers, moonbat insane much of it sounded.

The church was coming up on a big anniversary this year.

"August 28th, 2014, marks fifty years since the Emergence of the Beneficence," Charlie said, "See, MOR teaches that Earnest Seamark came walking out of the Pacific Ocean onto a California beach to launch his new order on that date in 1964. He never walked *in* to the sea, understand. He walked *out*, having been 'constituted and formed' at that moment, in the ocean. By God. He was found walking the beach alone and naked, a teenage boy here to bring the new paradigm into the world.

"When he was found he was incommunicative, and would be for a year. The church claims this as evidence of his spiritual enlightenment. He was undoubtedly a traumatized, abandoned kid. The social worker who received him into care gave him a temporary name, which became permanent, based on the 'earnest' expression that was always on his face, and the place where he was found wandering.

"A surf fisherman was the first to spot him in the predawn hours that morning. He gave a statement to the local news – 'The glow of the seamark revealed him to me.' That's like a small lighthouse. A seamark. I always wished the social worker had named him Earnest Glow. Maybe fewer people would have taken him seriously.

Anyway, the church fully endorses Earnest Seamark as his Earthly name. They have their own name for him, in their idiom. And he is called the Beneficence."

Matt thought it over, and said, "And nobody questions that he materialized in the ocean."

Charlie shook his head and continued browsing through notes, "... Nobody in the church," he mumbled. He took up another scrapbook.

The cover of this one had the logo of the church: An image of the head and shoulders of a man looking up and back at a towering mountain that rose behind him. It occurred to Matt that turning your head so far to one side and then looking up would be damned hard on the neck.

Certain show-biz celebrities were involved with the church. Washed-up pop singer Ricky Chance had his middling hit, "Mine Will Be The Mountain." A few movie and TV actors were in. There's also an anti-MOR stand-up comic, a former member who now lampoons the cult. Then came a bombshell. It had wormed its way into government. State Houses and even the Congress have active Adherents and people on the take to MOR. Charles expressed his worry that the upcoming 2014 mid-term elections could bring in a raft of cult-friendly politicians.

Hearing this backgrounder on MOR was like learning about the company where the arrowhead that entered your heart had been manufactured. It carried a certain dark fascination for Matt, but he decided that he would momentarily be shifting the subject to his fiancée, and all about getting her out of this thing.

Charles' radio voice rolled on. "So, in the early days, Earnest Seamark was a street preacher rambling about angels and extraterrestrials on small town California street corners. His syntax and spacey manner were hypnotic. A small-time motorcycle gang took him in as their trippy mascot. Soon enough, however, the cosmic one convinced the leaders of this bunch that he was for real. So much so that they disbanded the club and became his touring management."

Talk of planet Earth being hollow and full of ghosts was lucrative. More so every year. His worldview shifted regularly, as did his appearance, but not his compelling voice and haunting presence. One high point in MOR history was a gathering of news media to a location in the desert outside of Las Vegas, where Earnest Seamark was going to summon a flying saucer.

The few reporters who showed up were made to wait at a certain spot where they could just barely make out the great man standing on a ledge of a small mountain. He gestured to the skies, and a little wobbling disc with strobe lights came floating out from behind the mountain, hung in the air a few seconds, and went back the way it came. Bienville showed Matt the grainy video on a tablet, and said there were a few different ways they could have done it. But anyway, Seamark got a major bump in exposure. A year later he would declare himself the Shebbevunseh. God's regional manager for our dimension.

The big pivot came a couple years after that, when a cartel of nine anonymous Asian and American businessmen bought their way in, and Church of the Mountain of Transfiguring Radiance became a major religious media corporation.

The tabletop now held numerous photos of holy man Seamark, who always seemed to be staring directly at the camera, no matter the circumstances of the scene. Always the same hollow, haunted, staring eyes, always looking right back at the viewer. Matt was hit with the realization that Audrey would almost certainly be seeing these same old photographs, though in a vastly different context than how he was viewing them.

Charles said that following the buy-in, or sell-out, it was as if Earnest Seamark had become a mascot for a gang again. The group went through several phases from that point. They began their highly successful strategy of appropriating smaller cults, not unlike how big-time Mafiosi will take over smaller crime networks. No different from any big corporation gobbling up smaller ones. They had a profusion of front groups, funneling people in. There was a big one for Christians, called "Jesus Pointing The Way." It was quite enormous, especially in the South.

As the Church ascended, Earnest Seamark descended into figurehead status, for all practical purposes. Some scholars insist he has been kept in a drug stupor for years, or that it was a body double they were using.

"Could be!" Charles said, "He is never seen up close anymore. The facial hair materialized seven or eight years ago. All the real power seems to rest with the Council of the Nine, the bunch that bought their way in to leadership back in the '90s."

"Here's a funny story! As they got bigger, the cult picked up a nickname. Somebody coined the term 'Mo-rays' out of Mountain of Radiance. For a while the church experimented with adopting it. It didn't work out! Now they considered it a slur worthy of a fistfight."

Matt announced that he wanted to get down to the nitty gritty of extracting Audrey. ASAP. Charles had to explain a thing or two.

"She has been programmed first and foremost to expect and fear outside intervention, Matt. This cannot be any heavy-handed 'extraction.' Blaine said you were involved in liberating prisoners from Taliban caves, but those guys wanted out. She has to be actively involved in her own liberation for it to stand a chance. That is the toughest part of recovery from cult exploitation. It can't be done for her! She has to take an active part in exiting. There would be a benefit in your getting the message to her that you love her, that you and her family and friends want her back. But even then, she has to be open to making the exit.

"The optimal outcome is still that she breaks away on her own. But when and if that happens, her mind would still have to reconstitute itself. That will take months, at best. For the first month or two she would need mostly to rest! Sleep! Eat right!"

He said, "No two cases are exactly alike, and yes, she could show up at the doorstep of her home tomorrow. But in all likelihood, it will be a long-term recovery. She has to retake her mind. The locus of control has to go back to her. She has to heal and reconstruct her identity. You can't count on her mind popping back into place like a dented fender. It's possible, yes, but it could also take *years*. So, you have to understand something. The relationship you had with this woman may be destroyed forever."

Even though he had heard statements like this a few times now, it still elicited the blackest heartbreak in Matt. It had to show, he knew. Probably Bienville picked up on it, since he added, "There are examples of quicker recoveries in the literature. But usually, it's slow going. Also, when people exit a group, there can be a process we call floating. Just like it sounds, they aren't all the way back in the real world yet. Worse is what's called cult-hopping. It's like they become addicted to the life of cultic abuse, and seek out another group just as bad."

Matt cried out, "And the government will do *nothing* about this kind of thing?!"

"... Not our government, no. It all goes under First Amendment! Cults exploit constitutional freedoms! Lawsuits do happen sometimes. We get some wins. But in this country, there is very little legal remedy. And for the cults, it's all tax free. Remember that on April 15th. Church of the Mountain of Radiance won't be paying a dime."

Other countries can be tougher. "This was a case in France some time ago," Bienville said, "Thierry Tilley. He was a con man who basically enslaved a wealthy family after charming his way into their lives. He was convicted by a French court of 'abusing people weakened by psychological subjection.' He got eight years. Other cases have had legal precedent, too."

Matt exhaled long and heavy, and off-handedly pulled a random paper from the stack.

"Sexy Sadie?" he asked.

"The lyrics to a Beatles song. John Lennon wrote it after breaking away from the Maharishi in 1968. I consider it to be the first anti-cult statement in the history of pop music. And, sadly, one of the only ones.'"

Matt didn't sing, but read, "Sexy Sadie, what have you done? You made a fool of everyone. You made a fool of everyone ...'"

"Originally he wanted the title to be Maharishi," Charles said, "As he was leaving, the Maharishi asked him why he was going. Lennon said, 'If you're so cosmic, you'll know why.'"

A photo of a man ranting at a podium came next. Charles said, "Oh, him. A prominent cult apologist. That is, somebody who's well paid to argue that there's no such thing as cults or mind control. If ever you meet one, the first thing you do is ask how many case histories they need to see. How many decades worth of very similar scenarios does it take before they can perceive a pattern? From there you acknowledge that no two cases are exactly the same – it's not chickenpox. But the similarities are substantial. Enough to say that this is a definable problem, and not bigotry against people who are 'different.' It is definable enough that it's in the official psychiatric literature, the DSM-5. Under 'Dissociative Disorders,' it's called 'Identity Disturbance due to Prolonged and Intense Coercive Persuasion,' as I recall."

Charles collected his papers, "Okay, now let me ask you one. I want to know your intentions regarding Audrey if you find her." He got a little pointed about it, "... You find her. So, just what are you planning to do?"

Matt kept his cool, and said he just wanted to talk to her.

"Good. That's good. Now, what are you going to say?"

He stammered, and Charles said, "Here's a suggestion. You keep it very, very, *very* mellow! You smile a lot, but nothing big and phony-looking. You do not raise your voice. Ever. The most you can hope to accomplish is to counter what they have been telling her about you. Which would be something along the lines of – you hate her. You wanna kill her. You never loved her. All her family and friends hate her, too. Cults have to sever the person from all former attachments! And a big one, like a fiancé? Oh, hell yeah. What haven't they pumped her head with concerning you? Then, there's always the angel. The voice of her guardian angel says you're no good. Okay, so if you get to talk to her, what you are going to do is plant a seed in her mind that they have been lying to her about you. About you, or about anything. Once the seedling of doubt starts to sprout, it can put a crack in all those walls they've built around her. Something in your favor is that she will start wanting out pretty soon."

With a knock on the front door, Moultrie showed up. He said he just got a call from Blaine to say that he and Deidre were driving out to pick Matt up. He doesn't have to hike to any bus stop. They would arrive soon.

Craig concurred with Charles that Audrey is most likely assigned to a Singing Bell, which is a public relations and recruiting position. An attractive, enthusiastic newbie, not yet burnt out, she would get that for a first job.

When Blaine and Deidre showed up, Matt moved the conversation quickly to getting everyone assembled to pledge to do their utmost to recover Audrey. With other friends and relatives and some hired detectives, they would have a sizable network searching for her. But the people at this table would be the core. This was his "Go Team," he said.

O   O   O

About 250 miles from the Bienville home, Prindibin stood alone on the grounds of the MOR Service Center near Macon, GA, leaning against a lightless, derelict lamppost. She was deducting time from her dinner break, because she was hungrier for a moment's solitude than spicy rice and beans. This was a deeply difficult time. Despite all the resistance she could muster, she was starting to feel real doubts seeping in regarding her new life. Glossing over it was no longer possible.

As weak and inadequate as it made her feel, she could not restrain it. Shamefully, she could not block it out. The biggest part of the problem was the people at her level, and just above; she saw them as being utterly out of step with the stated ideals of the movement. She felt no trust for any of them, and wondered how high in the organization you had to go to find the wonderful super-people she had been promised at the start.

Her own commitment to the truth of the Shebbevunseh was rock solid and to-the-death, most of the time. But why did she feel so alone, when she *never was* alone? And what about this inner voice or presence that sometimes reared its head in a furious rebuke of the church? It felt almost like demonic possession, and was horrifying beyond words, not that she would ever dream of putting it into words. The internal impasse was agonizing, and she saw no way out. In the words of a gung-ho adherent she knew, the way out was up. Redouble your efforts for God.

Moments ago, she was informed that her timetable had been stepped up. She would be leaving for Florida before dawn in a van-load of Adherents, to depart on a ship for a yearlong mission to Brazil. She felt wistful on first hearing it, then as she considered what a big step it was, and how depleted her personal energy seemed to be, her mood was more like crestfallen.

A memory came to her spontaneously, as often they did in the rare moments when she was not kept busy. It was a visual of a double date. She and Matthias Pleasant and his sister Dee and her date Blaine were at a travelling carnival in the countryside near Fayetteville. There were colored lights and zany old music. They rode the Tilt-A-Whirl. Everyone was laughing. No glowering god was looking down on her, demanding obeisance. It was a time, just for the sake of itself. She would have it in her mind, to pull up and review whenever she needed to, for all the days of her life.

She knew they all hated her now, and there would never be any bringing them around to understanding her. Never would they understand the realities of the universe. There would be no making them see their downfallen position, and how to rise above. Though it was a waste of time, possibly evil, and certainly plainly to be seen by the ascendant entities who watched her mind, she could not help herself from wondering what those people were doing. What were they doing – *right now?*

○   ○   ○

After a deep pull on heavily sweetened iced tea, Bienville's mellow voice emerged from the white cloud of his beard, "I think we can locate her."

"Then it's on," Matthias said, "I do the heavy lifting, but all those helping me have my love."

He looked from one to the other, and said, "Hands in on it!" slamming his palm down on the table. One at a time they all joined in. The hands of Charlie Bienville, Jin Kyong, Craig Moultrie, Deidra Pleasant, and Blaine Wheeler stacked atop his own, and made for a moment that moved his heart.

Part Two

"The greatest weapon in the hands of the oppressor is the mind of the oppressed."

Steven Biko

Prindibin's sea voyage to Rio de Janeiro, Brazil, was to take ten days, with an initial stop in the coastal town of Natal. She and her Three would join hundreds of other Mountain of Radiance adherents from all over the United States, recruiting and singing at what was described to them as a major tourist hot spot. And this one was hosting the World Cup Soccer Championship!

"Okay! This one's ours," Zintopell cried out, "Home for the next ten days! We're going to make it count, sisters!"

Prindibin nodded her head as she gazed upon the converted cargo ship moored before them. Even though Zintopell was one of her sub-group, her Three, and was with her around the clock, she avoided unnecessary conversations with her. She had come to see her as self-centered and possibly two-faced. Zintopell had the seniority in their little group, but not by much. All three of this Three were brand new to the faith. The other member of the trio, Vetunsill, reverently pronounced the name painted on the ship, "... Mountain of the Water."

Clusters of other adherents milled around the dock, awaiting the boarding call. They were a diverse bunch, identifiable by the three-inch white plastic clips they all wore on the collars of their white dress shirts. Depending on how long one had served the church, various tiny decals would be stuck on it. Her own collar clip contained only a single red dot. Below her blouse, a simple pleated gray and white skirt reached to her knees. Her ensemble was completed by white, nurse-style shoes.

A lanky, bearded black man in blue dungarees, sea cap on head, sea bag in hand, was making his way down the dock. He paused to plop the bag on a bollard and began rifling through it. Vetunsill watched him a few seconds before piping up, "Are you working on our ocean liner?"

When he realized she was talking to him, he craned his neck to look at the ship behind her and turned back with a laugh, "That?! No!"

"The Mountain of the Water is one of the ships of our church's fleet," Vetunsill said, "We're just about to set sail outta here for Rio de Janeiro! Doin' some concerts down there." He continued digging through his pack and made no response.

Vetunsill said, "Sure is a gigantic liner. I can't imagine how big that must be."

"Two hundred feet," the sailor said, becoming peeved at not finding what he was looking for, "It's a single-deck feeder ship. Or it was, when it was new, which would have been ... 1970s."

Prindibin made eye contact with Zintopell, who cocked her head in the man's direction. The two of them made their way over.

Vetunsill said, "It has a presence about it, though. Can you feel it?"

He said, "It has paint. And rust. Up ahead is the ship I'm on. It's a thousand-footer ... Ahh!" He plucked a briarwood pipe out of the bag and bit down on the stem.

Zintopell said, "He knows where he is employed ..."

"But has he found his place in the universe?" Prindibin asked, smiling magnificently, as were the other two.

"Does he know where *God* wants him to be?" Zintopell went on.

Vetunsill cried out, "Deep down inside he knows! In his heart he knows!"

In a flat, businesslike voice, Prindibin said, "Your God has higher things planned for you. And you do know it. You have to know it. Katherine is right."

The Adherents were given worldly names to use for recruitment duty, or wake-up calls, as they sometimes termed it.

"It is clear to us that you do know it, friend," Zintopell said, "You don't have to say a word. In your case, it shines through like the sun from your spirit."

"Anyone aligned to see levels of spirit would spot it in your case," Prindibin casually stated.

He was looking from one to the other, his mouth eased open slightly and the pipe drooped. He began raising the sea bag to his shoulder. Vetunsill spoke in a pleading tone, "Do you know the special place where God needs you to be?"

He said, "Yeah. Until I set aside about another twelve grand, it's on that ship. Right there. Good luck, ladies."

He started walking, and may have been within earshot when Zintopell said, "Okay, you saw when he started blinking his eyes real fast? Right then he could have gone either way. I didn't think he was a winner, but the thing is, don't be shy with anybody. You try everybody! We're not here to be shy. So, always speak up. Okay, that was good energy. When we get to Brazil we'll be working tourists mostly, but if we're talking to any locals, you two just sing in the background and look good, because I'll be the only one of us who speaks their language."

A man whose voice needed no amplification jumped onto a bollard then, and bellowed at everyone, "We depart now! On the voyage of a lifetime! God is smiling! Your montralaveo are smiling! World Cup 2014 is June 12 to 13, and the world will be in Rio!"

The man, unknown to Prindibin, never once had she seen him, roared out to the assembly of adherents like a football coach, "This is going to be a big, big, BIG win for the church! Nothing but turn-overs, songs for God, sun and fun, in ... Reeeeeeeooooooo!!!" A mighty whooping cheer exploded from the adherents.

"Mountain of the Seas, I mean Mountain of the Water will be cruising for about a week! Seize this opportunity to advance your scriptural studies! Yes, everyone will have the chance to stand at the bow of the ship and feel the Spherules washing over you! Lemme tell ya, the BBs are a little different at sea, but I will let you find that out for yourself! First stop will be Natal. Rio is farther south. All right! Get with group leader and let's board. Berthing is to the left!"

Each singing different songs, they made their way up the gangplank.

Eight claustrophobic, nauseated days of little sleep later, Prindibin shoved her hip against a cabin door to emerge pale and wobbly on deck, with dozens of others, at the cry of – Land Ho!

She would have to be restrained from kissing that dirt when she set foot on it. The passage down here from Florida could not have been only eight days. Eight weeks maybe. She had spent most of the time in a dim, metallic-smelling interior hold, sitting on a hard folding chair listening to speakers teaching about Umyashuntopudda. Which was complicated.

The physical stress was compounded by a feeling of being stupid for failing to grasp this stuff. Though Prindibin felt no comprehension of it at all after mind-numbing tens of hours in the textual labyrinth, she was informed that she was well on her way and right on track. One of the instructors had held a small black metal box over everyone's head, one after another. He pressed a button on the cube and different colored lights would come on over each head. When he had lit up the scalp of the final Adherent in the room, this young man announced that everyone was progressing in the study at a thoroughly acceptable rate. This clashed not only with how she felt, but also with what Granavulid told her when he chewed her out at their Home Base.

Natal, Brazil, from off shore did not look much like what she expected. They were still pretty far out at sea, though. People were now filling the rusty decks of the ship. Loudspeakers, which usually carried only MOR religious music and fire drills, now bounced with the sounds of samba.

A couple of prominent hotels rose above the water's horizon, then came smaller, less distinctive buildings and assorted tropical trees. Someone had told her that Natal had not been developed as a tourist town until recent years. It was no Rio! As they would soon see! But Natal had also been tapped as a World Cup venue, and so here they were. Along with the world!

Hubbub and chaos attended the docking, especially as it was announced that they would be doing a vocal performance at a dockside amusement area just as soon as the Bell platforms were assembled. Leave personal gear in your berth and grab wigs and sashes! They had to take advantage of every hour of sunlight.

Prindibin, still almost bald, adjusted her Dolly Parton-style wig and slung the straps of a tote bag full of pamphlets, paperback books and CDs across her shoulder. Finally she fastened the Velcro on what they called a sash. It was stiff fabric in the fish-shape of the remembrance ribbons you would see on bumper-stickers. The looping part went around her neck and it crossed around the midriff. Men's sashes were in gold sequins, the women's in silver.

Make-up for ladies was to be kept minimal. Mountain of Radiance was not Vegas. Normal American amounts of lipstick and eye shadow were permitted, and Singing Bell women could put one small spot of glitter on their cheek. She and her Three began humming and softly singing the mix of old standards and original church songs that would make up the set, which they were told would be Set B:

1. You Light Up My Life
2. Oh Yes There is a Mountain
3. Wind Beneath My Wings
4. Radiant Face (My Heart Sings)
5. Day By Day
6. Mine Will Be The Mountain

Between songs 3 and 4 an announcer would do a brief blurb for the church, and call for a big round of applause for the dedicated adherents who were walking around helping people in the audience to understand their mission for God, and their love for their Shebbevunseh.

She took pleasure in noting that at least she would never be called to go through the miserable labor of putting the performance platforms together. Twenty men at least were scurrying in and out of the hold of the ship, hauling curved strips of aluminum flooring and the vertical poles that supported them. Circular stands, five levels high, slowly took shape on the quay. They were three in total, set up ten strides apart. Broadest at the bottom, and holding only one person thirty feet up at the top, the bell-shaped stages came to life when the sequined singers filed in and climbed to their assigned levels. Then, with no introduction but a signal from a flashlight, the Bells burst into song.

Choral harmonies alone filled the air. No instruments. Non-English speakers would have no idea of the lyrics, but it was an impressive and unexpected presence that spontaneously started up for any and all who were visiting the area. Folks at sidewalk bars, open-air shops, carnival game stalls and tour boats were soon swaying along with the shiny people of the Bells.

"Aaaaaahhhhhhhhh! ... Yooooouu Liiiiiiiiight Up My Liiiiiiiiiiiiiife!!! ..."

The weather was paradisiacal. Heavenly sea breezes attended every heartfelt note of the radiant, ebullient singers, and lofted Prindibin's pleated skirt. She relished the feel of the air moving through her legs. Clouds towered over the beach in psychedelic shapes, colored in pleasing shades of pink and white. A piece of blue sky stood out in the midst of them.

Prindibin could see sparkles from her sash sequins moving across her eyes and nose, like her own personal field of Spherules. Her body made sensuous movements to the music, which would not have pleased her superiors, but being up on the Bell surrounded by all the others let her lose a little control.

Her rapturous transport got another boost when the flashlight out in the crowd flashed two times at them, repetitively. It meant to stay on the Bell and sing another set after this one. She rolled her head back and sang directly to God.

After the next set she and the others would surrender their position to the next shift of singers and go out to work the crowds, pleading with them, wheedling them, cajoling them, and seeking to turn them over to the male recruitment managers who made the trip down here with them. It was for the good of the people, for their own good, she knew. But she saw the duty as dismal, and heart-shackling, compared to the Singing Bell.

As she and her compatriots began the reverent ballad, Radiant Face, she watched numerous Adherents emerge in a slow procession, from one Bell to the next, each of them holding up a giant placard with the face of Earnest Seamark.

While it was only another five hundred miles, the journey from Natal to Rio turned out to be as grueling as the much longer trip from Florida. Partly because they were given no time to recoup in Natal, but packed up the Bells and their gear and split after only six hours. She had heard different reasons why.

One supervisor of group leaders had said Natal was determined to be "dead." But she had seen multiple instances of Brazilian soldiers, in heavy military gear, engaging the MOR managers with loud talk in the local language that she didn't understand. They were pointing at the MOR paramilitary, about whom they were not happy, even though they had only their side-arms, no long guns. A rumor also ran rife amongst the Adherents that Michaelos G. W. Strennhaur, a Transfiguring Interlocutor of the Godhead, who had passed away in 2010, had informed the captain that they needed to make haste for Rio at once.

Haste had been made. A thin but piping hot chowder had been served. And, without reporting it, Prindibin had been able to sprawl across her bunk for thirty minutes. Soon enough Vetunsill was shaking her shoulder, saying the word had come down that time had to be put to good use in catching up on Ascendant Scripture study.

With that, she was back on her metal chair in the study hall, as a new instructor was intoning the otherworldly syntax of Umyashuntopudda, stopping here and there to note a point of interest with respectful cheeriness. The room was crowded, the air was stuffy, and very few hours had passed before Prindibin was in trouble again.

Scriptural studies were interrupted when someone stood and complained that "she" was repeatedly, and rudely, "swearing under her breath." Prindibin discovered, to her shock and mortification, that this was being said of her. On being compelled to stand, and soon thereafter to come stand in front of the entire assembly of fifty gender-segregated Adherents, Prindibin found herself interrogated.

94

Her denials were summarily dismissed by the group leader with angry snorts. Why was she seeking to sabotage Ascendant Scripture studies? Why did she hate Earnest Seamark? Does she not understand about the enemies, the forces of evil that stalk the church at all times? Was she working on behalf of "any outside-influenced or state-controlled academic body or organized interest?"

With some of the questions she seemed to lose the capacity to respond, and just stood there batting her eyes at this man, who had seemed so cordial before. His demeanor got darker as voices from various points in the room blurted out encouragements and agreements for him. She became aware of something that she had never experienced prior to being in the church: a near total inability to gauge the passage of time.

How long was she peppered with questions, and how long were the silent gaps in between, with only malevolent growling from her peers? It may have only been a few minutes, she was utterly unsure.

Group leader spoke inaudibly to the teenage girl who served as his assistant, and she went prancing out of the room, ponytail bouncing. Prindibin was left to stand in the soundless, hate-radiant stares of her peers, as the instructor poked his finger on the screen of a tablet.

She momentarily considered returning to her seat on her own, without being told to do so. In no time flat she had rejected it, and expunged it from her mind. She was held in abeyance, in a way of utmost strangeness that she had never experienced before in all of life's memory. But then, her memories were no longer applicable anymore. That life was gone. Flushed away.

The door of the room opened with the entry of a gray-uniformed Honors soldier. The perky assistant bopped in behind him. He made his way directly to Prindibin, and in silence took her by the arm to guide her back the way he had come. Her chin trembled but she did not cry.

As he marched her down the passageway to the aft of the ship, people stepped out of the way. Never once did he release his grip on her arm. Only when they arrived at the ship's laundry facility, he spoke, in an unnerving monotone, "This is going on your record, and cannot be removed by anyone but your Shebbovotan or the Shebbevunseh. Any further charges while on this vessel will mean brig time."

She was made to enter a hot, noisy compartment where a much older woman in blue coveralls was piling a gurney-load of damp, dirty towels into an industrial washing machine.

"Unload that onto that table," she said, in a flat voice, pointing to what had to be the largest clothes drying machine made. No greeting. No other statement.

Prindibin grabbed the metal handle of the thing, withdrew her seared hand, wrapped it in a towel, and grabbed it again. Though her heart was like lead, she moved at top speed. Fitted twin-size sheets, almost too hot to handle, she dumped in a heap on the steel table top.

After she finished, she stood motionless awaiting whatever was next. Still without eye contact, the elderly woman said, "Shirts are coming. Get your starch sink ready. Fill it to there and give it ten cups of the starch ... No, *that!*"

Later they stood folding the sheets, in the certain way they had to be folded to fit into the holds. They were at the same table, not far apart, so maybe it was inevitable that the woman would look up at her. When she did, the degradation in her dead eyes was such that it almost evoked a scream from Prindibin. She gasped. The old woman continued apace with the folding.

Before they were finished, she had words for Prindibin, "You just make sure of one thing. You do exactly what they tell you to do. You do it when and how they tell you ... *Exactly* what they tell you to do."

In a hushed voice Prindibin began murmuring in sets of three, "... Believe Only ... Believe Only ... Believe Only ..."

Gurney's came at steady intervals, shoved through the door. The nameless woman decided where things went, and had Prindibin putting them there. The netherworld of heat and laundry odors, ship's movements and mechanical noises, permeated every part of her cranium as the hours went on.

Prindibin awoke in her bunk, with Vetunsill shaking her hard as sunlight streamed in through a porthole. Supposedly, according to Vetunsill, this was the third time she had shaken her to get her out of bed. The ship was entering the harbor in Rio. Prindibin sat up, still in her same white blouse and gray skirt from last night, with zero recollection of how she came to be in the bunk.

She and her Three came to stand with milling groups of Adherents on the deck. Wigs and sashes in place, they looked down on a scene of chaotic uproar on the pier before them. This was less cheerful than the chaos when they disembarked at Natal.

"Can you see further up that way?" Vetunsill asked, "That white sand beach? That is Ipanema Beach! We'll be the girls from Ipanema! Or anyway, the girls in Ipanema." To Zintopell, who looked puzzled, she added, "That was an old song."

Zintopell said to Prindibin, "I have never known anyone who needs as much sleep as you do. There are probably types of bears that don't. I want you to start remembering, when you screw up, it has the potential to screw us up as well. We are a team."

She got no response from Prindibin, who hoped she was getting used to that by now.

Vetunsill handed her an apple. "You missed breakfast, so I grabbed this for you. You didn't really miss much. It was mostly just chowder."

The apple, soft with age, went into Prindibin's tote bag. "Thank you, Vetunsill," she said, curtly, "Believe only."

Men were hauling out sections of Singing Bell platforms from the hold and leaving them piled up on the pier. Rio police officers had showed up, and had definite objections to this arrangement. Shouting matches were going on in two languages. Prindibin's Three allowed themselves some amusement over it, since they were standing so far from it. But then whispers filtered in to them from others on the deck that there was a real problem. A box of parts was missing. Brackets for assembling two of the four Singing Bells were not on the ship. It was becoming clear that someone had left them in Natal.

Rio cops were pointing with batons at the heaps of structural aluminum on the pier, making themselves heard, and it would seem winning the argument. Guys began hauling pieces of staging back into the ship.

The vocal power of the man who had addressed them at the Florida dock was back, and again needed no amplification. Why was he not one of the singers?

He stood atop a crate on deck and bellowed out, "I want to make sure that every last one of you takes the lesson from this! You are in a church that has enemies! Everywhere! Enemies in the downfallen world, and – *enemies within!* Someone has sabotaged the assembly of the Singing Bell platforms!"

Everyone present shifted their gaze down onto the deck, and with uniform expressions of deepest dismay, they listened to the news.

"The evil-doers will stop at nothing to prevent the message of Earnest Seamark from reaching the people! And ooohhh, they think they have won a round with us today. Well, are we going to sit around crying? Like a bunch of soft, weak, weepy babies?!"

He seemed to take notice of the first ones to yell out, "NO!" Soon enough, everyone on the ship had joined in.

"We have two of the Bell assemblies. Okay! Half of you will be working as normal, in the prime locations we have reserved! The rest will be deployed in crews of six with folding tables! We have plenty of those. Three men will stand on the tables and three women will be standing on the ground in front of them. You do your regular set! And work the crowds when the next team of singers relieves you! Doesn't change a thing in terms of the work. You just have to sing a little better because you won't be able to hide in the voices of forty people!"

Prindibin tried to imagine how this would change things. It didn't sound as nice as the Bell performances. She was still shaken by last night's experiences, and had not yet processed the events in her mind. There would be no time to do so. Her mood went dour then.

The manager, or whoever he was, bellowed out, "I just want you all to know that the perpetrators of this crime against God will be found out! Honors has launched a full, in-depth investigation. All of you will be expected to cooperate with any questions they may have of you. If the saboteurs are within the sound of my voice, and I think they are ... you *will* face justice for this attack on the church!"

He offered a dark, dramatic pause, then continued, "We are renting vans that will begin lining up in the parking area by the flag poles. Group leaders will assign team leaders to each van. I want a nice parade with photo posters out to there. We will be singing Radiant Face. Some of you at the rear of the parade can hang back and work the crowds here by the pier. Looks like we got quite a few."

"That's what we will do," said Zintopell, "Just hang back to the rear and we'll mingle with these folks around here. I think it would look good if we could land a turn-over, or at least get some donations or some email addresses or something, especially after that scene we went through last night."

That scene *we* went through? She had been the one folding the shirts. She refrained from saying anything, but the time for that may be coming, she thought.

She stepped off to one side, far apart from them. Gripping the railing of the ship she threw her head up to the sky, then down, abjectly, slumping over to stare into the sea. Her wig slipped forward, and she just had time to catch it and jam it back into place. It almost fell in the ocean. Her body language would be worthy of a write-up to any group leader or supervisor who may have been watching. When she forced herself to stand upright, and pull herself together, she saw that none of them were taking any notice of her. But someone else was.

A woman older than her was sitting on the pier some distance away, with an easel set up before her. She had a little handmade sign, too far away to read. The lady was focused directly on Prindibin. As far off as she was, there was no mistaking it. She looked like her mother used to, in healthier times before she lost so much weight. She wore a kind of knit bonnet on this windy day, and a frumpy old lady sweater, even in the heat.

She would have been able to hear the manager squawling about enemies of the church. Her body language indicated she was paying attention. The two women maintained an eye contact for some time, though too far apart to see each other's eyes. When it became awkward for Prindibin, she turned away. About then, the droning strains of *Radiant Face* filled the air, and a slow parade of Adherents moved down the gangplank and off the ship, some of them holding up giant placards filled with the blank face of the gray-bearded man.

Prindibin's Three were the last to parade off the ship, and the last one of them was Prindibin.

The parade marched forward, and bogged down up ahead; word came that there weren't enough vans to haul all the singers and the load of folding tables, too. The cosmic wisdom of MOR did not extend to logistics, she thought. It became important for her to stop then and say to herself that this problem, and all the others, were due to ineptitude at the lower levels. The leadership was not at fault. It kept her thoughts straight to reaffirm this. Also, advanced entities were monitoring her mind. Down the gangplank, they moved out across hot pavement.

Prindibin was feeling sullen and letting it show. She denied it when Vetunsill came over to ask if anything was wrong. Vetunsill left, but quickly returned to say that Zintopell was talking about putting her on report. She shrugged it off, turned her back on Vetunsill, and made her way to the seated woman she had seen from the ship.

The lady's sign had hand-drawn, multi-colored 3-D letters that looked like Jell-O, and spelled out the word "Caricatures."

"We're singers!" Prindibin called out to her in an upbeat greeting as she drew near, "Here for the World Cup. I'm Prindibin, with Church of the Mountain of Radiance."

The caricature artist puzzled, and couldn't place the name of the church. Seemingly she had never heard of it.

"An American?" she asked in clear English, but with an accent Prindibin couldn't place, "My husband and I are now living just up the street, in Toronto, Canada! I'm Cynthia. My husband is off on a lunch run." She didn't sound Canadian, and then confirmed that she had lived all over the world. They travelled in retirement, doing caricatures to bring in a little cash.

She took up her felt-tip pen, "Strike a pose! Sling your arms back like you're singing! Okay! You're really belting it out!"

After only a short span of seconds, Cynthia said, "You can relax now. I just needed to get an idea of your face. That's the secret of caricature. Only the face counts. The rest is just cartoon."

When Prindibin said she had not requested a caricature, Cynthia laughed and said she was doing it for practice. "I haven't done one all morning! These World Cup people are cheap-o!"

She wouldn't let Prindibin see what she was drawing, but she chatted to her, "... I was ... ahhh ... struck by your parade just now."

"That's something the church does a lot. We would ordinarily have these big bell-shaped stages full of singers like myself. But an enemy of ... well, somebody didn't bring the box of brackets from Natal."

In a measured voice, Cynthia said, "Where I am from originally, there are also parades in the streets, with people holding up big pictures of men's faces. You would see that a lot, where I come from."

Prindibin thought for a moment as the sketching went on, then said, "The face you saw was Earnest Seamark. The greatest man who has ever lived ... I believe." She got a sudden strange, awkward, self-conscious feeling, not from telling her he was the greatest man who ever lived, but that she believed it.

"He is a saint in your church? A prophet?"

"A seer," said Prindibin.

Cynthia began drawing in slower, longer strokes, "What has he seen?"

"Everything."

Prindibin looked beyond the tourist traps of the pier, and off to the curving white sand beach with the surf rolling in. "I love him. His church has changed my life."

"You are a new woman?"

"That's putting it lightly," said Prindibin with a lilting laugh, "I can tell you, straight from the heart, I have been transformed. Our original name was Church of the Mountain of Transfiguring Radiance. They let us use the shorter name now, but it is transfiguring. The hardest part for me is just trying to put it into words! It's not just in the head. It is a physical thing, too. And celestial. The best part is, it's all scientifically verified and validated."

"You are happy, Brenda?" asked Cynthia, focused only on the sketch.

"Prindibin. With a P. Prin-di-bin. And I am happier than I have ever been in my entire life. Yes. Thank you for asking."

Zintopell caught her eye, and gestured at her from where she stood with Vetunsill, as in, do you want us to come help you?

With a forceful push of the palm of her hand, the answer came back – No.

"I can leave any time I like. Free to go, whenever I want," she said to Cynthia, and was suddenly unsure why she had said it. She went right on, with more urgency, "... When you come to see your true place in the universe, everything starts to resolve itself, all around you, like a miracle. And you can see your afterlife, in ascension. That's the Mountain. It ... it is a hard understanding, but as you study, it comes to you." Her voice took on the excited tone she'd had as a schoolgirl, telling her mother about her new project, "See, it is *already in you!* Always has been! It only needs to be *awakened!* So much of it takes shape for you as you study the texts. The Ascendant Scriptures of Earnest Seamark! I study three hours every day regardless!"

Why did it feel that these words were ringing so hollow all of a sudden? Her voice, it sounded forced. Cynthia had entered fully into listening mode, only occasionally looking up at her. Prindibin knew she had to deliver the invitation to a study session to this person soon, or call in a turn-over, but instead she spoke to the cheerful stranger in a voice that became steadily more relaxed and open, confiding more about herself, "As I said, I am happy. For me, the lights have come on ... But, I do have this one frustration." Leaning in a little closer to Cynthia, she said in a conspiratorial whisper, "It just seems like, at the middle levels of our church, an awful lot of people are either not dedicated enough to the mission, or they just don't have the right spirit. Not enough. Not enough. And I don't understand it. We have speakers and teachers that are so brilliant!

And then there's what I have to work with every day. Some of them. They are just so dismal sometimes. Breaks my heart sometimes. It is, I would say ... dereliction."

Out of the corner of her eye she caught a glimpse of Zintopell, making hand gestures of exasperation. As in, "What is going on?"

Cynthia said, "So, the low-level people are trouble and higher-ups are virtuous? I wonder! ... You know what I hope for you? Is that you be strong. And ... be true to yourself, Prindibin."

A man's voice sang out, remarkable for its light-heartedness, "Hey you! Looky what I got! Empadas!"

He was heading their way, a flabby old gent in a purplish suit, so heavily laden with pins and stickers as to seem clown-like. He wore a kind of nautical cap, with plastic flamingos sticking out of the head band. In either hand was a bulging white paper bag.

"Well, if it isn't Himself," said Cynthia, "Prindibin, I want you to meet Bryce, my husband. This is Prindibin! She sings with a musical group."

"Ahh, well it would be nice to have a little music around here. We had a guy yesterday assaulting some drums. Beat them up terribly. Actually, they were five-gallon plastic buckets ... So, this bag is the chicken empadas. I think you liked those, right? And I got little bottles of orange juice." He examined at the sketch on the easel, looked at Prindibin, winked, and said, "Looks as though she has captured your essence!"

"I'm not finished!" Cynthia said, "Almost ... Prindibin, have you ever had empadas?"

She shook her head. She had been preparing to launch into all the spiritual nobility that she sensed from her, and now from him. Only to get them to go to the study workshop, which was for their own good, and their own advancement. But in their case, she abandoned that. Her "mojo" was gone. Now she just sort of stood and looked at them, feeling that they were indeed spiritually noble, but not in the way that Adherents were supposed to talk about.

"Empadas are Brazilian, believe it or not," she said, with a sweet smile. "They are like little chicken pot pies! This kind has cream cheese. They're really good!" Then she said it, "... I would like for you to have these." And she held out the bag.

Like a movie clip that had a few frames missing, her hand zipped out to grip the top of the sack. She slipped it right into the tote bag on her arm.

Bryce said, "I thought you were so hungry."

Cynthia shrugged, "I'll get something in a minute."

He seemed to catch her drift, and changed the subject, "You know, I'm a musical kind of guy myself. I don't play anything, but I listen a lot. I'm into classical music. My favorite composer is Choppin'. Got a CD, The Best of Choppin'. Play that a lot. I'm also heavily into Batch."

No trace of a smile broke the faraway expression set in Prindibin's face. She registered that he had made an attempt at humor. It had been done just for her, to make her laugh. He thought it was funny. He was enjoying it, and enjoying sharing it with her. It redoubled the connection she felt to these two, and at the same time isolation, like one of those MOR spiritual physics conundrums wherein something was and was not, all at once.

Cynthia took the sheet off the easel, and said, "All righty! Bryce, we have something else for our new friend."

It was such a sweet, lovable thing that she had done. A singing cartoon Prindibin filled the page, with her preposterous wig and sequined "sash." Her smiling mouth was wide open in song, with little musical notes floating out. She tucked it into a bright yellow pasteboard frame.

The personal nature of it silenced Prindibin anew, and for the first time in some time, she felt watering in her eyes and a stinging in her nose. If she was going to avoid crying, she would need to get to work on it.

"Thank you, Cynthia," she softly said.

"It's fun to see yourself with a cartoon smile!" the older lady said, "One other thing. I wrote our phone number on the back. Give us a call sometime. If ever you want to talk. We're retired! Always around! ... Let us know how you're getting along."

She nodded in affirmation, her breathing not quite steady. Being speechless was not what she needed. She knew there was no point in trying to conceal it. But her mind was jammed and she couldn't choose her words.

Just then, a shrill woman's voice called out to her from behind, "Daniella! What are you up to, Daniella? We need to be going!" She looked over her shoulder to see Zintopell and Vetunsill walking toward her with a gray-uniformed Honors soldier.

She turned back to Cynthia and Bryce, who wore faces of confusion and alarm. "We sometimes use other names out in the ... world," Prindibin said, "Stage names! We use stage names."

The soldier moved in with a broad, toothy grin on his face, "What do you have here, Daniella? Why it looks just like ya! This will go great on the wall of our ship's study hall!" He took it out of her hands.

Vetunsill said, "Come on, Daniella, we have a van now!"

The soldier said, "Hi, I am Lieutenant Telford, with Church of the Mountain of Radiance. I am sure Daniella has told you a good amount about our faith, and our mission here in Brazil."

She made no words of parting, and gave only the briefest glance back at Cynthia and Bryce, who looked to her as if they might call out her name. She stepped back and turned away from them, as the other two of her Three guided her along.

"I sure hope you got more out of them than a cartoon, Prindibin," said Zintopell.

At a distance she gave a final look back at the couple at the easel, and saw that two other Honors soldiers had made their way in from different directions to form a triangle around them. Cynthia and Bryce were still focused on her, as the soldier addressed them. Then, Prindibin was whisked off into a crowd of the faithful.

They were crammed into an overloaded and under-showered van-load of sash-wearing Adherents. Prindibin heard murmurs of Believe Only and segments of songs over the many comments, complaints and overlapping conversations.

Feeling she should say something, she asked, "So, we still have two Singing Bells. We can't get on one of those?"

"Those were first come first served," said Zintopell, "We were bringing up the rear, remember?"

"It's okay!" Vetunsill said, "We're fanning out all over town, Prindibin! This is going to be better than the Bells! We'll be more widely dispersed! Make a bigger impact."

With all the best spots taken for the proper Singing Bell locations in the tourist zone, Prindibin's trio ended up being dropped off with three young men in gold sashes to warble in a park. Not a very big park, but heavy in foot traffic of strolling locals. She smiled sweetly for passing Brazilians, who looked her over with reservation and curiosity.

Two loud clacks and the table was unfolded. As soon as the fellows were standing above them, and a 1, 2, 3 was counted off, the six of them were vocalizing "Up Where We Belong," in heartfelt amateur harmony. Lyrics came in crisp, clear, perfect English. So, for this audience, they might as well have been singing in Vietnamese.

Approval came mostly from the youngest and the oldest in the crowd. Children danced immediately. Seniors smiled and clapped.

Those closer to life's prime years were more skeptical, standing and evaluating, sometimes through dark lenses of sun glasses or the smoke of a cigarette. A few people broke into laughs.

By the end of the third song they had quite a little cluster of folks, and it struck her what a brilliant way this was of striking up a warm introduction with people. Sing for them! When they finished singing there would surely be several people who would engage them in conversation. And then they could get down to business with them.

She passed her smiling eyes from one person to the next as she followed along in song, trying to spot someone who seemed like the most suitable for an approach. Only then did she remember it would have to be Zintopell doing all the speaking, in Portuguese. That was okay. Took some pressure off of her. She would be standing by, providing a light, loving ambiance.

As they were starting the final song of the set, Over the Rainbow, an unmistakable phenomenon played out in the crowd. Various people shifted their body language, suddenly turning and stepping back in withdrawal. Some walked away. And then three UPP cops strolled up. Unidade de Policia Pacificadora.

A group leader on the ship had told them the Pacification Police were a force set up just for the World Cup. Keeping the dope gangs at bay. Keeping the lid on. We of the church would have no trouble with them. If any of them have any questions for you, just get group leader. But these guys were an intimidating sight as they stood nearby. One in particular was a colossus. A body builder, his uniform looked like it might split at the seams.

For some reason she was reminded of something. She spontaneously got the memory of a man's voice talking to her in a relaxed tone, saying he never worked on his body for the sake of its appearance, but rather how it made him feel. His athleticism was entirely for the feeling of the oxygenated blood, the ease of movement, the calm mind. Why that guy should ever pop into her head anymore she didn't know, and she considered it a moment of weakness. One that may or may not be worthy of revealing to the Shebbevunseh during their next time of interstitial contact. She certainly wasn't going to mention it to any of these people she worked with. Esocush, maybe, some day. Everyone else only wanted to nag her about such things, and it was no help at all for her spiritual ascension.

The hulking Rio cop observed the singers with a broadening grin, which did not strike Prindibin as being entirely wholesome. He then bellowed something to the other two in their language, and they all shared a big belly laugh over it. The three of them drifted on over to the street and mounted their motorcycles as the last stanza of the set drew to its close.

"Biiiiirrrrrds Flyyyyy Over the Raaaaainnn ..."

Three choppers blasted their engines to life and sat rumbling for a minute before pulling away.

One of the men on the folding table snapped at Vetunsill, "Move, and let us down from here." The guys in gold sashes made straight for a young fellow who had been standing there by himself and started up an animated conversation with him. It was a little one-sided at first, then the Brazilian teen shyly offered them a few words.

Prindibin said, "Okay, Zintopell, you're on. Give up some Portuguese for the nice people."

Zintopell said, "Well, I speak Spanish. That's what I'll speak to them."

What followed next for Prindibin would be called a pregnant pause. Her breath stopped in her chest. She knew it was not a joke. She had never heard Zintopell make a joke, for one thing. For another, it was just such a perfect fit with the organizational skills she had seen demonstrated by her superiors since this trip began. It had to be true! They, or Zintopell, thought the local language here was *Spanish!*

She was not interested in whether the group leaders made the error on their own or if Zintopell had assured them she could speak to the locals. She was simply becoming furious.

"Brazilians speak *Portuguese,* Zintopell!" she blurted out, as Vetunsill began showing unmistakable anxiety, "Do you know any *Portuguese?!"*

Clearly thrown off stride, Zintopell said, "That's not the only language they speak! A lot of them will speak Spanish!" She broke away to engage someone in Spanish, without much success. The crowd began rapidly to dissipate as soon as the singing stopped.

Prindibin tried to reassert the smile on her face and salvage something from this. She called out, "Espanol? Espanol por favor? ... How about English? Anybody up for some English?"

Vetunsill said, "Why don't you and I sing, and Zintopell can speak Spanish ..."

"No we are not going to sing! We are going back to the ship!"

She marched over to her male counterparts and came as close as she ever had to demanding something from someone in the Church of the Mountain of Radiance. She wanted to use his walkie talkie.

They weren't using cell phones down here, instead they had these sleek walkie talkies to call in turn-overs and arrange transportation. They were said to have a five-mile radius. Only one person out of a Three had been given one, and Zintopell had theirs. Her church brother had just used his, and seemed loathe to hand it over to her. But she insisted, "We *need* it!"

She snatched the thing and slammed down on the key, "Prindibin to group leader! Come in group leader!"

A blast of static followed, with the words, "Go ahead!"

"Prindibin here, at the … park. We have a problem! There has been a mistake. No one in our Three speaks Portuguese! We can't work this crowd! We need a ride back to the ship! Over!"

After a silence of scary duration, the voice returned, breaking up badly, "…vans for … in use to … load up."

The much older church brother, with his golden sash and bloodshot eyes, said, "I'm going to need that back. Your Three has one."

She pressed the button and cried out, "We need transportation back to the ship!"

Static crackled terribly, and the only word she could pick out was – "Taxi."

The singer took back his radio, and addressed his new recruit in Portuguese. He then turned to Prindibin, "Lucas here says there's a hotel up this street with a cab stand. We're not that far from the ship. It won't cost you much to get back. Group leader said the vans are running full. One of them broke down, and you three are about the only ones who aren't bringing back a guest with them. They also need space for the folding tables."

Prindibin forced herself to embrace this current challenge as part of her service and sacrifice for God. She had to be strong! This mess was nothing compared to what the persecuted heroes of the church were enduring right now in the European Union. Still, deep down, she wanted so much to cry. Her voice had a quavering in it as she said to him, "I don't think any of us has any money for a taxi."

This set off the brother, who began berating Prindibin for her lapse of judgement and overall sloppy incompetence. She thought he might start screaming at her. She said, "If you could just lend me a few reais, we can pay you back as soon as we get on the ship."

It was utterly out of the question. The answer was no. There was no way they were coughing up one centavo for this trio of chumps. She couldn't tell if the guy was angry or hateful. At that moment of sharpest humiliation, she had an insight – *he* didn't have any cash, either.

Suddenly, the slender kid they had been working on spoke up, with a word or two of Portuguese. He pulled out his wallet.

Prindibin received a purple rectangle of paper with a stork on it, and the words Cinco Reais.

"For taxi," he said.

She just stood there looking down at it, finally up at him. She extended a hand and softly gripped his puny shoulder. Tears moved onto the dark circles under her eyes. She wanted to say thank you. But apart from not being able to find her voice, she didn't know the vocabulary.

"Okay! Okay!" exclaimed her Mountain of Radiance brother, "Five out of the donations bucket for you and yours! Now if you will excuse us!"

She said, "Please tell him we will repay him when we get to the ship ... Muchas Gracias, senor!"

She turned and signaled to Vetunsill who skipped over at once to join her. "Let's go, Zintopell!" she said, "We're catching a cab for the dock!"

Zintopell followed along in silence, having not encountered a soul she could talk to.

"There's a hotel up this street a little ways with a taxi stand," Prindibin said, "I don't know if five reais will get us to the ship, but maybe close enough to walk it." She had a feeling of power, having taken charge of the situation and extracted them out of it.

They went evenly-spaced in a line going up the street, which was a steep upgrade with steeper hills off to one side. Prindibin strode along in the lead, then came Vetunsill, and finally Zintopell. All three wore their outsized silver sequined sashes, and bouffant-style wigs on their bald heads. The rest of their clothing were identical, preppy-looking skirts and starched white blouses. This street would have seen a more surreal procession during Carnival, but only then.

A block of closed store fronts gave way to a more residential scene. Actively residential. Motor bikes zipped by, some with boom boxes blasting Portuguese hip hop – but no taxis.

The homes were built one atop another, going up the side of a slope. People sat on porches and stoops here and there, and no one missed the trio moving along the sidewalk. Bemused giggles and commentary filtered through the heat of the day. Children kicked soccer balls in the street, dodging traffic and shouting at one another.

"Okay, how much further, Prindibin?!" came a shout from the rear. Zintopell's voice was distinctive, and it sounded as if a mockery of it came floating down from the terraces. She felt like saying that since it was also her first time here, she wasn't sure how much further. She made no reply, but was somewhat concerned. The guy said it was up this street, and he gave her five reais after all, so he had to mean well. As she was pondering whether there could have been a loss in translation, her thoughts were shattered by a prolonged shriek.

"That little bastard squirted a hose at me!" Zintopell screamed. Prindibin turned to see a boy running across the street with a soaker squirt gun as Zintopell craned around to look past her sash to her bottom. Other kids gave out rowdy cheers.

"Okay, okay, let's just be cool and keep going please," said Prindibin.

She pried her eyes away from their forward fix, and saw ice cold stares coming down from the apartment houses. She smiled and nodded. Nothing.

The voice of a woman, much annoyed, cried out in Portuguese. Prindibin was horrified to hear Zintopell make some sort of snappy reply in Spanish. With a rictus smile bolted to her face, she muttered to Vetunsill, "Please ask our sister not to antagonize these people. Thank you!"

In response to the softly spoken request of Vetunsill, the voice of Zintopell, which carried, called out, "I am only wishing them blessings. That is all! Just sharing the love of Earnest Seamark with them. I did not travel thousands of miles to be silent. Not what we're here for."

Each step forward without incident had Prindibin sending up gratitude to God. She whispered "Believe Only" in sets of three. Children stopped chattering, grumblers on porches stopped grumbling, and there came something of the feel of a calm before a storm.

In the next half block ahead, she saw it, and her heart sank. A woman was standing on the opposite sidewalk dressed in such a way that she was either a hooker or someone who didn't care if you thought she was. Her focus was locked onto the approaching Adherents. Not only was she not smiling, she looked as though she had never smiled, except to watch something die. Her short shorts and halter top were jet black, and her neon lipstick was visible from thirty paces. Prindibin and her sisters of the Mountain continued their progress in her direction, with their sashes and bouffants sparkling in the sunshine.

The voice of the woman who had yelled at Zintopell sounded off again from down the block, and the woman ahead of them seemed to pick up on the statement, whatever it was. The final approach to the lady in black was excruciating. The street had emptied out, but for her.

Some dude in a sleeveless undershirt sat on stairs up above her. He rested his booted foot on a cement block. Apart from him, no one else was visible on the terraces.

Prindibin told herself that in a few minutes they would be in a taxi heading back, and that some things would be different from then on. She would be making the case that she was the one who handled a bad situation today, and she should be regarded as the senior Adherent of this Three. She silently stepped along past whoever this was glaring at her across the street.

So far so good. Except for her own footfalls, silence reigned.

Now Vetunsill would be passing her. Proceeding onward.

Peaceful seconds transpired. Their white, soft-soled nurses' shoes padded on the sidewalk.

An electronic sound popped and crackled, followed by, "... Zintopell to group leader! Come in group leader!" An explosion of static roared out into space-time, with the garbled words,

"... Go ahead, Zintopell!"

A staccato barrage of unknown words shot out at them from the woman across the street, much of it having the feel of profanity.

Zintopell addressed her walkie talkie, "Yes, group leader, we are *lost* on a side street here in *Rio!* We will be needing Honors in a transport to return us to Central! Over!"

Static roaring on both sides of the street now, as with hands on hips, the lady in black leaned forward to pelt them in abuse. The man above her laughed momentarily, then seemed to focus in with his full attention. His friend on the sidewalk had no use at all for the Three.

True to form, Zintopell was trying to address the Brazilian in Spanish, which was ratcheting up her outrage. Other furious female voices rang out from apartments on either side.

Partly because it seemed a good bit of reverse psychology, Prindibin waited on Zintopell to come to her, and spoke softly and gently, "Let's walk away. Come on. Let's not make it worse. Let it go and let's walk together."

They were in the process of doing so when an elderly woman and a teenage girl appeared on a low terrace. The old lady pointed a tremulous hand at the Adherents. The voice of group leader blasted out from the walkie talkie, and Prindibin said, "Let's mute that for now, please."

From somewhere a raspy voice broke out, "La hechicera!"

"Okay, did you hear that?" Zintopell asked, in irritation, "*That* was Spanish! Sorceress, they are saying."

"Let's keep moving."

She heard no men speaking, but there were more than enough women. A youthful-sounding voice came down from a nearby terrace, "... Cultista."

One more attempt in Spanish from Zintopell and then she was back on the walkie talkie, crying, as was Vetunsill. A Frisbee zipped over their heads. A soccer ball slammed down on the street next to where they stood. Looking back down the street, dozens of children were clustering up. One after another they threw plastic garbage, whistled, and jeered.

"Come on!" Prindibin said, and led the other two in a fast walk, "Just keep moving!"

The din of voices kept growing louder, horrifying and livid. A tin can clattered in a gutter. Soon Vetunsill shouted out, "Hey! That was a rock!"

The street made a curve and stretched out before them, with nothing resembling a hotel or taxi stand in sight. She was going to say again, "Just keep walking," but nothing came out.

A whooshing sound of thrown objects could be heard at intervals. Then came the crash of a glass bottle on the curb.

Zintopell let go a long scream, broke away, and began sprinting. Vetunsill took off in a different direction. Prindibin tried to catch up to her, but saw her dash around the corner of a brick apartment building. Incredibly, a louder gale of screaming followed, and when Prindibin cleared the corner, her eyes were met with the sight of

Zintopell sprawled on the ground, having tripped at just that moment over a little girl on a tricycle. The kid was flat on her back, too, scraped bloody on her chin, and shrieking with ear-splitting force.

A group of teenagers came piling out of the building and Prindibin ran as hard as she could make her legs go. Every muscle fiber of her body went into running for her life.

She clambered over a rusty chain link fence, to be pursued by a giant pit bull terrier. Back over the fence again, and she was propelling herself down an alley. Resolving not to look back, she just kept pouring it on, gasping for breath, executing a zig zag around old buildings.

Finding a regular street again, she went about a block before breaking left at an intersection, to be confronted by a military-style police vehicle with a burly UPP officer leaning against it, his foot propped back against a hubcap.

He lifted a hand, and beckoned with his index finger for her to come over.

Completely breathless, somehow still in possession of her sash and wig, Prindibin straggled over. He aimed his pointer finger at the curb, and she sat. Like a big game hunter standing casually by the lion he just shot, the stocky cop engaged in a chat on his radio. Several locals drifted over, holding up cell phones to record the bizarre, crestfallen, alien woman.

After the first couple of days in jail, three facts took shape in the mind of Prindibin. One, the food here was an improvement on what she had been getting. Two, she was able to get more sleep here. Lastly, it occurred to her that no American consulate was contacting her.

The charges against her were not specific. All she had been told was that a child had been injured. That would be the little girl on the trike that Zintopell had bowled over. She tried to get across the point that it was not her that had done it, but a Zintopell.

"Zin – To – Pell."

It soon became clear what the real problem was in her case. Her only ID was a passport in the possession of her group leader on the Mountain of the Water, and she didn't have so much as a phone number, or even a name for him, other than Murzwalladee. The idea of becoming separated from the group had never entered her mind. She was alone and undocumented.

An English-speaking UPP officer had spoken to her on her arrival. She told him the situation, that she was with the Church of the Mountain of Radiance, from the United States. He did not seem pleased by this. If he would just contact them, they would straighten all this out. She also asked him if he had found his place in the universe.

Being processed into the jail had been the most mentally disintegrating experience of her life. Rotund female jailers barked instructions in Portuguese. They were not so much mean as simply the most ice-cold people she had ever encountered, to include her superiors at Mountain of Radiance. Her wig, sash, tote bag and clothing had been confiscated. She was strip searched, cavity probed, and placed in a tepid shower. They were glad to see her bald head as they applied delousing powder. She was dressed in a bright yellow jumpsuit, given a banana and a peanut butter sandwich and parked in a communal cell with probably forty other women, some of whom seemed as if they would be entirely placid with homicide. An odor of bleachy mop water pervaded. There was one grimy toilet. Flies and mosquitoes landed on her. She could envisage no hope. She was about to vanish forever into the Brazilian prison system.

Nobody spoke her language. She kept saying, "Enguleeze? Enguleeze?" Vetunsill was nowhere to be seen, and she didn't care if she ever saw Zintopell again.

Then, there was someone from the church who visited, on the morning of the third day. She was sitting cross-legged in the holding cell, her back against the wall, eyes firmly closed, hands cupped to receive radiant gifts from the Mountain. She had no idea how many sets of three repetitions of Believe Only she had intoned. And there he was, facing her, eye-level with her, even though she sat on the floor.

The Beneficence. The Shebbevunseh. Earnest Seamark.

His wondrous, radiant face was perfect. His lips were moving rapidly under his lustrous white mustache. Though she could hear nothing, he was clearly pronouncing blessings upon her, in words of the Ascendant language, words of the Ummyashuntopudda.

She was rocking back and forth, eyes pressed tightly shut, fervently repeating "Thank you, Beneficence! Thank you, Shebbevunseh! Thank you, God of the Transfiguring Mountain!"

Rumbles of annoyance arose in Portuguese. She continued apace with the chants, and then saw with stupefying clarity the emergence of an additional figure, to the right of the Master. This one was a mere shape, like a four-pointed star from a Christmas card. It softly glowed in colors she had never seen on any chart of the spectrum. They were new colors. They seemed to transfer directly onto her visual cortex. She released an extended moan.

"Ayo! Cale-se!" someone bellowed indignantly.

She couldn't hear it, being agog with the visions taking shape before her. She groaned and gasped as a humanoid shape came into focus, standing on the left side of the Beneficence. It was skinny with a bulbous, bald head. Its indescribable face contained two massive black eye spots with a third, vertical eye on the forehead between them. This one had an iris and a perfectly round jet-black pupil that bore into her brain. Its tiny mouth made high speed pronouncements, in silence, but the experience of it being here delivered such profundity and wonder to Prindibin, she thought she might fall over and pass out. She was surely looking at an

Ellexataine, a being from another galaxy, millions of years in advance of humans, and now appearing with Earnest Seamark, in alliance with him and the Elemental who made them three. An interstitial celestial communion had been joined, all to help her in her hour of deepest peril.

Half sobbing, half laughing, Prindibin was making noises unlike that of anyone else in the cell. Presently she heard footsteps striding up on her right, and a sharp punch landed above her ear.

She toppled over, only to see the feet of a third woman now had been inserted between her and the person who struck her. These two inmates were raging at each other, swearing and declaring in livid, full-throated Portuguese. She sat back up against the wall.

The one who socked her released a growling denunciation, her bright red fingernail aimed down at Prindibin, before dramatically making her way back across the floor of the cell. The one who had stood up in her defense sat down next to her, and offered a cigarette that was already going and burnt down to its last inch. Prindibin considered refusing it, but then said "Gracias," and had a puff, her first in fifteen years. Only now was she noticing the absence of the supernatural entities who had seemed so solid a moment earlier.

Dressed in brilliant jailhouse yellow, like everyone else, the grim-faced Brazilian carefully retrieved the cigarette butt and took more draws from it. Presently she extended a powerful hand. "Diolinda," she said.

She blanked for a couple of seconds on what her name was, then she said, "... Prindibin." The woman nodded. It seemed like they might be close to the same age, but there was a hardened look to Diolinda, with many fine lines and cracks in her dry skin. Tobacco had stained her lips and teeth. In a voice that came across as disinterested, she said, "American?"

"Si! Do you speak English?"

"Un poco," said Diolinda, "Little." She waved a finger around as if trying to pin down some elusive point, "You got a ... religion? Or what?"

"Yes! Yes! I am an Adherent of Ernest Seamark! Church of the Mountain of Transfiguring Radiance!" She looked her right in the eyes and beamed a thrilled smile, her first one of any kind since after she stopped singing in that park, whenever that was.

The woman shook her head. Never heard of it. In her Rio accent she said, "So ... Protestant?"

She wasn't sure how to respond, and saw that she had rattled off too much high-speed English just then. She said, "No. Nuevo! Our church ... fifty years old!"

The Brazilian shook her head again, but this time there seemed to be a more sorrowful feel to it. She looked around the cell and said, "I think you be careful. While in here. Be careful. Get your American government get you out. Get American movie star get you out."

"I don't have my I.D." Prindibin whispered, with heartache, "No papers."

Diolinda thought for a moment, and said, "I tell you. Make sure one thing. You do exactly what they say. Just do what they tell you ... *exactly* what they tell you. OK?"

The joy at having someone to talk to was dashed as soon as it arose. She looked at Diolinda who stared out into space across the crowded cage, and said, "People die. Disappear. Maybe in your country people die held by police. It is more here. Lot, lot more." She turned her weathered face to drill into Prindibin's wincing eyes, "Officer want you, you go. You do it. Next day you live. You still alive. Stay living, to get out."

Prindibin was afraid she might start crying, but she snuffed it out within her. She said, "Thank you, Diolinda. Gracias, Diolinda." She closed her eyes. No apparitions this time. She was alone with

Diolinda, in this walled-off compartment of forty snarling and sighing women and girls.

She said, "I wish we spoke the same language. There is so much I want to tell you. I am grateful, happy, that you took the trouble to learn English. I guess it's a tough language."

Probably she didn't understand all of that, but maybe the gist of it got through. Her cellmate said, "We should write postal address. We get out, we send Christmas cards." She produced a pencil and a scrap of paper, which she tore in half. In big block letters she wrote out a post office box number in Rio.

When she took the pencil Prindibin got a sinking feeling. What address did she have? She had no idea where she could receive mail, next week or ever. She wanted to give her something. It was surprising at some level to watch her own hand writing out the address of Carolina Cattery, in Fayetteville, NC. At the top, in tiny letters, she added – Audrey Crane.

She handed it to her, saying, "I made two friends when I landed in Brazil, and now I have made a third."

The friendship was abruptly disconnected the next day. Day, night, no way to tell. At some point when she was sleeping Prindibin was awakened by the sharp voice of a guard, reading off names. Diolinda was called, and she stood.

"Remember what I say," said Diolinda.

She had no words, and they didn't speak many of the same anyway. Their resolute faces communicated well enough. "I will remember," Prindibin said.

Then, as part of a single-file line, her friend disappeared, and she was alone in a crowd again. Weeping might not look good here, and so she suppressed it.

Later, after a minimal lunch, she tried to meditate. Because she had written down that address, or for reasons unknown, images of Carolina Cattery came floating through her mind. She saw the old place distinctly. She would make her rounds of the pens, talking to mewling cats, looking for veterinary issues to report. Then the best part of the job, coffee klatching with the other volunteers. They solved the problems of the world. Jolly voices. Heartfelt comments. Silliness. Profundity. All of it was so day-to-day ordinary, but looking back on it now gave it the feeling of a rarified paradise.

Imagery of Fayetteville and elsewhere in North Carolina came unbidden to her mind's eye. Then came a full-body memory. She was riding on a man's shoulders, laughing like a mad woman. He was trotting right along and she bounced and bucked and held tight as she could to him. More than one such romp made it into her memories, in more than one setting. She was not supposed to engage in reminiscences of this person, and had been counseled more than a few times to block them out. She needed to work harder on it. Once she had ridden on his shoulders at a white sand beach, heading into the ocean. Another time was in a leaf-strewn park. She rode on him with some frequency, looking back on it. He also had a way of lifting her up off of sofas and beach towels as if she were so much Styrofoam.

It was not all physicality. He could hold his own in conversation as well, though he had made clear he was only now, over thirty years on, starting to put real energy into developing his intellectual life. He loved hers, and the worldview she had then. They could talk on a world of topics, and he always seemed so interested. Sometimes she would trowel it on a little thick, because he seemed to like it. He always kept up.

Sometimes they spoke about complexities of their relationship. It was so physical and sexual. But it was of the heart as well, and the intellect, too. The way they could shift gears was effortless and natural. They spent as much time discussing psychology, biology, history, novels, astronomy, styles of music, and classic films as they did in splintering bed frames in hotels across the Carolinas.

123

She recalled a breakfast conversation where she had made the offhand comment that human minds were as complex as galaxies. Maybe more so.

She added, "... And people in love are two galaxies rotating around each other, moving always closer." It seemed to strike such a chord in him. He told her about being wounded in the war; when shrapnel hit him, he was left lying helpless on his back, staring at the arc of the Milky Way. He had identified that moment as a great turning point of his life. For whatever reason, he found something powerful in her remark about people being like intricate galaxies.

He could also reveal a dark side. At the time, he had said, "I guess two rotating galaxies finally crash and annihilate one another."

She had had the presence of mind to say, "... Or they merge, and create a super-galaxy."

Within days he had given her a necklace, with two little silver galaxies. She declared it her most special, prized possession. Now it was in that box of jewelry, wherever that was.

Early in their dating, she recalled testing him. Needling him. She said he had an undistinguished face, like a mannequin. She said if she ever had to describe him to a police sketch artist she didn't know what she would say. He said only that he would never give her cause to describe him to a sketch artist. Then he said mannequins have to be at least a little bit good-looking. And he smiled for her. It was impossible to unnerve him.

The memories of him did keep on returning, when least expected. Probably because they were, so often, full body memories. But they would have to fade in time. She had a new body now. Hers was the new, ascended body of the radiance of the Eternal Field of Spherules.

On the sixth day, Prindibin was suddenly, summarily extracted from her cell and told she was being released. She was given her old skirt, blouse and shoes, and incredibly the sequined sash. No wig. She was led to the front gate and out into the sunshine with no explanation, dumped into the custody of a sour-faced man and woman who had plastic MOR collar tabs packed with insignia. A dirty white van was sitting there, with a glowering young man behind the wheel. Judging by his gray jacket, haircut, and overall visage, he was Honors. In the back window of the van, the weary, drawn face of Vetunsill peeped out at her.

Several blocks away from the jailhouse the van pulled over, and the two Adherents were separately removed and questioned by the driver and the other male MOR functionary as they stood on a dusty, gusty, trash-strewn roadside. These men repeatedly demanded to know if Prindibin had been raped in the jail. At first, she was pleased that her church cared so deeply about her well-being. But there was something in their tone. The questioning became accusatory. She saw that they were more interested in whether or not she had been rendered unclean for becoming a procreator for the faith – a Channel of Passage.

If she had been violated, a low-ranking husband might still be possible. But she would be rendered forever unfit for carrying the seed of someone of consequence. And that was the great hope the church had for any female Adherent. The message was made clear. Her uterus was church property. If she had allowed it to be contaminated, she was unsuitable for further ascendancy. They made it very clear that lying about this would be the worst possible course of action for her. Lies would be found out.

"So ... one last time ... *were you raped?*"

She stuck to her story, which happened to be the truth. No rape. The men jotted it down. Then they got blunt with her about how she was still in hot water, well apart from any future reproductive life. Her superiors would make no allowance for the fact that her

125

Three couldn't speak Portuguese. If they were strong in their faith, they would have had inter-dimensional interdiction, and a successful day. Any problem was their fault, and their spiritual weakness.

As they said it, "Don't blame God for the weakness of Prindibin!"

The reception was frigid on the ship as well. Nobody wanted to speak to her, and it turned out that while on the ship, she and Vetunsill were not allowed to speak to one another. Her immediate supervisor on Mountain of the Water, Murzwalladee, silently handed her a mop and a bucket. It spoke eloquently to her status for the remainder of their time at sea.

It struck her again how brand-new members of the church were loving and warm – mostly. But the farther up you went the more hard-hearted they got, until apparently there was a breakthrough point, very high in the order, beyond which everyone was a serene, advanced superhuman. Above them, it was all demi-gods and deities. Most likely it was set up that way by Earnest Seamark and God for a purpose.

Esocush would later agree with these observations. They were reunited with their old "den mother" back at the Macon, Georgia, Service Center, and had several tearful conversations with her right away. She said Prindibin's opinions about the other Adherents, while valid, must be kept absolutely confidential. Never speak negativity of any kind about any aspect of the church.

Esocush said she had put in a request for her and Vetunsill when she heard they were coming back. The name of Zintopell was no longer to be spoken. They would serve in solitary status for a time, but Esocush reassured them that after a while in "The Penalty Box" for their debacle in Brazil, they were sure to be placed in a newly-created Three, and continue their ascendancy as before. For now, work! Study! Recruit with street teams! And Believe Only.

That was exactly how the muggy June days unfolded.

One evening while ironing uniforms for Honors soldiers, Prindibin and Esocush chatted about their lives, and how things were surely getting better. At one point, Esocush made a comment about the "tab" that everyone was running here. It was something Prindibin had heard before, but wasn't clear about it, and thought it might have meant the collar tabs they all wore. Now she asked her bland-faced supervisor about this business of "running a tab" in the church. Surely it didn't mean being charged for things, on account?

Esocush smiled and said, "It's like it isn't even there. They just denote a little bit every week, based on things you do. I haven't even looked at mine in years. Don't see the point! They aren't going to demand it all at once. If you live at Home Base you get your room and board all taken care of. And, some day, when you pass on to the Mountain, you don't have to pay what's left on the account!"

Prindibin was set back a bit, and tried to process this. Later she asked the gentle woman, "How long have you been in the church, Esocush?"

She said she came in at the age of fourteen, when her parents joined, "I have given the church six children. Six fine Adherents. Or, anyway, they were healthy babies when I gave them over. Nine is the ideal number. Three times three. Nine babies to the church and you begin eternity two thirds the way up the Mountain. But I couldn't have any more babies." After a long time with only the sound of steam irons, Esocush said, "... I was Diane Beverly Callister. I was from Sacramento, California."

Silence returned, and many dozens of gray military trousers were processed. Mechanical movements allowed Prindibin a period of deep thought. It wasn't often she was assigned a task that granted her some time for thinking. She slowed down a little, to extend the thinking time, and found herself reviewing in her mind the good reasons why she was hanging on with all this, despite very real hardships.

She reviewed how much she had invested in it already. She had entered into the ultimate commitment of life that day in her whited-out bedroom. Abandon it? Never. She had to see it through. All that was unthinkable was failure. And the proof of the teachings had been laid out for her in Spherule alignments and Ascendant group sessions, all scientifically vindicated.

Another thing, she was getting feedback from her instructors that she was progressing mightily now in her studies of Umyashuntopudda. If she still didn't *feel* the progress, that may actually be a good sign, Esocush told her. It meant she was pushing herself hard toward excellence. She's not self-satisfied! She yearns for Ascendant Engulfment!

Another part of the situation was pure *fear*, though she would never use that word for it, even in private thoughts. She well understood that she had nowhere to go. The loved ones of her previous life all hated her now, at a visceral, animal level. Besides, if she ever left the church she would be cut off from alignment with the Great Field of Spherules. Both she and her guardian angel would be cast into an afterlife of perpetual quantum damnation. It was something about being devoured and defecated, and then devoured and defecated again, forever, by giant swimming things with crushing jaws that dwelt below the base of God's Great Mountain. It had been screamed at her once by a group leader, but she had been so shot through with terror and dazzlement at the time she couldn't take it in.

She rejected the idea of there being any intimidation in the presence of the Honors soldiers, and wasn't sure why such an idea had come to mind. Surely, they were only there to protect everyone from the many enemies of the church. They were her first line of personal defense.

She knew the feeling of uncertainty that would come over her at times, and hated that haunting sensation. But most of the time Prindibin was committed. Seeing the Beneficence and his allies appear before her in that jail in Rio, and then emerging from that place to regain her life, she felt reconstituted. She could imagine herself advancing in the faith now, and being a far, far better leader than any of these people who were ministering to her. No turning back. Brazil had been a disaster, yes. But that was history, or would be when they decided that she had been rehabilitated. Likely as not, the whole thing was just a test from God.

Her moment of introspection was shattered by a trumpet blast, the signal for an assembly. Only now did she remember that a celebrity speaker had been scheduled to address them today. Her superiors had seemed thrilled out of their minds when they announced it. But there were people speaking every week or so, always being given a big build-up.

She asked, "Am I allowed to attend the assembly?"

With a note of irritation, Esocush said, "Prindibin, you more than most of us, need to attend." She abandoned the laundry and sprinted for the assembly hall.

A crowd in white and gray MOR uniforms were gathering out front. They formed a line, orderly as always, and made their way into the same auditorium where Prindibin had first appeared on stage after her initiation.

Lights dimmed, and rapturous cheering accompanied a heavily decorated officer of God's Army of Eternal Honor as he ambled into a stationary spotlight. He stood in front of the podium, and raised a hand, instantly stifling the applause.

He spoke so loudly into his hand-held mic that it distorted the words, "I am Defense Marshall of the Range, Jordan Bissonell. Yusselleon, in the Ascendant ... Believe Only."

In two separate groups, one hundred and fifty men and women murmured in unison, "Believe Only, Yusselleon."

He continued, in a voice with more snarl than warmth, and a bit of an edge, as if he resented being made to address this bunch.

His feet were shoulder width apart and his right hand rested on a chrome-finish automatic pistol on his hip.

"Defense of the church is the first obligation of Adherency," he said, "And it would be, even if the church was NOT besieged on all sides by enemies. But enemies ... *enemies* of such monstrous evil that I will not describe it here ... stand hiding in wait for us at every turn. *Whenever* you are outside of church property, sharing the teachings with the downfallen, you are *in the cross-hairs!* Never forget it. They want us dead. They want us thwarted and humiliated, if not dead. They *hate* you for your Adherency, and their red-eyed hatred of Ernest Seamark and God motivates their every move."

A fearful quaking came over Prindibin as he went on a tear about how certain enemies of the church were in amongst us. As plants. As double agents. He seemed to be looking right at her, but she shook off the notion as he was too far away. He said, "We know you are out there. We're watching you. Don't ever get smug. Our vigilance will be triumphant in the end."

He fell silent for several seconds. Prindibin didn't understand. This guy wasn't even supposed to be the speaker, as she recalled. When the woman in front of her moved her head she could see he had retrieved his pistol, and pointed it up over the audience.

"God ... Triumphant ..." he said, and a concussion like the Earth cracking apart filled the auditorium. From a spot on the ceiling, plaster particles drifted down like heavy snowflakes.

The shock took a moment to overcome, then scattered applause and whistles popped up, and a wave of rowdy male voices rang out in celebratory cheers.

Yusselleon casually holstered his gun and spoke over their noise, "Protecting the church and all of you is the biggest part of the job for me and my men, but we are also honored to defend the lives of some of the greatest minds of our age. I mean men who are pillars of this faith. And one such man I am proud to introduce to you at this time ...

"Bergstrom D. Milantar is an author, a cleric in service, a philosopher, a warrior, an academic, and a bridge to Almighty God for the downfallen and downtrodden through Ummyashuntopudda. This incredible Deheshacom was in consultation with Herk N. R. Beyrhan during the years in which he wrote *Pristine Flagship of the Sciences!*" He paused for thirty seconds, allowing a full grasping of that.

"We are fortunate that our life paths have touched upon his! I proudly present, a Founding Professor Emeritus of the Earnest Seamark University of Advanced Learning, Boston, Massachusetts ... Bergstrom D. Milantar!!!"

A cacophony of acclaim erupted, sounding like far more people than what made it. Prindibin was all in, giving her full voice, hurting her vocal cords in celebration of this person she never heard of until now.

The flabby, balding man emerged from stage right. He moved at a stately pace toward the podium. Twice he stopped to raise a hand in recognition of the frenzy of the audience. The Honors officer, Yusselleon, was clapping his hands so hard and fast it had to be painful.

Milantar went to the edge of the stage, center, and made a gesture she had seen from one other speaker. He held up cupped hands, as if receiving divine treacle from the stars. Then, he thrust his palms out at the crowd, as though drenching them in – whatever it was. The people gasped in delight. Prindibin felt a wave of Spherules cascade over her, and her head rolled in a fleeting ecstasy, just like the other time it happened.

He made his way to the podium then, with the confidence that comes from slaying the audience before starting to speak.

"I have always had a special place in my heart for your Home Base. Ahhh, you can feel the spirit here, every time. The BBs. Wow. You can draw in the fragrance of God's Mountain."

Probably it was not the best analogy to use for this crowd where everyone saved precious minutes by skipping the shower. Prindibin was thinking of how pungent it was here, jammed in shoulder to shoulder like this, and then immediately got mad at herself for noticing. It was a sign of the strength and dedication of these Adherents.

"How about our Defense Marshall of the Range!?" he cried out, to great response, "He knows what time it is! Hey, not everybody on the street has back-up like what you got!"

The soldier was worshipfully celebrated for two or three minutes, with Milantar leading it. Prindibin wondered if the guy was going to fire off another shot into the ceiling or somewhere, when suddenly she saw the two men react with excitement to a vision they had spotted backstage. Unexpectedly, and with no introduction, Emzharotav ambled out, in a lime green IZOD LaCoste golf shirt and black slacks. He shook Milantar's hand amid frenzied cheering.

The Shebbovotan, Randolph Poleander, spoke only a few words of thanks, then gave the stage over to Milantar. He raised his hand for quiet, which he got, like shutting off a faucet. He and the Defense Marshall stepped backstage.

"Emzharotav. God, what a great man," Milantar began, "We have such men in our church. Men of strength. Men of will. The will of Earnest Seamark. The strength of God. We don't teach weakness here ... AND THAT IS WHY THE DOWNFALLEN HATE YOU!!!" He screamed it, startling everyone, "AND THEY DO HATE YOU!!! THEY HATE YOUR GU-U-U-UTS!!!"

He instantly calmed down and said that outreach to the downfallen was the most important part of their lives. Then he shouted, "But you can feel their hate when you first start talking to them! As soon as they hear what it's all about, that's when the hate starts flowing. You know what I'm talking about!"

"They hate you because deep down inside, in their heart of hearts, they know you are ahead of them. You are ascendant of them. You are, essentially, *better* than them. And although you are offering them what they need more than anything else, they are going to hate and spite you for it. That is the way of the downfallen. They are dying of thirst, and they will not sip from the overflowing fountain you offer. Such is their nature."

"It's okay to feel some pity for them. Hey, you were once like that, ya know?! Before the light of the Mountain reached your brain, you were one of those shambling meat machines. Just always remember, bringing downfallen up to Adherency is the prime, number one mission of your existence. We must win them. So, NEVER apologize for your faith! Never show anything but proud confidence to those empty shells. They are more than willing to run down your church all on their own, without you helping!"

Slowly turning his head, it was as if he were making eye contact with everyone here. Or at least all of the men.

"And what do you really have to do? You just have to run your mouth a little! Because let me tell you, a percentage of them are NOT hopeless. Just as you were, they are yearning for the guidance of Beneficence. They only need to have it awakened within them! But you can't tell at a glance which are hopeless and which will make fine Adherents. You have to talk to everybody. So do it! And every morning when you rise, I want you to stop and bow your head and thank the living God inside of you for showing your life to you! Don't resist Him for a second! *Be* his sock puppet, with his timeless hand providing your talk and movement and personhood."

It was warm in here. No air conditioning. Only a few fans. She knew he must be sweating in the spotlight.

"Aside from the basic hateful nature of the downfallen, there is another problem with them," he said, "This so-called free society we live in has hardened their hearts. They are bombarded with sales pitches all day. Then here you come! They have probably been pestered by Jehovah's Witnesses and Hari Krishnas and Christians and who knows what. They won't want to hear from you. Oh listen,

133

let me tell ya, this country has a terrible problem with cults. Must be hundreds of them. The cult problem is an underestimated stumbling block for mankind. But you have the solution, the one great hope, right there in your tote bag. And that is the radiant word of Earnest Seamark, as revealed to all mankind in Ummyashuntopudda."

"Now, the downfallen will want their 'science,' of course. Just remember, your church defines what that word means. *Proper* science supports Mountain of Radiance teachings. When I was working on Pristine Flagship ..." he paused for scattered applause, "... we learned that science is like a tree or bush that grows and progresses and branches out. But like a bush or a tree, it can be trimmed back. As needed. Everything is subordinate to God, even knowledge. Especially knowledge! Otherwise, what's it good for?"

As if to give an example of knowledge, he launched into an extended exploration of the interlocking interstitiality of Ascendant Physics, and its applications to human spiritual psychology. Prindibin began to feel a lack of blood flow in the soles of her feet. Her knees, as well. Then there was the situation with her back. She had been on her feet all day. All day every day, for that matter.

This concrete slab floor was taking shape as a monster assaulting her body. She recalled with sudden horror that the other speaker she attended here spoke for four and a half hours. She didn't remember his name, only that he was extremely elderly, and had a voice that mixed droning with mumbling. And his subject had been: The Shebbevunseh, Understanding Why He is of Critical Importance to Your Life. And he spoke for four and one-half hours.

She closed her eyes and her head rolled slightly in the river of words passing over her. Don't lock your knees, she thought. Soon she was whispering Believe Only, in sets of three, in sets of three, in sets of three.

Later that afternoon, how much later she couldn't say, his voice took a turn. He was suddenly intense, and doing some yelling again.

"Do not let so-called 'evidence' determine your experience of God! Let your experience of God determine your judgement of the evidence!"

The audience lit up in response as the subject matter shifted from ethereal cosmic to nitty-gritty spiritual existentialism. He wanted it made clear that people who failed or quit the church faced unspeakable eternal destruction in an afterlife below the base of the Mountain.

Off Mountain, it was called.

"They came so far!" he shouted, his voice breaking, "They spent years working with the teachings, bringing in the downfallen, building a life! Then, they, they ... lose everything!"

He meant that some Adherents join the downfallen, through sheer negligence, weakness, and worthlessness. Prindibin wondered why there were so many sermons about the horrors of people leaving the church, or backsliders lapsing into unbelief, when everybody always seemed so frantically gung-ho about everything.

"They forget that the Mountain is real!" he screamed, "But IT IS REAL! And they go rolling and falling, bouncing and tumbling down its lower slopes! By the millions! The hundreds of millions! BILLIONS of them! Rolling in hopeless disaster! Spilling over one another in their hundreds and hundreds of millions! Falling and falling! Like an avalanche of bodies, down, down the slope! *Over the precipice!!!*"

He looked out into space above the heads of the assembly with a wide-eyed face like a dying man, and he let out an extended scream that silenced everyone. His arm shot out in front of him to point to someplace above them. Maybe he was actually seeing it. The man was said to be a visionary.

He wasn't done with the damned. They had fallen off the Mountain, but now came the bad news. Enormous, unspeakable beasts "swam" down there.

"Leviathans!!! They ... I ... I cannot say it ..." He clasped his hands over his eyes, and blurted out, "They are not true LIFE! They have departed from ... LIGHT!"

Sobbing filled the muggy air in the auditorium. "They are the unnamed!" he bellowed, "They engulf the multitudes in their maws and they grind and destroy with heavy, heavy jaws. They devour."

He fell silent for a long time, staring at the floor. Ultimately, he said, hollowly, "... They devour."

Soon he was weeping brokenly, sprawled across the lectern, spitting out something about monsters defecating the downfallen out to be devoured anew by lower monsters, and so on for eternity.

"Only the Beneficence stands in the way of it. *Only* that one figure. Earnest Seamark." He stared straight up at the ceiling, trembling, until he croaked out, "Thank you, Shebbevunseh! THANK YOU, MY BENEFICENCE!!!"

The audience fell right in, giving repeated thanks to that one man, the founder of it all.

The speaker's weepy breakdown about the heavy-jawed leviathans at the base of the cosmic mountain was a performance reminiscent of one she had seen on a Broadway stage. It was also one that worked, and worked brilliantly, in the case of Prindibin.

For so long she had been looking only at the other people around her. This speaker got her looking *up*. She had been nursing all kinds of resentments and questions. But not now. Not anymore. At this moment, this speaker awakened her as never before, to see that her Adherency to Mountain of Radiance was the only important part of her existence in the three-dimensional quiddity. She screamed her gratitude to the Beneficence with a force that shook her body.

O   O   O

Budget Suites, Fayetteville, NC. In the smallest unit they had, a budget suite within Budget Suites, Matthias Pleasant sat saving money.

He could have saved even more staying with his parents - and brothers - in the trailer. But his mental health was as marginal these days as he had ever known it to be, so this was better. Had the poisoning of Audrey's mind contaminated his own by extension? He pondered it as he took a break between phone calls. The inactivity of this downtime had its own challenges for his psyche. The doldrums. His only option was to keep busy and push through it.

He snatched up the phone and soon plunged into a contentious call with a rep from a facial recognition detective agency. He hired them over a month ago, and they had spent the time scanning crowds at MOR events around the Southeast. Their technology dazzled him. Working from a photograph it could spot a specific face from a crowd of thousands while being carried around discretely by individual operators.

They had come up empty.

"I'm cutting back on the service ... That's right. Coffers are running dry at the House of Pleasant."

The salesman tried to defend the lack of results, "I think we have determined something. She was not at any events held by this church or ... uhhh ... group, in this part of the country in the past five weeks. If she showed her face at any of them we would have spotted her. So that tells us something. Unless she has been swapped off to another US territory of the organization, which you said was unlikely, then she's probably not in the United States at all."

Matt gave a testy reply, "As it turns out, I am not able to have you scan all of planet Earth for her. We had you working the most likely locales, and you got nothing."

"It makes it tough for us when you can't focus the search any better," said the rep.

He could have gotten obnoxious with the guy; it would have felt good to blow off a little spleen. But he couldn't, because what the man said was the crux of the matter, and maybe the downfall of any attempt to ever find Audrey. This so-called church was a black box of secrecy, they operated in multiple countries, and were known to randomly shuffle their people around on the whim of some Great Pumpkin. She wasn't in the territory where she had been recruited. In point of fact, Audrey Crane could be anywhere in the world.

He had known going in that it might play out this way, but had charged forward anyway. Now, chastened by the situation, he adopted a more businesslike tone, and informed the rep of two events coming up. First was a festival in Alabama, but then came the big one, the Fiftieth Anniversary All Worlds Convocation at Trailblazer Bank Stadium, in the California wine country, over near to where Earnest had walked out of the ocean. He would spring for their facial recognition service at that one. He and his Go Team will work on their own at the thing outside of Montgomery, Alabama. They arranged to fax new contracts, and he ended the call.

Even cutting back on the detective service, it still came to a brutal financial bite. Matt had some savings, and some free time. He was resourceful, and in top physical condition. But even he was struggling at his limits. How in hell would an average family deal with something like this? How would a low-income family deal with it? They wouldn't. The cults would just win, again, in the Land of the Free.

An email had arrived this morning from Yvonne Crane, and for the fifth time he read it. She had received a letter from a guy Audrey had been dating four years ago. This dude had subsequently ended up in Mountain of Radiance, he said, in writing, to Yvonne. It had been required of him to draw up a list of names of people he felt would be ideal prospects for recruitment into the faith. He had immediately thought of his ex, Audrey. He had gone for extra brownie points by telling them about the gemstone collection she owned.

This individual had broken away from Big Church, and now wanted to confess to the Crane family what he had done. The cult had asked him follow-up questions about Audrey. They were clearly interested. Now he was hoping he had not done a bad thing, and that Audrey was okay.

Yvonne ended the email by saying that it really doesn't change anything, but at least some of the mystery of how Audrey got targeted in the beginning had been resolved.

Matt was pleased by how quickly he had dispensed with fantasies of manually strangling this man. He was growing in his knowledge of cult tactics and depredations. It was pointless to blame Audrey, or now this old boyfriend of hers, for what happened. The blame can fall where it deserves to fall, higher up, but only when the time comes. Until Audrey was found, and at least offered help for regaining her life, blame games were irrelevant.

His eyes fell on the framed photographs on his desk. Some carried memories of "the 'Stan," others were all Audrey. Not a day had passed since she disappeared that he hadn't thought of her. He wondered how many years of such days might await him.

Next to the little display of his Purple Heart, a languid image of her gazed out at him from a frame. George Washington on the medal seemed to be regarding her. The photo had been snapped shortly after they had made love the last time, which was the last time he had had sex with anyone, other than himself. How long had it been?

His thoughts drifted to a local singles bar, among the other things it was called. The club was not far from here. He had patrolled it with his fellow MPs looking for soldiers getting out of line. Prior to meeting Audrey, he had patrolled it off duty, looking for something else. The women there were after the same thing. Matt would do his push-ups show for them.

Asking a group of rowdy ladies to please do him a favor and keep count for him, he would go into the push-ups. Sometimes he would do them on the bar, depending on the bartender. After an impressive enough series, which he could judge by their laughter and vocals, he would stop and say he really preferred chin-ups. On spotting the most likely-looking prospect, he would ask her how many chin-ups she could do. Whatever she said, he would say, "Here, let me help you. Just hold onto my arm." Then, as she gripped his outstretched arm, he would brace himself on the bar and lift her just barely off the ground, once, twice, and three times. In many cases, with some follow-up conversation, she or one of her friends would be up for leaving with him. He never went with anyone he deemed excessively drunk or mentally ill, and he considered himself a good judge of both conditions.

In his mind he traced the route from here to that club. He looked at the clock. Then he glanced back to the photos of Audrey.

It took several minutes of thought until he arrived at the idea that the club would still be there if he decided it had come down to that. As of yet, it had not. He put on one of Audrey's jazz CDs to kill the silence.

It was good that the war photos didn't outnumber those of his loved one. It was close, though. Too many were of snow-glazed, gleaming mountain landscapes, and too few showed friends who had changed his life. One group shot of MPs showed Terrence Hyer, now with the FBI, with whom he had reconnected over the internet recently.

"Might have a hot tip for you later this year, Terry," he had said.

You never know who you will encounter in the cross-section of the population that was the Army. Some of the guys in these photos were among those who first got Matthias thinking, and reading, and beginning the process of intellectual advancement that he later planned to continue with his new wife. In an ethereal jazz piano piece by Bill Evans, he closed his eyes. For him, trying to meditate usually led only to a review of old, bad memories.

Of the combat he had been through, so much was at long distance, firing into rocky crevices and rough terrain where you may or may not ever know the results. Roadside bombs were a big dread, and he had driven in plenty of convoys where they were a factor. Once he was at the wheel of the lead vehicle and felt an intuition about a half-flattened cardboard box that sat alongside the route. He had the entire procession come to a stop while he leaned out the window and fired a single shot into it, which created a fireball the size of a parade balloon.

One incident had been the most up-close-and-personal. Easily so. It involved a Taliban fighter who had been separated from his cohorts. Matt would always believe it happened because the guy had fallen asleep.

There had been this quiet period after a long firefight in some abandoned housing on the edge of Kabul. As the sun rose, Matt was walking around the corner of a house and the bearded young dude came flying out of a side door, not fifteen feet away. His gear was all over the place and his gun was in hand but not at the ready. They made eye contact. What Matt saw was someone who had just woken up and found himself alone in a war zone. He had tried to raise his weapon but Matt's was already there, and an arc of five holes appeared in his chest in a matter of about a second and a half.

He had not intended telling Audrey about that one, but it came spilling out one morning while they were talking in bed. He was going to say something about how it was "him or me." She was more interested in hearing about how it might still be affecting him, so he tried to talk honestly about how he felt about it, which still ultimately circled back to it being him or me. He talked for several minutes, as he recalled. Audrey mostly listened. She concluded it by saying, "At least for you it wasn't just a video game."

He had told her earlier about the video game mentality that he saw in so many soldiers, which did not sit well with him, especially when he contemplated what these robotic shooters could be like back home after the war. He had a clear memory of the chirpy, twerpy voice of one of them saying, "Five points for Pleasant," as they gathered around his kill.

The frame that held his Purple Heart was next to the photo of Audrey because the two had a certain link. The medal had come his way after he survived a piece of shrapnel zipping through his left armpit, in the one square inch of his body that was not armored. It had happened during a raid one night on a bomb-making factory in the countryside. Bombs were definitely going off, as were guns, and something or other went in and through the flesh under Matt's arm. He registered no pain, but he was spun around a third of a turn and pulled backward by his heavy pack. Like an up-ended turtle, he was left gazing at the mottled arc of the Milky Way on a cloudless, moonless, freezing night.

His mind was on the way to unconsciousness. But for the briefest moment he found himself understanding that he was looking at both life and death in that star field. Both at once. Life came from stars. We are made of stars. But there is no living out there. No air. No warmth. Pressures to blow you apart. Death only, where life comes from. He chuckled to himself, and then he was laughing, there on his back. The guy who heard him and dragged him to safety said it was insane laughter. Matt didn't remember how it sounded, just that he was laughing and couldn't stop. The inexplicable laughter had saved his life, because they said he had lost so much blood he would not have been laughing long.

It flashed back to him when Audrey said what she said about the two of them being like two galaxies, orbiting each other, drawing closer. When he was at a flea market and saw the silver necklace with the two hurricanes or fireworks or whatever spirals they were supposed to be, it had practically jumped into his hand.

And there it was in the photograph, the two spirals centered just below Audrey's throat. He wondered if she might be wearing it right now.

Probably not.

He took up his phone again.

Charlie Bienville never claimed to be an expert on mind control, but he knew of people who were, and referred him to them for phone consulting.

It was something of a relief when this call went to voicemail. Suddenly, he was not feeling up to talking to a stranger about exiting his fiancée from her cult, and the aftermath thereof. The various specialists he had spoken to so far had all broken his heart by telling him she would need extensive, long-term psychiatric care when and if she ever climbs out of something like Mountain of Radiance. More than one of the experts had mentioned the dreaded abbreviation, PTSD, which Matt had seen so much of in fellow soldiers.

He had also read about it, extensively. Post Traumatic Stress Disorder was ancient. It didn't always have that clinical name. In World War II they called it Combat Fatigue. In the "Great War" it was Shell Shock. Then, going back to the Civil War was the name that struck Matthias with the most feelings of cynicism and poignancy – Soldier's Heart.

He never thought he might have it himself. Not until some of his times with Audrey, when she seemed to relieve a hurt that he didn't even know he was carrying.

For him it was like a jagged labyrinth of hyper-alertness that his thoughts had to make their way through from time to time. But it faded in her presence. It had been part of him for so long he had become accustomed to it, until it became conspicuous by its absence. It had less importance when she was there. His way of dealing with it had always been through crass humor and rude jokes – not unknown in the military. But Audrey was not used to hearing it.

Once on a park bench he told her a supposedly funny story about the Battle of Bunker Hill.

"... So, an amazing thing happened during that battle, you know. This officer shouted an order at the top of his lungs, and a bullet zipped right between his upper and lower teeth without chipping a single one. Passed right through!"

Audrey said, "What a miracle, huh?"

"Well, no," he said, "It didn't pass from side to side. It went straight in. Blew the back of his neck away. But it didn't chip any teeth!"

He put a big wacky grin on his face. But Audrey wasn't buying it. She said nothing, but in time her searching expression found one of the same in him. She held open her arms, and Matt went in for the clench, his muscles seizing up all around her. He might have hurt her. She stroked the lone lock of hair on top of his head. He relaxed. She kissed him softly under his eye. And then, with what seemed like the greatest wisdom and insight – she *let it go*.

She didn't belabor the moment at all. It was left there, on that park bench, and in the memories of Matthias.

Apart from his love for her, which may have been the first one of his life, Matthias felt that he "owed Audrey one," for her help with his readjustment to civilian life. Even though he had been stationed at softer duty stations after his injuries, ultimately here at home, he had the war rotating in his head more than he ever let on, even to himself. Always saying how fortunate he was to be free from PTSD, he never saw how it wasn't entirely so, until his days with Audrey.

The next time the Reverend Moultrie or old Bienville tried to find out if he was still committed to all this, still really intent on going through with what it would take to find her and bring her home, he planned to reply, "She would have done it for me."

Bienville always maintained a list of the upcoming public functions of Church of the Mountain of Radiance. For the past month Matt had been attending small workshops and lectures they held around the Southeast. The next major event was to be at a fairground outside of Prattville, Alabama.

He called Charlie, to go over details of getting out there with his "Go Team" and scoping it out. The unmistakable voice that answered said he was delighted to hear from Matt; he had all the information they would need. He insisted on going with them. Although he was a known quantity to the security apparatus of the cult, he would color his normally snow-white beard and put on some hippie-style clothes he had.

"From back in the day?" asked Matt.

"This outfit is a lot more over-the-top than I ever got back in the day. This one is worthy of Doctor John the Night Tripper. It's called hiding in plain sight ... I've done it before."

Matt wasn't thrilled at the idea of hauling the massively obese Bienville along with them on a road trip in his worn-out Volkswagen Jetta. Craig Moultrie was coming too. Deidra had told him she and Blaine would drive it in their Ford Focus. That was the only thing making it doable.

With the calendar marked and the details jotted down, Matt determined to spend as much of his downtime as possible studying up on anything that might be relevant to the situation. Anything that might be helpful later, he wanted to know. Charles had supplied him with a box of articles in three-ring binders.

He reviewed a piece on the Asche Conformity Test, where 65% of test subjects conformed to a staged scenario which they were told was an optical experiment, but was really a psychological one. A group of people seated around a test subject would repeatedly declare that a line on a chart was the same length as three other lines. It wasn't. It clearly wasn't. But better than six in ten caved in to the pack and said it was. No mind control regimen was used on them; *none at all.* This was entirely peer pressure and group-think.

65% was also the number that went along with the Milgram Shock Test. Subjects thought they were inflicting electric shocks on other subjects to train them to remember data. The shocks weren't real, but the screams of their fellow human beings were. Rather than walking out, these American citizens applied what they thought were increasingly painful electro-shocks, because some bland authority figure in a white lab coat kept telling them to do so.

In a bright orange binder labeled "Examples" he saw case histories of mind control cults, with the worst being grouped in a section in the back. Heaven's Gate: thirty-nine dead in ritual mass suicide. Order of the Solar Temple: seventy-five dead in ritual mass suicide. Movement for the Restoration of the Ten Commandments of God: five hundred and forty followers died after being locked in a church house that was deliberately set on fire; the death toll rose to nearly eight hundred following the discovery of mass graves in the countryside. Aum Shinrikyo, who attacked the Tokyo subway with nerve gas in 1995, were found by Japanese police to have a compound stacked up with high explosives, chemical weapons, a Russian Mi-17 military helicopter, laboratories for manufacturing LSD and methamphetamines, a safe with millions of dollars in cash and gold, cages containing live prisoners, and enough sarin nerve gas to kill four million people. Jonestown, 913 dead in the worst one-day loss of American civilian life until the 9-11 attacks, which were also perpetrated by a religious cult.

Church of the Mountain of Radiance was in the section second to last. What great news. Audrey wasn't in Bienville's rock-bottom worst! Only second to worst. Matt pored over print-outs on MOR, and the mafia-like structure of the organization, with its commission of nine bosses-of-bosses at the top, thought to be in control of burnt-out, figurehead leader, Earnest Seamark. The report stated that while no actual murders had been proven within the group, disappearances had happened suggestive of homicide. No bodies found.

Dozens of front groups were running all kinds of gross malfeasance. Child labor. Child abuse. Elder abuse. Coercive intimidation and psychological abuse of basically the entire membership. False imprisonments. Stunning financial frauds ... Mountain of Radiance was perpetrating life-wrecking horrors on an industrial scale at an international level. Matt sat reading, and reeling, thinking that the government he risked his life to fight for would do exactly *nothing* about these people, except to grant their monstrous enterprises a tax-exempt status.

The afternoon was slipping away. Another day, passing away. He glumly decided to read a few chapters of Bienville's book, then take a break and do a hundred pushups, run five miles, and take a bath before he went out to dinner. His fugue was interrupted when a black stretch limousine rolled to a stop outside his window.

Nobody else had a room down on this end. Whoever it was, they were here for Mr. Pleasant.

He sat motionless and watched through the sheer curtain as a young woman in a chauffeur uniform came sprinting around the front of the car and knocked sharply on his door.

"Mr. Matthias Pleasant?" she asked, with a bright, chipper smile.

He looked to see she wasn't holding anything, and nodded.

"Ms. Della Crane would like a quick word with you. It won't take long ... Right here."

He was glad he had some clothes on, not that he would look any better than most vagrants. He made his way to the rear door, which the driver opened. On climbing inside he found himself opposite Audrey's older sister, Della. Her mode of dress was all-business expensive. The driver eased the door closed and remained standing by as raindrops appeared on the window.

He was mildly stunned by this visitation. He had not seen or heard from this lady since the day Audrey disappeared, and only on rare occasions prior to that. He knew much more about the younger sister, Yvonne, very little about this one, except that she was some sort of a businesswoman.

She began in a blunt tone as soon as he was settled in, "I was in Fayetteville to visit my mother, who continues to improve ..."

"Yeah. I visited her not long ago," Matt said.

"I heard," said Della, "I'm not apologizing for my statements that night in April, but I have done a bit of research, and I am seeing things a little differently now, so let's leave it at that." Her cell phone rang and she looked at it and turned it off. She said, "I have re-evaluated some things, including you. I can see your sincerity in wanting to help Audrey. So ... that's good. I have also come around to seeing that Audrey was conned into whatever this is. She was not acting entirely of her own will."

Matt sat nodding his head. He had the talent of knowing when listening was the better way. She dug into her purse and tossed a business card into his lap. Next, she drew out a folded slip of paper, which he immediately eye-balled as a check.

"We'll keep in touch," she said, flatly, "Keep me posted on your progress. The email address there is best for reaching me." She leaned forward into the spacious area between them and thrust the note at him. He didn't examine it but tucked it into his shirt pocket, and said, "Thanks, Della. I will keep you apprised on developments."

The driver seemed to telepathically get it that the meeting was over, and pulled the door open. Della said "Good luck" as he climbed out, and the driver closed the door and dashed back to her steering wheel.

Della Crane's limo crept forward, turned out of the parking lot and disappeared down the street. She left him standing in a drizzle with a check for twenty-five thousand dollars.

Doldrums were concluded. Matthias Pleasant was back in business.

The next morning over breakfast he spotted a sharp customized van in the Auto Trader that looked to be an ideal mobile office and camper. The lady who owned it told him it had belonged to her ex-husband and she just wanted to be rid of it. Raising a carport door revealed a heavily modified, burgundy Chevy van. She said it had always reminded her of the van in the Scooby Doo cartoons. Matt muttered, grimly, "The Mystery Machine."

He had to smile when he lifted the hood. It was immaculate, throughout. Gas mileage would be the only downside, but it would be capable of transporting five people in comfort.

Sold.

At 4 am on the appointed day, the "Go Team" took turns driving it to Alabama. Seven and a half hours, one way, loomed before Matthias, DeeDee, Blaine, Craig Moultrie, and the weighty Charles Bienville, who could not be dissuaded from making the trip despite his unsteady health.

As the sun began illuminating the Carolina countryside, DeeDee called back to him in the wide seat at the rear of the van, the only place that could comfortably accommodate him.

"How ya doin', Charlie?"

She asked what he thought they might encounter as they worked the crowd at this festival. Apart from trying to spot Audrey and noting general impressions, which was all she had been asked to do, what else might be happening?

"The main thing to remember is that the group has a face for public consumption and an entirely different one for back at the compound behind closed doors. What you will be hearing today is whatever they think you want to hear. And at this one they will have their front group for recruiting Christians. 'Jesus Pointing the Way.'"

Dee and Blaine looked to each other with some amusement, more from the old man's regal tonations than anything. She said, "So, go with the flow, talk to them, and learn what we can."

"That's it. And don't leave with anyone," Charlie said.

Matt was intending to do most of the driving. He was still at the wheel when Blaine and DeeDee began a wide-ranging conversation with the Reverend Moultrie. His teeth went on edge a little as he heard the discussion move from the Greek philosopher Seneca to a big wrangle about religion. Secular humanist Blaine wanted to know "why" you believe in the supernatural. Not so much the ethical teachings – the supernatural stuff. It perturbed Matt a bit, only as he didn't want any quarrelling getting in the way of the operation. Not that the tone was disrespectful, but Blaine had a way of coming to the point that could get a little blunt. Craig was being paid for his time here, but not much.

Moultrie said he just had a feeling about it in his heart. It's not entirely an intellectual thing. He felt the presence of God.

Blaine said that, according to the doctrine, Moultrie would not be permitted to have an intellectual reason anyway. Or it would be irrelevant if he did, as that wouldn't be taking it on faith. Debates about reasons and rationales are beside the point. You aren't supposed to have a reason. You aren't supposed to weigh evidence. That would make you a Doubting Thomas. You are just supposed to hear it preached, believe it, and make it the center of your life. On faith.

Deidra backed him up, "That's what I hear most often from people!"

Moultrie said that was the fundamentalist approach, which he didn't hold with, but anyway, faith is not a hard intellectual experience. To him it was more of a transcendent state of mind, which involved some reason and some emotion, which is hard to describe, but when it's a peak experience it is quite beautiful and fulfilling.

Blaine said if it was for real it wouldn't have so many intellectual problems. Too much of it just doesn't make sense. If it was truth, it would be more than a good feeling. It would make sense consistently.

Moultrie said placidly that he works with people in his congregation to get them into more fulfilling lives, and without their church community many of these people would be quite isolated. It is simply all that they know. They carry on the way of life as best they can. It is a tradition that goes back more generations than he could guess.

Matthias had had this talk with Blaine and Dee in past get-togethers, and he knew that when the subject of the antiquity of religion came up, Blaine would make the point that in the Good Old Days, if you weren't enthusiastic about the local religion, you got a visit from the King's men. Those were the guys with the lances.

Heretics were burned.

Maybe he was going to say something like that now, but DeeDee spoke up, and said she had a theory on it all, "... For the sake of argument, say that the mind comes in three parts. The rational, the non-rational, and the irrational. The irrational is pathological. Mental illness. Everybody has some of that, because there's no perfect mind. The *non*-rational mind is different. It's healthy. You need it. It evolved. But it is very different from the rational, analytical mind. It is the area where you get creativity, dreams, emotions, fantasies and imagination."

"The unconscious mind," said Blaine.

Dee said, "Part of it is unconscious. And it's probably a much older development of the brain, closer to the animal world. Well, that's where religion comes from! Seems obvious to me. It is a transcendent state, with visions and passions and the whole package. But it is part of the mind, not outside of it in a spirit world. Everyone has it, even though religions themselves vary from one place to the next. The root of religion is universal – the non-rational mind, which every person has."

Moultrie said, "So, atheists can say religion is all in the mind, and theists can say the mind has a component that lets you experience the Divine."

The three of them seemed to take some amusement from that, which came as a relief for Matt, who was not up for any hassling whatsoever during this trip. Looking back, he could see Charles gazing out the window, stroking his white beard like some Renaissance painting of God.

At the next rest stop they pulled over, even as idling eighteen-wheelers monopolized the parking. Everyone piled out, and Matt stopped Craig and held him back for a second.

"I just wanted to say that I hope you weren't peeved or annoyed or anything by that little debate back there. Blaine has never hesitated to speak his mind, as far as I know."

"I've been through worse!" said Craig, "He's young! He should speak his mind. They're both great kids. I can tell."

When Blaine returned from the restroom, Matt asked him, "So are you still highly suspicious of Moultrie?"

"Him? No, he's okay. We were talking just now at the vending machines. I think he's a humanist, just from a Christian tradition."

A couple of hours later, with DeeDee at the wheel, a pop-up thunderstorm like none he had ever seen threatened the van. It was the first time he had seen walls of rain so heavy people were turning on their emergency flashers as they drove, and some were pulling over. It was only early evening, but the sun was gone.

He sat across from his sister, and would have been advising her, but there was nothing to say. Water standing at a certain stretch of road made for a grim passage. He would have insisted she stop and not attempt to pass through, if only he had seen it coming. But it had risen up all around, all at once, and suddenly they were in it.

He heard water slapping on the underside of the van like the palm of a giant hand. It was all the more audible as he was hearing nothing, not a word, from any of them. To himself, Matt thought only how glad he was that DeeDee and Blaine weren't out in a little economy car in this. He was glad that if they were fated to be here, all of them were together in a vehicle with higher clearance, and he was with them to do what he could if it came down to disaster.

She inched forward, until, with excruciating slowness, they attained higher ground. It really started raining then. But within minutes the pop-up storm was gone as suddenly as it appeared.

Originally, he had the idea of not getting motel rooms. Just drive straight back after the event. Matthias might have done so if he were on his own, but the others wouldn't be up for that. Outside of Montgomery he pulled into a no-name lodge that didn't look too gruesome.

In his cigarette-smelly room, late into the night, Matt sat poring over books and articles about MOR, bent on learning as much as he could. He was particularly intrigued by their paramilitary wing. How had he never heard of this thing prior to it grabbing his fiancée?

Around dawn, he was knocking on Charlie's door, and stood blank-faced for a moment when he opened it. Matt held up a print-out, and stammered, "You mean ... these freaks want a nuclear weapon?"

Charles said, "They would like to have one. Very much. They don't, as of yet. But, yeah ... maybe a real 'mountain of radiance' someday, huh?" Matt raised a hand to his forehead. Charles said, "C'mon in. I'm making coffee."

At 9 am sharp the van came to rest in a parking lot of many acres by a boarded-up strip mall not far from the fairgrounds. The plan was to walk over separately and mill around for a few hours, meet back and compare notes. Possibly they would go at it again until the thing shut down at sunset.

Charles needed some time to get into his costume, he said, and would make his way over with Craig at his own pace. They were to listen for the name Prindibin, but never *ask* anyone about her. Never let on that she has people searching for her. Matt, Deidra and Blaine soon found themselves separately exploring "Faith Family Festival 2014."

Carnival tents came into view. School buses with the names of Christian churches were lined up nearby. A few decrepit carnival rides were lit up and in motion. Apparently, some parts of the fairgrounds remained year-round, for anyone renting it. For today's event, only one was chained off – a walk-through attraction with big, zany, multi-colored letters – "CRAZY HOUSE."

A small but well-lit stage held five musicians that looked like they could be a Heavy Metal band, but the sound they were making was innocuous enough for the cartoon rock 'n roll of old Saturday morning kids' TV.

Matt bought a paper cup of greatly overpriced coffee, and stood alone on gravel, sawdust, and cigarette butts. Out of nowhere he found himself being chatted up by a flirty teen-age girl, far too young to be talking to him that way.

"All by your lonesome, huh?" asked the spindly kid, who could not have graduated high school yet, if she had even entered it. Her clothing style was not unlike that of prep school. White blouse, pleated gray and white skirt, institutional-looking white shoes. She looked him up and down with an inappropriate smile, and said, "You sure don't have to stay that way. See that tent? And the gold-colored one down there? Those are for people who know what time it is."

Matt gave her a semblance of a smile.

"So what time is it?" she asked, with an eerie, phony expression that was more a baring of teeth than smiling. He was so taken aback by the weirdness of it, he had to work to avoid grimacing. He wasn't sure what to say.

She said, "... Time to take your place. Time to be a part of something." She leaned a little closer, invading his space a bit, and whispered, "It's hero time."

Yet again, he was thrown. In all that he had experienced in life, this was something of a first. He then decided to resist being thrown, and said, "I'm keeping God waiting. Is that it?"

Her freckly face went into a more natural-looking, laughing expression, "You're the one who said it, not me!"

As she laughed, in a way that had a derisive edge, Matt saw for the first time the placement of two other girls in similar outfits stationed at nearby points, forming a rough equilateral triangle with her. They were sweetly engaging other festival-goers, of which there were suddenly more and more walking about. He zeroed in on his sister and Blaine in the distance, talking with a man in a gray military uniform who was showing them the long gun he carried.

He had a sip of truck driver coffee and tried to look nonchalant, as he said, "Yeah, I just happened to have a day off today. Some friends of mine told me about this. They're stopping by later. Thought I'd check it out."

The girl smiled knowingly, and said, "You're here for a reason."

She spoke in such a forceful manner. It was making him nervous.

She declared, "Nothing happens without a reason."

He began an awkward process of halfway trying to disengage from her and halfway offering small talk. He said he was definitely going to check out the speakers in the tents. She gushed that there were brilliant musical groups, too, along with speakers he will never forget. And later would be Singing Bell. She gestured at an empty, bell-shaped set of risers.

It was then, through lack of sleep or being knocked off stride by this person's bizarre manner that he made his mistake. Looking at the Bell stage, he asked her if she knew a Prindibin.

Immediately he caught the error and tried to backpedal out of it, "I think that was the name she gave. I was talking to her earlier, right over there."

She locked her eyes into his, and said, "There hasn't been anything earlier than right now. We just started up."

Fully realizing his blunder, he silently cursed his stupidity. "No, she was just there," he said, gesturing over a wide area. He changed the subject, talking with her a minute more before claiming he was hungry and abruptly moving on.

He circulated around. His cup of coffee became a nice prop to help dispel any sense of awkwardness. He was cool, just standing here having a cup of coffee!

Foot traffic expanded by the minute. More buses had pulled in, not just from churches, but now various local corporate groups were here. Dozens of cars had filled in a parking area. Families were out in force, with squealing kids pointing out a little Ferris Wheel.

He came upon a man and a woman dressed up as generic comic-book superheroes, greeting the crowds. They had red nylon capes and brightly-colored costumes with insignia on their chests, and wore raccoon-type masks around their eyes. They stood at either side of a booth, staffed by a pair of teenage boys with clipboards. He saw the sign:

"Mountain of Radiance Summer Camp! Building Healthy Ascendant American Youth. Grades K thru 12. Three Week and One Month Programs. Reserve Your Spot!"

Three gray-uniformed troopers of God's Army of Eternal Honor came drifting slowly through the growing mass of attendees, semi-automatics at the ready. Too late he caught himself staring in a cold way at them. One of them spotted him, and returned the glare. It seemed to go on and on. He had committed another klutz move. If he looked away too suddenly that would look more suspicious than if he kept on giving them the stink eye. The one who was visually engaging him said something to the other two, and the three of them stopped short.

Matt still had his prop, and he used it to break the eye-contact in a more natural-looking way. As he took a big swig from the coffee, he pivoted and turned his head.

Then his salvation came. Moving in at a stately pace from the right, Charlie Bienville and Craig Moultrie came into sight. Bienville was a sight, indeed. The superheroes at the booth could not compete with what he was wearing. Elton John couldn't.

He had on a sky-blue top hat with a feathered band around the base. He sported wire-rim sunglasses with round, pink, mirror lenses. His once white beard was now deep red. A green velvet cape was fringed in white, and his waistcoat was electric paisley. The navy-blue bow tie was the most dignified thing he had on. His deep blue crushed-velvet pants ballooned out above square-toed boots.

Craig Moultrie was in regular street clothes and black, wrap-around shades. He did the initial talking to anyone who came over, which included the Honors soldiers.

Matt could hear Craig saying, "His Grace is a cultural leader from Florida who is aware of the presence of Ernest Seamark in our world, and wishes to hear ascendant sermons. He grants karmic blessings, but asks no autograph requests at this time."

Charlie said, "Namaste," or something.

Matt took his leave, and ducked into a tent up ahead that had an open entrance and an amplified voice spilling out from within.

A man in a sweat-soaked white dress shirt spoke passionately to a sparse audience. Matt was debating whether to retreat back to the van when a gentle sound reached him. So incongruous with the ranting from the stage, this was lovely. It was singing.

Mostly female vocalists, they were singing One Hand One Heart, from West Side Story.

It was a Singing Bell.

He pushed through the crowd to the far side of the tent where an open slit let the sun in. There he slipped out. Only a few strides away it stood. A five-level bell-shaped stage with men and women singing, segregated by gender. Urgently, he scanned the female faces. They wore wigs that, to him, were beyond ridiculous. Giant bouffant wigs. They were a distraction, but they didn't obscure the facial features.

He had to slowly circle the structure. There were people on all sides and he needed to see everybody. They all wore the most insipid smiles. It was a wrenching moment. Audrey could be here. Indeed, that was the great hope! There were dozens of them, crooning, "One Heart! One Hand! Only death will part us now!"

Matt imagined he saw Audrey more than once. He couldn't be sure. It was hellish, as now it hit him that his memory of her face had faded, ever so slightly. He could feel it; he had a diminished sense of certainty over whether or not a woman in the distance was his fiancée.

The singers went into a third number, Radiant Face My Heart Sings. Each of them turned and raised a hand in the direction of the largest of the stages on the fairgrounds. Immediately, it was lit up in spotlights, as a booming announcer's voice introduced a former Alabama State Representative. He didn't catch the name in all the echo, and didn't care, but watched glumly as a gray-haired chap in a suit and tie made his way with a cane to the podium.

Matt was apparently the only one here who didn't know of this patriarch, judging by the welcome he received. When he finally made it to the mic, he said, "I'm sure glad to see ya."

Ear-shredding feedback followed.

MOR techies in gray blazers scrambled in a frenzy around the stage and fixed the problem.

The hunched old man said, "On a day as beautiful as this one, and with the sheer beauty of the voices we all just heard, I have to thank the Lord that he has granted me another year. Let's all be sure and thank all our new friends at Jesus Pointing the Way Ministries, and Church of the Mountain of Radiance for bringing this wonderful event to Autauga and Elmore counties ...

"I was not personally familiar with the ministry of the Reverend Earnest Seamark, who I understand was unable to join us here today. But I can sure vouch for the fact that there's no 'enthusiasm gap' amongst his congregation!"

Explosive applause revealed who in the crowd was MOR.

The speech gave Matt a great opportunity for a prolonged examination of the faces of the female vocalists, who remained standing on the Bell. The statehouse veteran launched into the kind of boilerplate speech that both parties figure the people will never tire of. Matt had to shake his head at the empty pandering the guy started doing to the military. How many times had he and the guys had to stand by while some probably crooked politician used them as background props for a speech?

"Talk a little longer, old man," Matt thought, as he narrowed his search to three of the singers. The rep did talk, quite a bit longer, and in time there came a shift in his tone. It got angrier. Darker.

"People of faith have never been under the kind of merciless attack that we find ourselves in these days in the USA. I remember like it was yesterday when they robbed our children of the liberty to pray openly and unashamedly in the classroom. I'm sure that Minister Earnest Seamark would agree with me that the day is coming when we will restore that vital freedom to America."

The crowd gave it a warm round of applause, with MOR Adherents being particularly vocal. Matt turned for just a minute to listen to this individual. He recalled Audrey saying once that fundamentalist religion always wants to indoctrinate kids early, because otherwise people don't usually get involved with religion later in life. Ironically enough, she said that.

"I recently spoke with the Mountain of Radiance regional director. Mr. Poleander. I want everyone to know we saw eye-to-eye on all kinds of issues. He is one respectful and agreeable young man. And especially when it comes to securing religious liberty, let me tell you, he has the right ideas ... Like *what*, you may ask? Well, say hello to the Honors Heroes!"

He pointed to the side of the stage where three of them stepped out and nodded briefly to the crowd that was suddenly going nuts for them.

The retired pol yelled out in a voice that cracked with age, "If the evil-doer does not recognize a Superior Being, let him recognize superior firepower!" Big raucous cheers. "They're not going to give us freedom because we ask nice! This is the kind of support we need! Time will come when the Tree of Liberty needs be watered with blood of tyrants! All right! All right! Here's the caliber of men that can make that a reality!"

Matt thought of what Charlie said, that a big wave of cult mentality could be arriving with the upcoming 2014 mid-term elections.

The state house veteran received the acclaim of the crowd for a full minute. He said then that he wanted to introduce a man "the likes of which America needs more of ..."

Randolph Poleander.

It was him. Poleander. Emzharotav. The Shebbovotan of the Southeastern United States Service Region. Matt had to assume this was an unbilled, surprise appearance. Charlie would have mentioned it if he had known. This was the boss who ran Church of the Mountain of Transfiguring Radiance from North Carolina to Louisiana.

He came jogging out to the podium in his trademark golf shirt and black slacks. The rock band from earlier in the day stepped out in an array behind him, shaking their big hair and giving him a rousing instrumental. Curtains were pulled away to reveal four towering photo placards; four giant, unsmiling men's faces stared out from the background.

He respectfully shook the hand of the retired state rep, and signaled for someone to help the fellow off the stage. After much waving, grinning and gesturing to various adherents in the crowd, he snatched up the mic from the podium.

"I have started seeing ol' Jelly Belly, my driver, showing up more at church services!" He cried out. The audience tittered. "I said, JB! Been a while since we seen you at the church house! He said, well I been waiting for six strong men to carry me in."

Scattered laughs.

"I said, let's save that for your final visit!"

He had more on the adventures of Jelly Belly, "I said JB! You a lucky man. You have something even Adam didn't have in the paradise of Eden. You know what you got that he never had? ... Ancestors."

Matt remembered what a comedian told him at a USO show. People want to hear themselves laughing along with other laughing people. It's not complicated.

Poleander pointed out the church buses, also the corporate buses, and, "... alllll those station wagons and mini-vans with the families of the area. Hey, grab a brochure for Mountain of Radiance Summer Camp on your way out, Mom and Dad. Sure wish I'd had it when I was a kid."

He then paused, and spent a good thirty or forty seconds just looking his audience over, with the widest of grins. He said, "Everybody who's with us for the big event at three gets fed, you know. Gonna have a big spread afterwards. What is it today? ... Hamburgers? Well, that's good protein. We're gonna nourish soul and body here today."

Following another awkward if not eerie silence, he gestured to a gold-painted tent.

"... Right there ... Gold tent ... Three o'clock sharp ... Tha's when and where life changes."

People craned their necks to look at it, and with no explanation he left the statement hanging and rolled right along. Still with the same giddy grin, he said "I know everybody knows who this is," as he gestured at the twelve-foot photograph of Earnest Seamark's face, "But how many here today know this man? Hmm?" He moved to stand before a jowly, pock-marked visage that seemed to be burning holes in him with its blazing, bloodshot eyes. He looked up at it for a long time. He looked at the audience for a long time. He then dashed to the edge of the stage and bellowed out, "*Men* make a church! God comes in, but it takes men to *make* a church!" He turned and straggled back to the photo and seemed to mumble something to it.

The two other wall-sized photos got his personal attention. He grew increasingly agitated as he reflected upon these saints, and ranted into the mic about how their sacrifices had been so much heavier than anything this slacker generation is ever asked to do. He got mobile, too, and dashed around the stage like Mick Jagger.

In between the strange pauses, his presentation was wide-ranging. Was it stream of consciousness? That was the term Audrey used for one of the novels they'd read together. In Matt's estimation,

Poleander had simply lost it. Drugs? At one point he seemed to be struck mute, and shuffled like a condemned man back to Earnest Seamark's giant face, raising his hands before it as the confused crowd slowly began to cheer. It couldn't be the content of his words, Matt thought. Maybe just the sheer theatricality of it. They were also being stoked by handlers down front, gesturing for applause.

Later, when he could speak again, Emzharotav belatedly acknowledged the former State Rep, and what an honor it was to meet this gentleman, "who they say knows everybody worth knowing" in the state.

His attitude reverted back to the jovial, even cocky, like a frat boy at a big party. It looked as though he might be chewing gum. He sang out, "Anybody here believe in *God?*"

The festive crowd roared in the affirmative, as he stood with the broad, somewhat wacky smile on his face. He was indeed smacking gum.

The smile suddenly wilted. His face locked into a dismal mask. He snarled, "... Are ya *sure?*"

That was unexpected, and seemed to throw the audience a little. Scattered mumblings followed, amid mostly silence.

"There's kind of a lot riding on it, you know," he said, "... I don't *believe* there's a God. I know there is. And I know Him. We are on speaking terms. Now let me speak something to you. God doesn't care what you believe. Neither do I. What you know is what matters. But a lot of you standing here know nothing, or next to nothing. Especially concerning God and His universe."

Matt scanned faces in the crowd. From Jelly Belly to this? Was this going over? If so, how?

"You gotta know," said Emzharotav, the Shebbovotan, his face a joyless cipher, "And without all that 'Mystery of the Lord' stuff, please. If it's a mystery then you don't know it!"

For another tidbit of enigma, he blurted out, "Give Jesus credit. He tried." A few people in the crowd got up and walked out following that one – but to Matt's surprise, only a relative few. Poleander pressed the microphone flush against his lips, and murmured, "... Gold tent. Three o'clock." He pivoted again, to speak at length on the defense of religious liberty, though with more subtlety than the gun-slinging rhetoric of the one that preceded him.

After a stretch of speechifying that the Christians in the crowd could approve of, he went more specifically into his own theology: The ultimate, final goal of human life is the Mountain, he said. The intermediate, or long-term goal is Earnest Seamark, or rather mastery of the knowledge and wisdom of Ummyashuntopudda.

"... But the immediate future, for all of us here and now, is entirely ... *military!*"

He hauled out the Honors trio again, and tried for another little spasm of soldier worship. Many in the crowd went for it. Again. Matt had to wonder if any of the guys on that stage had ever made it through so much as the Cub Scouts, beginning with the Shebbovotan.

Poleander's address went on rambling far and wide. But he seemed to be wrapping things up when he roared out a promise that he would be fighting, alongside "the right-minded among you," to establish a constitutional amendment to "... prohibit, criminalize, and prosecute *blasphemy* in these United States of America!"

Matt remained on the gravel watching him and grinding his teeth. At one point the two men seemed to make eye contact. He had no interest in standing through ten minutes of mechanical applause for this nut, so he turned and started walking.

Drifting, he circulated the grounds a while longer, probably looking pretty suspicious. After convincing himself that his fiancée was nowhere to be found here, he entered a state of impotent rage. Finally, he headed back to the van, wishing it could be a longer walk.

He soon slowed down as he spotted Blaine Wheeler up ahead. He was engaged in conversation with a portly Alabamian in Bermuda shorts and a ball cap by the pretzel booth.

"… Yep, down here from Raleigh, North Carolina! I'm a full-time student at NC State. That's the Wolfpack!" Blaine said.

"Oh, I know that! You can't tell me nothin' about college sports!" said the guy, whose shirt bore an image of Jesus Christ pointing skyward, amid giant letters – JESUS POINTING THE WAY!

"I'm majoring in … engineering," Blaine said, seemingly unsure about it. Probably didn't want to tell the dude he was an English major, Matt figured.

In the kind of voice that so many country music stars try to emulate, the festival-goer proclaimed, "My home-school boy is majorin' in Book of Revelation! He's only eight, but can that boy ever preach! I mean he can preach and preach and preach and preach and preach!"

He was ebullient, until something suddenly occurred to him that seemed to flatten his mood.

He said, "One of our pastors arranged this trip, for some of us to visit this church. That's our bus. But I've been here for a while now, and I'm not hearing much mention of Jesus at all!"

"This is Church of the Mountain of Radiance," said Blaine.

The man in the cap said, "But it's also Jesus Pointing the Way." He tapped on his chest.

"That's Mountain of Radiance," Blaine said. Seeing Matt amble away, he said, "Excuse me."

He trotted up from behind and called out, "Hey, they got a Tilt-A-Whirl here!"

Matt replied, grimly, "They sure do."

Blaine said, "Deidra and I figured we could cover more ground separately. She's in one of those tents listening to a speaker or something."

Matt said, "Okay, but don't talk so much to me. I don't want them to see us together. Remember? Talk at the van."

They walked on, spaced several feet apart.

Matt was stewing, boiling, by the time they climbed into the van. Only later did the mood lighten a bit when they spotted Bienville leaving the fairgrounds in his get up. Craig was at his side helping him as best he could.

Blaine said, "Hey, did I ever tell you what he does for a living? He only works ten weeks out of the year. He's a *Santa Claus* at a shopping mall in Atlanta! His wife told me when we were there the second time! I went to use the bathroom and I passed this room with all these framed photos of Charlie dressed up as Santa Claus! She said he's been doing it twenty-five years!"

"His wife talked to you? She never has much to say to me!"

"She told me she relates to you," Blaine said, "Maybe she has so much she wants to tell you she can't choose one. You know, she and her brother were in one of these cult deals once."

With the testy voice of his rapidly declining mood, Matt said, "Okay. Let's compare notes on what we saw over there while we wait on Deidra. Please."

Blaine said, "I saw this woman walking around taking photographs, and she didn't look like a tourist. She seemed to take a few of you."

Reclining against a headrest, Matt closed his eyes, and said, "I'm sure I have been photographed more than Beyoncé by now. I'm not going to worry about it. So I'm in their photo album." He neglected to mention how he had slipped, and asked one of them about a Prindibin.

"They had videographers roaming around, too. I don't know if you noticed," Blaine said, "Of course, having data and interpreting data are two different things." He blocked the sun with his hand and looked back at people leaving the fairgrounds. He said it was nice to see so many people leaving early, but he wondered what was keeping Dee.

Moultrie and Bienville returned and climbed into the van. In the tight space in back Charles struggled to extract himself from his costume. He assured everyone he had on a T shirt and jeans underneath.

"Some truly fascinating chit chats out there just now!" he said, "Hey! How about Emzharotav popping in!? That was only the second time I've ever seen him in person!"

Matt yelled back, "How about him?! This event has been another *bust!*"

He lowered his voice, and said that all he had come away with was deeper disgust over how people accommodated groups like MOR, if that was possible. Seeing how he was squashing the atmosphere in the van, he apologized.

Matt was simmering until Charles extolled the promise of the event coming in three weeks. "The Big One." The MOR Biennial All Worlds Convocation, Trailblazer Bank Stadium, Central Coast California. Fifty years of MOR! Their Messiah himself will be there, along with ten Singing Bells.

Matt perked up when he heard him say it was a near certainty that Audrey would be present in that stadium somewhere. He thought there was a good chance she would be at this thing today, but the next one is a virtual lock. He gave him a resolute look and said, "She will be there. I'm calling it. This next one is 100%."

Momentarily, Matt softly said, "Okay." He was ready to go. Checking his watch again, he cried out, "Where the hell is DeeDee?!"

He shoved open the driver's door and clambered out. Along with Blaine he squinted into the glare up the street where people were walking in all directions.

"Where did you say she went? The gold tent?" he asked Blaine.

"I'm wondering if she could have gotten turned around and took the wrong way back. These roads all look alike," Blaine said, with affected calmness in his voice.

They stood there watching, occasionally spotting someone in the far distance who resembled Dee. Moultrie came to join them, glancing at his watch.

Blaine said, "I'm going to give it another minute and go back and find her."

Young women would sometimes appear walking alone, looking so much like Deidra from a distance. One by one they turned out to be someone else.

A figure emerged from a cluster of people, as if from a fog bank, and strolled nonchalantly down the sidewalk. She could have been DeeDee. But she was moseying along so slowly. If it was her, she would know she was late and would shake it up a little.

The distant woman was biting into a giant pretzel as she sashayed along. Drawing gradually closer, she eventually resolved into the image of Deidra Pleasant. She made it to the van, walked around the guys, climbed in and got seated.

Blaine said, "You were in that gold tent, listening to that speaker. Right?"

She nodded, biting off another big hunk of pretzel.

"What did you learn?" he asked.

Seeming lost in another world, she replied, "... The importance of being Earnest."

Then she added, "And something else ... It's great that you are working so hard to find her, Matt. Because we really, really need to get Audrey out of this thing."

○   ○   ○

Having never been in Alabama, Prindibin sat 165 miles away, where she worked ten-hour days telemarketing for the church in Pensacola, Florida. Not that they identified themselves as MOR. Heart's Lighthouse Fellowship was the name used. Columns of phone numbers in tiny print on a sheet went into soft focus as her eyes slowly crossed a little. It was several hours into this shift. For many seconds just now she had felt paralyzed, sitting before the wall of phone numbers, her mouth hanging open a little. A drop of her drool appeared on front of her blouse.

After the disaster in Brazil, she now sold supplemental health insurance and mail-order vitamin subscription plans to senior citizens over the phone. Ascendant scripture studies were before and after work. Sometimes she accompanied recruiting teams on the street.

The air hung motionless in the telephone trailer. An array of white boards stood above the cubicles with big words scrawled in black and red marker, "Get SS Numbers!!!" ... KEEP DIALING!!! ... Ask about their *heirs!!!* ... DO THEY HAVE DESIGNATED *HEIRS???*"

Curled over by tedium and hunger, Prindibin presently heard her name called. She stepped quickly to stand before the director of the boiler room and receive a dressing-down about her dialing rate. In general, she needed to shape up. As her ability to dial a telephone was "lethargic," she was being dismissed from the remainder of the shift to accompany a recruiting team that would go late into the evening. She tried not to show her excitement at the prospect of some breathable air.

Within minutes, she set off with a vanload of hyper teens to roam the streets of Pensacola, talking Ummyashuntopudda and selling energy bars. Which would be expired energy bars. The Adherents had fastidiously snipped out the expiration dates from the flaps of the wrappers.

It was different doing this solo, not in a group of three. One of the kids called it "free-style."

In any case, there she stood in the evening darkness of downtown Pensacola, alone on a sidewalk in front of a closed shoe store, broaching the subject of Ascendant Scripture to passers-by. One lady remarked that it was "a funny question to ask" if she had found her place in the universe, and for the first time it occurred to Prindibin that it was.

She knew she had brought in next to nothing for her spiritual family since becoming one with them. Since that time she had heard nothing from her superiors apart from how no life is possible for her beyond the church, and that she truly needed to get it together, as in now. When she spotted a scrawny, unkempt young man drifting down the sidewalk, her greeting was effusive – "Well, hi there!"

She had to tag along with him for some time, peppering him with personal questions and comments before he finally stopped to contend with her, his face a mask of confusion. She talked at him for several minutes. When his weak, faltering voice began answering her in the affirmative multiple times, she hit the speed dial on her church-supplied phone to call in a "turn-over, male." With that, the baffled guy was set upon by three other young men who started talking him up in a highly energetic manner.

Prindibin left them standing there and went back the way she came. She was met by her new supervisor, a powerful, stocky young fellow with a crew cut. He was the replacement for Granavulid, who had since been condemned and banished for disloyalty to Earnest Seamark.

"Wow! Prindibin!" he said, "I am trying to remember when I ever heard a better lead-in to turn-over, and I am not coming up with anything! Girl, that was outstanding, throughout! I sure wish I had that one for the training video."

She demurred modestly, with plenty of smiles for him. But he was not finished, and said one of his colleagues had told him of witnessing other impressive recruiting encounters from her since she had been in Pensacola. Now he was seeing it for himself. He told her to report to his office before she turned in for the night. He might have some ideas for her.

After all that she had been through, his few words of praise gave her a feeling like the love-bombed first days of her new life.

On returning to the residential compound, Prindibin made her way to his office. She was warmly greeted. His name was so hard to pronounce, she just called the younger man "Sir."

After some small talk, the supervisor adopted a professorial tone, and told her, "It is possible to move up fast in MOR, Prindibin. Perhaps your talent lies more in the field of in-person recruiting. Sure looked that way tonight. Maybe that thing in Brazil was someone else's fault, like you said."

If only she wasn't at the brink of keeling over from lack of sleep the meeting would have been wonderful beyond describing. As it was, she only did a lot of smiling and nodding.

He said they had all noticed that she appeals to men, and that can have no end of benefits, "Not least of which is that women who appeal to men have a greater likelihood of bearing sons." He did not elaborate.

He concluded the encounter by telling her that she was off of telemarketing duty and reassigned to full-time in-person recruiting. He added that he would recommend she attend the All Worlds Convocation in California. A whipsaw of emotion had her spinning inside by the time she was allowed to meander away to her bunk. It seemed like such a breakthrough; would it vanish tomorrow, by some fluke, or someone's whim?

Prindibin had often been plagued by nightmares since entering the church. It had been explained to her as God's punishment for her various failures. This night, after skipping a shower to collapse like dead weight into her top bunk, she immediately began dreaming of an enormous, scary, mobile machine that rolled around and around.

It looked like one she had seen years ago that gathered up golf balls on a driving range. In the dream, horizontal gearing was gathering up multitudes of odd little objects, just like the golf ball gobbler did. When she saw these little things resolve themselves into living human faces, Prindibin sat up gasping in horror.

It was only scant minutes after she settled back down that she had another vision. As she shifted on top of the sheets, in the twilight zone between waking and sleeping, her mind became filled with an image.

Two mountains of impossible size appeared across a great distance. One was *upside down,* and resting peak-to-peak atop the other, brighter mountain. With their points grinding together, they slowly rotated in opposite directions, casting off rocks and dust. After the briefest view of this dream world, her muscles seized up all over. She sat bolt upright in the dark barracks.

Hyperventilating, drenched in sweat, she released a shout, "... I have seen the Mountain!"

The memory of the image flooded her head, intensifying like a feedback loop. Was this her moment of death? Why else would she have seen it? Her chest heaved convulsively as hysteria seized her.

"*I have seen the Mountain!!!*"

Another adherent was just able to break her fall from the top bunk. Surrounded by church sisters in cotton gowns, she shrieked at the top of her lungs from the floor –

"I HAVE SEEN THE MOUNTAIN!!! ... *I HAVE SEEN THE MOUNTAIN OF RADIANCE!!!*"

Within an hour, the directorate of the compound and the two primary male and female superiors of Prindibin, along with Esocush, were intensively interrogating her about this possible miracle. No detail was too minute to be pinned down, and precise wording was of the utmost importance. Two video cameras recorded every millisecond.

All of them thrilled at the thought of it being recognized as a miracle, which would work to the benefit of everyone at the Home Base. Everybody associated with Prindibin could be considered at least fractionally blessed, which would help with advancement. That's if the event stood up to investigation. It would entail specialists being flown in from the Council of the Nine. Excitement crackled in the room, as Prindibin stood wavering in euphoria and the withering weight of sleeplessness.

She heard them say that the vision would almost have to elevate her in status, almost immediately. The church had to be somewhat deferential to her, at least for the time being. She may have personally received the favor of God Himself. Merely by taking the report seriously enough to investigate it, her superiors, even those of highest-rank, will have invested something of themselves in it.

The following morning, she was told only that higher-ups were evaluating her experience. Apart from going through another grueling, video-recorded interrogation for them, she should "just keep doing what she is doing." And wait.

It became clear that the vision and the hubbub surrounding it had given Prindibin a boost within this society, but also within her own morale. She felt as though she had finally received something of a pay-off from God. It showed in her demeanor, and the way she carried herself.

The next morning on arising, Prindibin was greeted by a teary-eyed Esocush, who had news.

"Prindibin, Prindibin, beloved of the Shebbevunseh, you are being reinstated to Singing Bell while your Inquiry continues! You are flying to Atlanta today to begin rehearsals for World Convocation! You are getting a clothing allowance because ... you are now classed as a *Public Image Adherent!*"

Extended shrieks of joy peeled out of the women's barracks, none louder than Prindibin's.

◯　　◯　　◯

August 28th, 2014, with dawn just brightening the sky, Charles Bienville drove a rented SUV toward a parking deck entrance by the curving wall of an enormous baseball stadium. Pleasant slouched in the passenger seat. Even at this hour, there was a protester on the sidewalk.

A slender, scowling young woman in a business suit held a sign that towered over her head:

"HEY MOUNTAIN OF BULLSHIT!!! WHERE'S MY BROTHER???"

"I think I may know her," Charlie said, "If it's who I think it is, she'll be there all day."

They rolled on by, and Matthias muttered, "Hey, Mountain of Bullshit, where's my wife?"

Further up, around the curve of the circular building, Prindibin and the two women of her new Three stood before towering twin sculptures that bracketed the main entrance of Trailblazer Bank Stadium. The two heavily stylized statues were supposed to be cowboys on horseback, but the horses were almost abstractions rearing up under the more detailed, gold-plated men, who completed the verticality of the pieces with upthrust arms pointing at the same spot in the sky.

174

"They do seem to fit our event," said Prindibin, with a confident resonance in her voice. The other two agreed, one after the other. What a step up these ladies were from the two nebbishes she had been with before. It was no accident. She had ascended in the church.

The two new women, Deprellex and Nevrelun, were awake and aware and would be going into real estate where the money is, they said, after the church secured them their husbands. Prindibin told them her plan was to remain rising in the church. She might start a podcast or a TV program geared toward introducing women to the teachings of Earnest Seamark.

Better dressed than average adherents, the three of them walked on with heads held high between the two trailblazers, past the shuffling huddles of the downfallen, up the ramp and into Gate D of the dramatic, dynamic stadium.

Surprisingly the place had adequate signage, and they were able to make their way to rendezvous with the assistant director of today's extravaganza. This man, whom she had never seen before, thrilled her by calling out, "Ahh! Prindibin!"

They each received a little map showing their dressing room, and the field entrance closest to their Bell stage. Bell #5. That would be 5 out of 10. The map also had directions for accessing the glassed-in VIP boxes on Level 4. The assistant director confided that when ladies aren't singing on a Bell, it would behoove them to circulate amongst the VIPs. They thanked him, and returned to the corridors of the bright, modern facility.

"What a brilliant venue to showcase the faith," said Nevrelun, the most serene of the Three.

"It's so well laid out you don't need a map," Prindibin replied. She added, "And in three hours, we get to see ... *Him.*"

The Three would periodically remind each other of the fact that today was the day they would be seeing the greatest man who had ever lived, Earnest Seamark, in the flesh. Whenever it was mentioned, it always led to a moment of weak-in-the-knees and hearts-aflutter. Everyone who was on a Singing Bell during the time the Shebbevunseh was onstage would be allowed to promenade in a rotation so that no-one would be facing away from him the whole time.

They strolled past three uniformed stadium workers pushing carts of soda pop syrup. These whiskery dudes were unmistakably gobsmacked by the Three, though they said nothing, only stared in wide-eyed wonder. When they were some distance away the giggling began amongst the women, and became belly laughs when Deprellex blurted out, "I'd say they know *their* place in the universe!"

Smiling radiantly, Prindibin thought to herself that this new Three knew what time it was. They didn't need to be constantly keeping tabs on one another and reporting on one another. She told them she would catch up with them in the dressing room, just because she could, and drifted away to a portal to stadium seating.

Leaning on a rail outside, she let her gaze play across the heavily decorated ball field, balloons and banners everywhere. Chalk marks showed the parade routes they would take on the promenade to the Bell stages. Techies were in motion everywhere, getting the set-up just right. An enormous Mountain of Radiance logo was chalked on center field, with the minimalist figure of a man looking up and back at the jagged mountain rising behind him.

"Fifty Years 1964 – 2014"

A big part of the outfield seating was partitioned off with blue fabric panels. This she found sad in that they had been unable to fill the place. But in front of the closed-off section, with a great view of the action, stood a platform for television crews. Logos of big news organizations hung all over it.

Up front, the home plate area was covered by a stage that had been built out from the stands. Multiple levels and peripheral risers were to be seen, and dead center, hard to miss, was a gold-colored throne. Suitable for a giant, it was heavily ornamented and heaped with red velvet cushions.

As warm breezes washed over her, she sensed the holiness of this scene. That's when she felt the Spherules. Like never before, trillions, octillions of Spherules flowed through her like a great warm ocean current. She hung onto the rail and swept her head back to look up at a clear, sun-splashed sky. Two words spilled out of her, over and over:

"... Believe Only ... Believe Only ... Believe Only ..."

Two levels below her, Matthias Pleasant stepped out from a portal. His expression was dismal in extremis as he regarded this place, built seventeen years earlier for a Major League expansion team that didn't make it. Thousands of dark spots could be seen all over the floors where people had spat out their chewing gum over the years. He told Bienville that the trailblazer sculptures out front looked like two guys getting thrown off their horses.

A sense of contagion that he felt hanging over the place was made worse by the hokey cult trappings he saw all around him. What a big budget had gone into those balloons, he thought. At least they had put some money into the photographic placards on the stage, which dwarfed the ones he'd seen in Alabama, but to him still resembled mugshots of serial killers.

He looked around, and up behind him at a strange woman standing two levels above with her head held back, displaying the underside of her chin. She swayed side to side and seemed to be talking to herself. Weird, but no worse than the kids who should have been in college but were haranguing him in the passageway about EU spy satellites deployed above this ball field in geo-synchronous orbit. They weren't the first who wanted to talk to him. Too many people did. The phony media credentials that hung around his neck might be more trouble than they were worth. Chatty Adherents, including Honors troopers, all wanted to put forth a good face for this correspondent of the Fayetteville Observer.

The lady upstairs was still staring up at the sun. Whoever she was, she couldn't be Audrey Crane. He ambled along, trying to get a feel for the lay out of this circular maze. Their sound system seemed a little buggy. Reverent violin music droning out of the stadium speakers would cut out now and then with a pop.

Half an hour of walking around and Matt still felt lost. But Charles had advised him on two areas where he might encounter Audrey – the Singing Bells, and the glassed-in VIP suites.

As the music turned upbeat and blasting, the seating areas started showing signs of life. All eyes shifted to the costumed singers, now parading in formation by the hundreds to where they would ascend their Bell platforms. With this distraction, he hastened down the steps to the lowest level, and made a surreptitious little jump onto the field at the far end.

It looked like half of the stadium's seating sections were empty and blocked off, the empty seats concealed from TV cameras by panels of blue fabric. At least their best efforts hadn't been enough to get this place more than half full, he thought, with deep satisfaction.

He planned to contact the real journalists at the platform in the outfield. From time to time he planned to drift back in proximity of it, just for appearances' sake. He brought a voice recorder with a little microphone into which he would pretend to dictate a news story. It wasn't total pretense. He actually recorded some observations of the scene, with syrupy tributes to "this church that has long been part of the Fayetteville community." It might be helpful to play it if anyone challenged him.

He had high hopes for this fake ID of his. Charlie's network had come through with it. A certain magazine editor had sent a reporter to the Convocation, and not being a big fan of Mountain of Radiance, this person had obliged by emailing Charles a picture of what the press pass looked like.

A perfect fake ID it was not. The bar code was a dummy. If it got down to somebody wanting to scan that, he would have to do some fast peddling. He would say it was what his editors had sent him, and that's all he knew.

He had gained access to the stadium in the first place the same way Bienville did – by buying a ticket at the gate. Unlike Charlie, he had no intention of remaining in the stands.

MOR members had been shipped in by the thousands from multiple countries. A third of the population of the sect was in attendance. "Interfaith outreach" efforts had resulted in busloads of people from fundamentalist Christian churches, New Age groups, corporations and private schools. Matt was rankled to see an Army band. This crowd was already pretty damn big, and soon thousands more would be parading on the field and milling about in the stands.

The event was to be considered underway when the JumboTron cranked up, which happened as Matt checked his watch. It was going out live on MOR's internet TV channel, with clips to be hawked to major media, tabloid TV, local news shows nationwide, on down to Youtube channels. The sight of all these big network TV logos had to be a breath of life to the church, he figured, in regards to maintaining a sense of legitimacy. No famous journalists were here, but up-and-coming second-string correspondents could be seen on the screen doing interviews with Shebbovotans from around the world. The network logos took up more space on the JumboTron than the reporters' heads.

Why, there was Randolph Poleander himself up on the big screen. Emzharotav was telling some pretty face with a microphone that this was not only a pivotal day in his life, but also in hers, and in the lives of everyone who was watching.

It would be a two-day event, but this first day was the big one. Senators Rigby and Merquar would be speaking today, bracketing the appearance of the Beneficence. Some of the bigger names from the MOR stable of B-List movie and television actors were here. A long-term Adherent, shockingly underweight bygone pop star Ricky Chance took the stage beneath the empty throne. With no introduction apart from riotous applause, he began lip-synching his maudlin, middling hit from years ago, "Mine Will Be The Mountain."

Prindibin sat at a long table in a noisy, crowded dressing room. The other two of her Three sat to her left. Before her, the mirror. Which became a problem. She was suddenly a little unclear as to how long she had been seated here, confronted by herself framed in lightbulbs. In a very few minutes, the experience of being in the church had taken yet another, new, whipsaw slice. Looking into her face, she entered a kind of slouching ennui.

"Oh, I just love this song," Deprellex said, in a way that was both gushing and void of emotion.

"You can really feel how it comes straight from his heart," Nevrelun replied as she shifted her wig around, "Such a classic. Just love that thing."

Prindibin glanced at the TV on the wall, turned back to the mirror, and said only, "... Yup."

The fabulous mood of minutes before had vanished. She wondered – what happened? At some level she was still thrilled to be here. But something had struck her, and like dirt in her eye, she couldn't ignore it. It was so crazy, but there it was in the mirror.

She didn't look like herself.

Not even close.

She had rarely seen herself in a mirror since her entry to the church five months ago. They didn't have that many mirrors. The other two of your Three told you if you looked okay.

In the past, which was over, she would often get ready for school or work with a little fixing up at the mirror. Before dates with Matthias Pleasant, she remembered there could be quite a bit of mirror time. She knew what she looked like in a mirror. Now, only months later, she didn't look like that anymore.

Granted, her hair was as short as it had been since her birth, so that was one difference. Just now she had seen herself with both the two-inch hair and big blonde wig. But it wasn't the hair.

It was her face that was different. The whole cast of her face was altered. She may have lost a little weight, but that didn't explain it. The very flesh of her face was different. There was no glow. It was slate gray under her eyes. Fine lines had appeared around her eyes and mouth. A sagging quality predominated that she had never seen in herself before. She looked diseased, if not deceased.

The sight was increasingly stupefying.

On the wide screen TV on the wall, it was holy men and movie stars. Someone described as a "star of the daytime drama, Vineyard's Landing," would now be speaking. As this well-coiffed fellow gave his testimonial about getting off of drugs due solely to Mountain of Radiance, there was a knock on the door.

The assistant director, going from one dressing room to the next, had an announcement: "There has been a change in the schedule! They don't want new singers climbing onto the Bells while the Shebbevunseh is on his throne."

For Prindibin and her comrades on the second shift of singers it meant that they would remain on the Bell the entire time he was sitting there! And they will perform *a second set as he departed!* This will stand as the privilege of a lifetime, for all of them.

Assistant Director said they will do a promenade around the Bell stage, making gestures to shift focus to the Beneficence. He demonstrated the gesture he wanted, with an amusing fluid movement of his arms, like a hula dancer. Everyone will be gesturing to the throne this way, he said. Prindibin wondered silently to herself how that could possibly be necessary. *They* were to shift focus to the *Beneficence?* So stupid. Anyway, she would get a nice long look at him.

It would be restorative to see the giant of the faith, and his closest luminaries, after so much time spent with those unworthy of him, at the lowest rungs. Her thoughts were entirely superficial to the convulsion she was feeling over the state of her face.

The harried assistant gave them their new call time, which would immediately follow Senator Merquar's speech. Later they would be cued when to parade back. He cried out, "Just be sure to hustle back and do a quick change. We need you in those VIP suites!"

As he departed, Deprellex looked at her with a sort of lewd grin, and said, "The V-I-P suites!" Prindibin remained impassive, even as she heard her say, "Who knows, Prindibin, maybe you'll meet your future husband up there."

She watched as the depleted woman in the mirror pressed a bit of glitter on her cheek.

While Ricky Chance pretended to sing, the first shift of costumed singers had paraded out to their Bell platforms and ascended them. Matt was agitated, feeling she had to be here, but the solar glare, chaos and crowd noise was overwhelming. It was dizzying; he feared it might trigger a recurrence of the tinnitus and vertigo from his war injury. At the same time, ironically, it afforded him a kind of a hiding place. He was just one more guy with a laminated press pass bouncing on his chest as he ran around with a microphone. Nobody looked twice at him.

He strode around Singing Bells, one at a time, attempting to size up each one as quickly as possible. But there were ten of them, holding forty people each. Only twenty women, each. Still, that came to two hundred women!

A musician he had interviewed on the fly told him the singers would only stay on the Bell for just so long, then be swapped out with others. How many sets of two hundred women he would have to sort through he couldn't imagine. Based on what he saw in Alabama, he figured they would do six or eight songs before leaving. They would change-out all ten Bells at the same time. So said the man he spoke to.

He felt he should have just barely time enough to scope out each one before they rotated. If only he could spot Audrey early on, he could tag along with her group when she left. If she went to work the crowds, like Bell singers typically did, then he would be there to say hello.

Beyond hello, what would he say? He hoped he would know when the moment came.

Singers and speakers, and speakers and singers, and then came a break in the pattern.

Senator Merquar was a towering, broad shouldered, musclebound fellow with a squeaky falsetto voice, "... People of faith in America today live under greater oppression than any slaves on any plantation in history!"

He was fairly screaming into his microphone, which distorted wildly, but he was more than washed out by the explosion of acclaim from the crowd.

He was soon talking about himself, his humble origins, how much evil he had overcome to get into the Senate, and how indispensable he was to that institution. Funding for his campaign was also indispensable, if he was to continue fighting for your lives. He gave his website and 800 number, twice, until the booming, God-like voice of the unidentified announcer rang out over stadium speakers, thanking him, and blasting the words, "If it's not a riveting speaker it is the most accomplished musical talents on earth! This is Mountain of Radiance, Fiftieth All Worlds Convocation!"

Without a pause, teen heart-throb Vanny Monet was introduced, and dashed onto the stage beneath the empty throne, belting out his version of "God Bless America," as a colorful, sequin-spangled, parading shift change took place on the Singing Bells.

Prindibin had never known such a moment – of ambiguity. Simultaneously she was thrilled to her core and wanted to crawl into a bed to sleep for twelve hours.

Thousands of people screamed their love and support for her. It was also for the other hundreds of singers, but it seemed solely for her. Strolling to Bell Five, she was floating. The intensity of this sunlight had her brain ablaze in photonic overload. She bared her teeth in her most theatrical smile and gently waved a hand at the endless, dreamlike sprawl of roaring, loving humanity. The parade around the field to the Bell stage seemed without end, but then came the surreal and further disorienting experience of climbing the interior spiral staircase. When she was at last in place, it was on the dizzying fourth riser.

Vanny Monet had launched into his most recent hit, "Wanna Be Your Wannabe." He was scheduled next to perform "Everything is Beautiful," during which Bell singers would slowly come in and take over the singing halfway through, and then go soaring right into "Radiant Face My Heart Sings." Looking out over the roiling scene, in its near-deafening cacophony, Prindibin in her dizziness suddenly had the sensation that it was all moving. Her Bell stage was moving, like a stately ship underway. She whipped her hands up to grab tight on the railing.

On the field, by Bell 6, Matthias was reminded how sometimes NFL quarterbacks would complain to the refs about crowd noise. Beyond a certain level it could be dangerous, like standing too close to a jet engine. He was reminded of that somehow as he stood here.

The angle of the sunlight was just perfectly wrong for allowing him to see large portions of the Bells. Much of the time he was looking up into a blinding sheen. He wore sunglasses; it didn't help. A welder's mask wouldn't help. He moved into the shadow of the Bell, where at least he could see something.

As he did, the sound of four-hundred Bell Singers began rising from stadium speakers all around him, joining the kid onstage in the religiously-themed pop tune of the Seventies, "Everything Is Beautiful ... In Its Own Way." These vocals had to be pre-recorded, he thought. He wondered if the singers even knew they were lip synching. In this sustained thunder, how could they?

The sun's glare was becoming a psychological blow that felt somewhat like the last straw. He had come all this way, over all these months, to be positioned in precisely the wrong spot, astronomically speaking, to accomplish what he most wanted in life. The sun would shift away later, of course. After it was too late for his purpose. He was utterly thwarted. He had to figure something out.

A minute or two into the next leaden ballad, he perceived a change in the crowd noise. It rolled like a wave from awe-struck oohs and ahhs to a building crescendo of the loudest uproar yet. He looked around, all over the stadium, and came to see that an enclosed sedan chair was being carried by six uniformed bearers. They were approaching the golden throne.

They stopped in front of it for a full minute.

When they moved away, there he sat.

A diminutive little old man, he seemed even smaller in the enormous chair. His arms had to splay out slightly on either side to reach the arm rests. Should have gone with a smaller throne, Matt thought. Somebody in the public image department blew it on that one.

He was clothed in loose-fitting silk of a gold color. Lank gray hair and a gray beard hung about his face. He had on wire-rim sunglasses with jet black lenses. A microphone on a boom had been positioned near his mouth. The crowd noise shifted lower as he continued sitting there – completely motionless! Silent, too.

This was the scene for the next full minute or more. As Matt wondered if Seamark might lose the crowd, he heard them all around begin softly and slowly to intone, and moan, "Beeelieeeve … Ooonly … Beeelieeeve … Ooonly …"

The phrase kept gently wafting out from the myriad spectators. Matt stood in the outfield trying not to be unnerved by it, and thinking to himself how redundant it was to send out a call to higher powers when the highest one they had was sitting right in front of them.

"Beeelieeeve … Ooonly …"

"Beeelieeeve … Ooonly …"

This tableau, unlike any experience of his life, suddenly struck him as being religiosity without the least trace of spirituality. It was a set piece. It was what they were supposed to do.

Another minute passed, then Seamark's right hand rose up from the arm rest. He exposed the palm of his hand to the stadium crowd, and a quavering voice spilled from the stadium speakers, emitting ten or twelve syllables of nonsensical gibberish.

The masses of people gasped, and in their thousands seemed to swoon slightly at the realization that he had just projected his blessing upon them. In person. In the flesh.

The hand drifted down again.

Prindibin had been facing away from the throne when first he was revealed. Now her neck was getting sore from wrenching it around to see him. Everyone on the Bell was leaning out over the railing and jockeying for position to see him. Someone fainted on the level below her, slipped under the rail and fell to the level below, triggering screams.

She wondered if she might pass out as well. Her head was like an inflatable toy. She was drifting in a sea of Spherules in a shimmering sun storm. Her mouth hung open, and breath came in little gasps.

The voice appeared again, "... What is your name?" he asked, "... Do you know?"

The JumboTron filled with his image, going out in a live stream, internationally. A crawling caption at the bottom rotated in different languages. It said, "EARNEST SEAMARK SPEAKS."

"Do you know your real name? The name by which the eternal God calls you? And He does call you ... But maybe you do not know your name."

The assembled throng seemed to appreciate this. Although, as was the case at the Alabama festival, there were crowd handlers stoking the applause.

He seemed so frail, as if he were too weak to move. Essentially, he did *not* move. Apart from the brief raising of his hand he was completely frozen. His wispy facial hair concealed his lips entirely. The voice, which did not seem to go with the person, continued to echo from the stadium speakers.

"... Fifty years ago, near to this place, I was encapsulated to this form that I might provide sustenance to you all. Today, know that you are worthy ... You are worthy ... You have my love."

The crowd noise took on a sound like that of relief. First they had been blessed, and now it sounded as if he was going to let them get into Heaven or something. Prindibin was not certain exactly what it meant, but it sounded so positive, tears pooled in her eyes. Here at last was the man that her new life was all about. As her mind began drifting into a zone of adoration, a grating voice from below screamed up, "Rotate!"

Next to her on the stage, Nevrelun barked at her, "It's the rotation! Move!"

They all began a measured stepping around the Bell, each one holding their arms out toward the Beneficence as he came into view, albeit hundreds of feet distant.

He sat still as a mannequin as his voice intoned, "Today is for you to create the peace you longed for yesterday ... Smile in your suffering ... Our lives today are as nothing ... Tomorrow, on the Mountain, is all."

Around and around Prindibin slowly stepped, doing her arm gestures when she had an unobstructed view of this man who remained silent and stationary. Circle after circle. And with each rotation, it became harder for her to deny that he was not what she had expected.

This was not the presence that had manifested itself before her in that Brazilian jail.

No musical accompaniment was dared, lest it impinge on his spoken message. His long silences would sometimes roil the crowd, with people reacting in a multitude of ways. Rough, guttural, baritone voices screamed, "I love you!" A cluster of shrieks circled the stadium, like "The Wave." Fainted people were left where they lay, and sometimes this meant sprawled on concrete steps or slumped over a railing. As he was rotated out of Prindibin's view, Earnest Seamark said, "Joys are shadows cast by sorrows ... Live with eyes open ... Happiness is an activity ... First things first ... Look into your heart's home."

What a load of fortune cookie crapola, thought Matthias, as he continued his scans of the Bell platforms. He had squinted at the bearded scarecrow for thirty seconds or so when he first appeared.

Now he was back to the Bell Singers, and hoping that the guy on the throne would continue to serve as a diversion for everyone.

"Go not where the path may take you. Go to where there is no path, and make a trail," said the God Man. That cliché is older than I am, Matt thought. He's plagiarizing old homilies now!

The Beneficence delivered at least one miracle. He had started all the people on the Bell stages moving in rotation. This moved them out of the sun's glare for several seconds. It was perfection. The singers were presented to him in full face, three-quarter view, and profile as they toddled around through shaded sections of the platforms. Matt stood with his retinas out of the glare and had a good look. He quickly concluded Bell Six had nothing happening, and moved on to Bell Five.

The voice from the throne, or somewhere, said, "Let your deeds speak. You will never be known for anything else ... Our deeds determine us, as much as we determine our deeds ... Do the work of today in serene humility ... Tomorrow the Mountain will be there still ... You are never a failure until you give up. Never give up."

Cheers broke out amid what otherwise sounded like a muttering, or grumbling stadium.

On the fourth riser, Prindibin was suddenly tired of doing the presentation poses.

The Shebbevunseh was talking on and on, and she was sashaying around doing these idiotic movements. It was absurd looking. Like bad comedy. She released an irritated sigh as she came back around in view of him and hoisted her arms up yet again for the undulating gesture.

Around she went, in another circle. Grimly now, without smiling, and without doing the gesturing anymore, she looked at his faraway image.

The JumboTron had him in close-up. Maybe too close. He did not appear to be talking. His voice rambled on, but he appeared catatonic. No jaw movement was to be seen, as a person has when talking. No breath shifted the gray walrus mustache that covered his mouth. Within her mind, she made excuses, angrily insisting that this is simply how supernatural demi-gods look and behave.

His voice broke out again, "... Upward movement initiated in time can counteract fate. We are here to master the universe."

Reaching the far point of opposition, she circled back, on her way to face him again. She would not be doing the gesturing anymore. She raised her chin with determination and dignity.

Stepping out of the sun-drenched section of the stage, she entered its shadow.

Matthias' squinting eyes locked onto her face.

The voice in the sound system said, "I give you a grain of sand, and I have given you the Mountain ... You and I shall weep in joy ... Man is born to live, not to prepare to live ... Remember, everything happens for a reason ..."

One hundred percent positive identification. It was her.

Twenty feet beneath her, Matt was looking up, as if at someone ethereal. She glided slowly, looking straight ahead. Everything she had ever meant to him was still intact. Her presence was re-imposed on him.

He stood motionless, just feeling it for a moment.

He waited until she completed another circle of the Bell stage, and with her location pinpointed, he drifted off to the side of the field so as to be less noticeable to those who might want to throw him out, hoping he had not already pushed his luck too far. He maintained focus on her position and the people surrounding her.

Earnest Seamark talked on at great length. He finally wound things up by imploring one and all to study Ummyashuntopudda, and especially the charting therein, where all the greatest secrets resided. Study until understanding seeps in, with the helpful intercession of angels, star brothers, and Ascended Light Masters always there for the asking. Let understanding happen. Your brain is designed and built for receiving Ascendant teachings.

"I am hopeful for your victory!" he cried out, in his first departure from monotone, "May we see you on the Mountain! On that day! And until that day ... We will see each other in our dreams!"

The sedan chair was hauled back in front of him, going the other way, and when it moved again, he was gone.

As the Beneficence departed the sound system cranked out a trumpet concerto. No more singing? Prindibin and company got the signal to depart. They wasted no time heading off to change into evening wear, and get to work in those sky boxes. Movie stars and senators were upcoming.

Though her mind was compressed, compacted in mixed feelings, as she walked across the field she pushed it all aside and went over what she would be saying to the VIP people. It would all be upon her in a few minutes. She could work out internal conflicts later, during charting, or at night before she fell asleep. High pressure schmoozing with rich prospects was dead last among things she felt like doing right now, but she had to get through it.

She had been given certain phrases to use, but didn't remember many of them now. One that stuck in her head for some reason was that being up on the Bell meant she was eye-level with the Shebbevunseh, gazing upon his precious face. She was now a different person from being eye-to-eye with him. She would say that to them.

Matt followed her at a distance he hoped was safe enough. He entered the stadium's passageway behind them. While he watched, her group went through a double door down in the guts of the building which he took to be the circus dressing rooms, based on his map.

It took twenty minutes of waiting, which he spent pretending to text and talk on his phone, until finally he saw her emerge in a cluster of mostly women. Certain frantic guys tagging along babbled orders at them. From what he could make out they were being told what to say, and above all what not to say. They moved down a corridor to a public area where a pair of glass atrium elevators were coming down. Matt waited, pretending to use a vending machine, until he saw her enter one of the lifts. He counted off the floors as it rose.

Fourth floor. That was the VIP suites, and that was where they departed the lift. Matt hastened to the fire stairs and started legging it up two steps at a time.

He stepped out to see the suites, and the broad passageways linking them, all swirling with masses of people in motion, people laughing, and people enrapt in deep conversations. There were high ceilings and lots of bright lighting. It was expansive, with all manner of restaurants, and meeting rooms. The side facing the baseball field had plexiglass walls; the other side was lounges and dance floors. The glass elevator she rode up on was right here, so she was close at hand, and he was going to find her.

O   O   O

Prindibin and her two female counterparts were led around by church brothers and introduced to various businessmen, as well as entertainment types and purported sports celebrities. She said she found all this to be so exciting. She said it to everyone they met. In time the three women were separated, taken away to speak individually to clusters of mostly men.

Executives of the new Centaur Athletic Footwear Company were standing outside the seafood buffet, listening as a Mountain of Radiance speaker told them how Clock Tower Executive Management Advisors could remake their workforce into people as appealing, dedicated, and manageable as – Prindibin, here. The seminars would reshape the lives of everyone on team, upper management included.

"My name is Prindibin," she began, looking each man straight in the eye, one after the next, "... And since beginning my studies of the words of Earnest Seamark I have been, as we say, transfigured into such a more effective and fully-realized person. Now my understanding of life dwarfs what it was before. What has happened for me can definitely be replicated at your business. I *know* it can."

"Earnest Seamark?" one of them asked with a grin, "The guy we just saw speaking? I can't say that was exactly a dynamic motivational speaker, ma'am!"

Prindibin didn't back down. "Were you in a place where you could hear the crowd?" she asked, "Have you ever heard any motivational speaker get a response like that? How many super-humans have you seen in your life? You saw one today. If you saw him speak you received his blessing. The benefits of that will become apparent to you, beginning tomorrow morning. Being up on the Bell I was eye-level with the Beneficence. I gazed upon his precious face directly. I am a different person for that, for being eye-to-eye with him. That's the energy you need in your workforce at Centaur Athletic Shoes."

With the mood having turned a little confrontational, a smiling church brother swapped Prindibin off for Deprellex, and took her over to where she would be meeting a Mr. Denken.

She was still miffed at the reaction she got from that corporate knob as she bared her life to him, and she said so. She and the brother stood together at a wall-sized aquarium tank, and he said, "Pull yourself together, because we may have a problem. It turns out there's going to be a procession of an Ascended Child through here in a minute. I don't know whose idea that was. That kind of thing is better for Adherents, not downfallens.

Anyway, we need to talk to this guy without all of that going on, so when he gets here, we kind of guide him into those double doors on the right. It's a big lounge. You should be able to talk to him. We might be swapping you out again, I don't know. We have had a request for you. Might get crazy. Be flexible."

Denken was elderly, and then some, but he puffed out his chest and tried to seem suave for her when they met. After some introductions and formalities from the brother she smiled languidly at him, and said, "Being up on the Bell meant I was eye-level with the Beneficence. I gazed upon his precious face. I am a different person now, from being eye-to-eye with him."

She then gazed into the aquarium as they spoke, feeling his eyes going up and down her. Prindibin looked past the smallish, bald-headed figure, and saw the procession of the Ascended Child moving up the passageway. Moving up fast. They must have emerged from a suite. She and the church brother both saw their predicament. The parade was coming from the wrong direction. They were coming from where Prindibin was supposed to be leading Denken – not the brother's plan.

The procession was surrounded by such a swarm of people, it was going to get hard to maneuver around here in a minute. Two flag bearers led the way, chanting Ascendant verbiage. Behind them, a tiny girl of about three years was borne along on a great cushion by four muscle-bound men. This drooping, listless creature Prindibin knew to be a direct offspring of Earnest Seamark. His bloodline. Despite the theatrical show of security for the Child, nobody was fending off the Adherents who swarmed around her cushion. They were trying to speak prayers and foist gifts and slips of paper to the lethargic little figure, and kiss her hands.

Deep within herself, something struck Prindibin – the kid seemed drugged. Images from her former work in child psychology were impossible to block out. Male voices were babbling all around. She floated for a moment, torn between feeling the need to do her job and get through this, and being disgusted to her core at the treatment of this girl. She decided to move Mr. Denken away before he saw it.

As she was talking to the wrinkly VIP, Prindibin's eyes came to rest on a figure in the crowd across the distance. So far away, but it was somebody who looked like Matthias Pleasant. The image gripped her.

He saw her, too, or thought it could be her. That was the way to go. But the procession was almost upon them, on track to block him off from her. He was about to lurch in front of them, but they were too close.

He saw a chance. A gap of six or seven feet had formed between the flag bearers and the men carrying the child. Matt would zip right through and not stand waiting on the train of people following behind them.

Prindibin took Denken by the arm, a gesture he returned with gusto. Two brothers and now two Honors soldiers accompanied them as they turned to move along to the lounge.

The flag carriers went by, and Matt made his move. But with his eyes searching for Audrey, he didn't notice how long the flag poles were. They dragged the floor. First one then both of his feet hung up on an aluminum pole and he started stumbling, nearly falling flat. Both flag bearers screamed at him, and yanked their flags forward.

His momentary entanglement led to an abrupt, jolting stop of the bearers of the Ascended Child. She was jostled, pitched forward, and had to brace herself on her cushion. As the bearers regained their coordination, Matt tried to continue on without looking back. But the noisiest of hassles ensued.

The humble petitioners to a three-year-old goddess gasped and cried out in horror. Matt kept going.

"Do you know what you just did?" someone shouted at him.

"Excuse me," he said.

Prindibin heard the racket but couldn't see what it was about. Glancing back over her shoulder, for all of two seconds she saw the boyish yet incisive features of her one-time fiancé. Mr. Denken had her gently by the elbow. She was borne along by the group around her, who nattered on and on with comments and questions. She spun her head around for another look back into the swarm of people.

In an intersecting passageway, the Assistant Director appeared suddenly, told her she was doing a great job and it wasn't going unnoticed. He and the pair of Honors troopers eased her away from Denken, introducing another woman to take her place. They spun her away in another direction, walked her into a crowded ballroom, across a dance floor and finally to a dim, intimate lounge on the other side. Here, she was seemingly abandoned by them. They walked off and left her there.

She stood alone for a moment until she saw the approach of a jowly Asian chap in a peach-colored business suit, with a peach-colored cigarette and a silvery necklace. He had stepped away from his retinue to walk directly toward her. Addressing her warmly as Prindibin, he said he just wanted to shake her hand. No introduction was required to know that he was well placed. She offered a vacant smile to conceal her puzzlement when he told her what an inspiration she was to him. He then wanted to ask a couple of questions about her vision of the Mountain of Radiance.

She spoke at length about what she had seen, still without any idea who he was. Her narrative of the experience was well-memorized, but she stumbled once or twice, when another vision, that of Matthias, minutes ago, kept appearing in her mind.

The unknown man listened with great concentration, sometimes with fingertips on his lips, until suddenly he smirked and nodded. He called out a few words in an Asian language, at which point Prindibin's superiors reappeared as if by teleporting. He had nothing more to say to her, including goodbye, and they led her away back across the dance floor, where a gaggle of Adherents stood by. The buzz started up immediately all around her.

"Prindibin! ... Do you know who that *was?!*"

Matt felt certain that no one could identify him in connection with the little incident with the kid on the cushion. He was going to resume his search for Audrey and not give it another thought, until a sound of turmoil spilled out anew from the room where it happened.

Word must be spreading about it. He tried to move through the crowds as quickly as possible without shoving people or looking suspicious. He found that Audrey had vanished, utterly. Although in this shifting mob she could have been right next to him.

Even before the hassle with the little girl he had been nervous about being challenged on his phony credentials and ejected from this place, or worse. Now he was sweating over it. He knew nothing attracts suspicion like believing that people are suspicious of you. Standing near a bar with a panoramic view of the baseball field, he imagined security people swarming this level.

He rejected the idea of leaving. Audrey could be in the next room over. But he reconsidered again when it occurred to him that he could easily walk right back up here, after things cooled off. There was such a thing as a tactical retreat. It would be different if she had been here for hours, and would be leaving soon. But she just got here.

The pop and crackle of a walkie talkie sounded from somewhere in the crowd, which could only be Security. The sound of it grabbed him, like ten thousand volts.

He briskly withdrew into the Fire Escape staircase. Entirely alone on the steps, he shot a text to Charles, "Meet me at the bar and grill. Second level. ASAP."

He made his way downstairs, texting as he went, "I don't recall the name of it," he typed, in an agitated state, "It has the doors with the big wooden handles."

Bienville replied, "OK."

Big wooden door handles, like bars have in every shopping mall in America. Matt got there first, climbed onto a barstool and ordered a non-alcoholic beer. Numerous tables in the dining area behind him held chatty people, but there was no one else at the bar, so maybe he could have some privacy to talk to Charles.

The big man made it in a few minutes later, huffing and puffing and leaning heavily on his four-footed cane. He had the foam neck brace, mirror lens sunglasses, and other disguising accoutrements. He settled in, balancing himself on a barstool.

"I saw her," Matt said.

Charlie's eyebrows shot up over his shades.

"It was her. I know it."

He then recounted the heartbreak of losing her again, due to a clumsy incident with some people carrying a little girl on a pillow.

Bienville said, "That was an Ascended Child. That child is direct bloodline of Earnest Seamark."

Matt thought it over, and just said, "Okay ..."

He said Audrey had changed into an evening gown when he saw her, and now was on the fourth level doing PR duty. Since she only arrived twenty minutes ago, she was almost certainly still there.

"You were right, Charlie. She was singing and then went up to schmooze VIPs. I hope they are keeping their hands to themselves. I am going right back up as soon as things settle down. My press pass seems to get me around pretty well. I'll give it half an hour. They won't expect me to come back. And this time I am going to talk to her."

Charlie advised against rushing back, "They won't forget somebody slamming into the Ascended Child. Not in half an hour. This thing goes on all day tomorrow, too, you know. She'll still be here."

"Nope. No way am I taking a chance of losing her again. They didn't see my face. I kept moving. And it's not like I knocked the kid to the floor! I bumped into someone at the head of the procession. It caused a slight delay. That's all!"

Bienville was wary, "They won't see it that way, Matt. You might as well have punched out the Shebbevunseh himself."

"But again, they didn't see my face. Okay? So, it could have been anybody. Everyone was looking at the little girl! By the time they saw there was a problem I was almost out the door. Then I turned the corner in that passageway ... and Audrey was gone. I couldn't see which way they went."

"Did she see you?" Charles asked.

"I can't be sure. I think so! But it was such a quick glance, from a distance."

The bartender became gregarious. Too much so. He broke in, saying he wanted to show them something. He poked on a tablet and held it up for them to see video of a stand-up comedy club. Matt quickly saw it was that comic Charles had mentioned once. A former Adherent, he now lampooned the cult for a living. He would be all that most people knew of MOR.

The bartender cranked up the volume and Matt and Charles chuckled as the guy in the video cried out, "... Morays and Gentlemen! ..."

The paunchy bartender sang out, in a laughing voice that carried, "The Morays! They're all over the place in this town. You know, the beach down the road is where Ernie walked in out of the surf ... I just laugh at the idiots."

In the few seconds after he said what he said, Matt became aware of a silence. Not sound, but silence caught his notice. The mumbling conversations at the tables had ceased.

He felt a pang of anxiety. His talent for reading a situation had gone active in his mind, with a definite alarm claxon.

He thought it would be better not to turn around, but he did it anyway. Every eye-ball in the dining room was trained on the bartender and the two at the bar. Everyone remained seated but for one young chap who stood by the chair of a wide-eyed, white-haired fellow. This one had a face that was crinkled in deep offense, and sputtering fury.

Silence reigned, apart from the apoplectic geriatric spouting orders to his youthful counterpart. No doubt in Matt's mind, that was what was happening. He noticed the young dude was wearing a gray suit jacket. With broader comprehension, numerous similar jackets became visible, each about midway on the gray spectrum, like car fumes.

"Let's turn that off for now," Matt told the bartender, who squinted, understanding nothing.

The young Honors recruit raked a chair out of his way and strode to the bar.

"You have made an extremely insulting slur against the people of my faith," he growled.

The bartender said he didn't know what he meant, as he shut off the video.

"We are *not* morays!" he barked.

Matt interceded, saying, "You may have misunderstood him, brother. He was talking about a movie."

"I heard what he said," the kid shot back, "We are not here to take disrespect. From him, or *you*, or any others like you! Especially not *today!*"

"All right," Matt said, "I'm sure the old boy meant no disrespect to your church. Did you?"

"Me? No!" the bartender said in a breaking voice.

The gray jacket wasn't appeased. "We are not *morays!*" he screamed.

Matt said, "Okay, well, I think the local police should resolve this. Let them negotiate a settlement! Talk it through! Maybe a proper apology and a discount on the tab will help."

The bartender said, "I'm not authorized to do any discounts." Matt's head did a slow pivot, just to look at him, in casual disbelief.

"Nobody is calling any police," said the young man with the strong voice, "Security at *this* event is provided by God's Army of Eternal Honor!"

From one of the tables a much louder, deeper voice roared, "And thank *God* we're here!"

Matt had not considered that, and was unsure if it could possibly be true. But he nodded, shrugged, and scratched his head in a kind of comical, hapless manner. It allowed him to turn to Charles and whisper, "Get to your car and meet me at Gate D."

Charles rose from his stool, and the Honors soldier said, "You sit right back down."

When Charles continued on his way toward the door, the young man in gray moved after him. That was when Matt's hand came to rest squarely on his sternum.

"Now, now. That is an old guy with medical issues," he said calmly.

As the kid drew up a fist, Matt had it pinned behind his back. Braced against the bar, he propelled him back from whence he'd come, knocking a table over on the way. It was then that he saw for the first time, clearly, how many of them there were.

The oldest one was aghast, beside himself, babbling inaudibly. Three other tables held gray-jacketed youths. All would be new recruits with something to prove.

The bartender was gone, and fortunately so was Bienville. Hopefully one of them was calling the law, if there was any civil authority in this place. None was immediately present.

As he was wondering when they were going to attack him, the old man at the table started rocking back and forth. Everyone was looking not at Matt, but at him. They were awaiting the word from grampa, who was sitting there deciding how this was going to go.

Suddenly, the loud one who yelled in support of the first one hollered out again, "Hey! That's him! That's who assaulted the princess! I knew it looked like him!"

He held up a phone with a blurry photo of Matt's profile.

The old man stopped rocking as he exploded in nonsense words. None were coherent, but chairs went over on the floor and eight mostly screaming young men started advancing.

Matt knew to keep them from surrounding him, to keep them all on one side, and to try to keep an open path to the door. There were windows, but this wasn't the ground floor, and he was unsure how far of a dive it would be.

Thinking at top speed, he identified the psychological leader of the group. It was not the old man, but rather the loud one, who now stood at the center of the group, bellowing nonsense. If he could be taken out it would demoralize the others, whose body language was revealing more bluster than any special courage.

That door could open with cops any second, he thought. Or with reinforcements from MOR.

Two of them lunged at him, swinging away, and he dropped them one at a time as they entered his space. They lurched back to their comrades. If only they all rushed him at once it would have been impossible for him to prevail. But they seemed to want to take turns, and after the first two went down they were all waiting to see who would go next.

The loud guy was speaking, or shrieking, in plain English now. Matt picked up one of the four-legged bar stools, and as he had a clear path and nothing to lose, he put all his power into an overhead throw. Like a giant tomahawk, it went end over end, directly into Loud Guy. He stumbled backward, fell down and scrambled to his feet again. But he was quieter after that.

Matt snatched up another bar stool and whipped it side to side in front of him. The legs made a light whooshing sound that seemed to unnerve them.

Why couldn't somebody walk in that door? He considered making a break for it, but they were too close. He had thrown them off stride psychologically, but it couldn't last.

He held a bar stool horizontally and charged them, crashing into two of them with it, and knocking them down. He started whipping it around like a baseball bat.

The final, feared, group attack came down on him at that moment, but there were fewer of them. He was able to execute a couple of judo moves, but they came right back, and then they were all over him.

Staggering back under a barrage of punches and kicks, he braced himself against the bar and surprised them with his adrenalin-charged strength. Three of them he shoved to the ground, or they simply went down because they didn't want to fight him any further.

The first ones he incapacitated were regaining their footing now, and he saw no further hope for the fight. He grabbed another bar stool, dashed out the door and wedged it into the ornamental wooden handles. It would buy him only ten seconds or so, but Matthias was a runner, to include sprinting when necessary. Numerous people, adherents and downfallen, stepped out of his way.

Lacking a handkerchief, he used his sleeve to wipe the blood off his nose and mouth. The only good news in this catastrophe, apart from the fact that he escaped without being arrested or crippled, was that he managed to cover for Charles until he got away. He texted him and changed the pickup point to a gas station he had spotted on the way in. No point remaining in the stadium now.

Charlie showed up in his rental much later and gave Matt a lift back to the hotel. He said he was not feeling well, not well at all, and would be taking the next available flight to North Carolina. He had just spoken to his wife, who informed him that he would not be doing any further travelling. Ever.

Anyway, he had seen Audrey.

He knew it was her. But he had blown his chance to make contact, and now there was no way he could set foot in that stadium again, not even tomorrow. He decided to fly back tonight as well. No other option. The local cops might even be looking for him over that barroom brawl.

Times that try men's souls. Matthias made a silent vow to himself, and Audrey, to soldier on.

o   o   o

Later that night, in the van going back to the local MOR center, Prindibin tried to take stock of her experiences of the day. She was marveling at why God would send her a vision of an old, downfallen lover. Matthias Pleasant could not have really been there, so it was just an interstitial image, sent to her from higher powers. But how was she to interpret it?

She considered going to her group leaders and seeking their counsel, and immediately rejected it in her mind. Instead she resolved to contemplate it on her own, while referencing key charts in Ummyashuntopudda. For now, she would not openly broach the matter with any other being, of any cohering dimensionality.

The next day at the stadium was less eventful for her, except at the end, after it was all over. She assumed she would be taking the van back to the dorms where they were staying, but was surprised when church brothers called her away, to load her and five other female Adherents into a spacious, luxury SUV. The brothers politely, almost sweetly, told them to shut up and enjoy the ride.

The five other women were her age or younger, and whispering soon broke out amongst them. Prindibin spoke in a louder voice, saying the guys up front only meant them to shut up in terms of not speaking to them. She went further, saying that she wouldn't want to anyway, which gained her a certain standing among the ladies. The big question of where they were going, and why, remained hanging. Nobody knew.

The scenery got more interesting with the passage of an hour or so – definitely more upscale. These were small seaside towns, and none looked remotely affordable.

They arrived at a hotel, which was no Super-8. The six women were herded by the church brothers into an elevator, and from there to the top floor. One of the guys said, "When we get where we're going, stand side by side in a line."

Prindibin found herself in what must be the Presidential Suite. The carpet was Haitian Cotton. A balcony had its doors open, and breezes of a visible sea wafted the sheer curtains. The art on the wall was not hotel art. The man in a recliner before them was not low ranking in Mountain of Radiance. Not that she had ever seen him before, but as with the man in the peach-colored suit, it was self-evident. He also sported a necklace like that of the other man.

He said nothing, but stared at them, examining the row of women with a mild interest. Two other men, younger, and in high fashion business suits and sharp hair styles, stood on either side of his recliner. One of these addressed the women, "We have a big announcement this evening for those of you who pass our initial examination. First Doctor Gulpathoa wants a moment with each of you. Remain standing right here."

From the far side of the room, the man who was called a doctor stepped into view, with what was presumably his nurse. Neither were dressed in medical attire. He smelled strongly of moth balls, and that was with two women standing between him and Prindibin. The nurse directed the first woman in line to, "Open your mouth."

Dental exam? She craned her neck to see what was happening, but when the nurse met her eyes, she looked away again.

The flat, blunt voice of the nurse sounded again, "Give him your right hand."

Uneasy seconds crawled by, made worse by the change in breathing that was audible in the woman having her hand examined. She was puffing her breath in and out in a way that could only have been from some sort of distress.

He moved to the next in line.

"Open your mouth," said the nurse.

Within a minute he was standing in front of Prindibin. His jaw had a dark shade of stubble, as if charcoal had been rubbed on it. His staring eyes bored into a place above the bridge of her nose, as though he were looking right into her cerebrum.

"Open your mouth."

She was startled to see him raise an ungloved hand in front of her face, with the index finger pointed in, pointing at the back of her throat.

Slowly, the fingertip moved into her mouth. He touched nothing, just held it there. She struggled not to have her tongue touch up against it. For perhaps ten seconds, the finger remained positioned there, as his eyes twitched slightly. He produced a phlegmatic grumble. Never did he say a word, but as he withdrew his finger and sighed, the nurse said, "Give him your right hand."

He had it, and put all ten of his fingers into an intense tactile examination of the joints and bones of her hand. Twice he popped a knuckle. He tested the range of mobility of the outermost joints of each of her fingers, and rotated her thumbs around.

It wasn't painful, but it passed the point of discomfort. What was agonizing was not knowing if it would start hurting, or how long this would go on, or just what in the hell was he doing? In no time she dispensed with the idea that this was okay because it was a doctor's examination. It was a violation, and shock and simmering anger led a sudden swarm of emotions within her.

He finished with her, and without eye contact or a word or grunt, he was on to the next in line. When he finished with all of them, he had a few whispered words for the sallow figure in the recliner, who smiled up at him. Doctor and nurse departed the suite. The man who had spoken before stepped forward.

"All of you are still with us," he said, "You may yet be eliminated from contention, but you are going to have a chance to be what almost no other women ever will be. If you successfully complete the second examination, you will attain the highest position a woman can know."

The man who stood like a bookend on the other side of the recliner said, "Most female Adherents are married to male Adherents, and they have their children. That's all. But you are to be of the Avrovalas ..."

Her eyes popped as a shout erupted from the recliner, "Your bloodline is going to rule the world!"

The women in line broke out with theatrical, if not over-played expressions of joy and gratitude, and possibly fear. All except for Prindibin, who stared impassively at the nameless mystery man reclining before her. He struggled to get the thing into a sitting position, then barked out, "You are going to be Channels of Passage! Your offspring will be the only ones who matter five hundred years from now! *Rejoice!*"

The other five did rejoice, or acted like it. Prindibin stood in silence. She felt his eyes land on her, and stay there, looking. Evaluating.

One of the bookends cleared his throat, "Final evaluation will be up to your Shebbovotan. You will be returned to his care now. God has blessed you ... Believe Only."

Five female voices chirped, "Believe Only," as they turned to file out of the room.

As they stepped into the hallway, two more sets of six women were standing there, waiting to go in.

The elevator opened to disgorge six more. Like the six that included Prindibin, all of these ladies were attended by church brothers. On seeing each other, the guys immediately launched into a noisy laugh riot with their counterparts. Clearly, the boys knew each other. Had it been a locker room they would have been whipping towels at one another. Once this started, the groups of women began loud gabbing sessions amongst themselves, standing in the corridor.

Alone among them, Prindibin was not taking part in it. She drifted around the yammering groups. Slowly she sidled toward the elevator bank.

Pressing the button to summon one was not in her mind at all. Not much was in her mind, apart from a logjam of thoughts and emotions that she felt might have led to a seizure had they been much more extreme.

High-spirited, idiotic yelling from young men and mindless jabbering from women flooded her head. She just wanted a little space to stand alone.

An elevator opened.

No one stepped out.

Prindibin stepped in.

She jammed her thumb onto the wide button at the bottom that said "Lobby."

It was as if she was merely observing this, like a movie. She didn't seem to be actually doing it. She had every expectation that a hand would zip in to stop the door closing, but none did. The elevator doors met with a soft clack, and the car descended with Prindibin feeling it in her stomach.

Alone, apart from her ever-present, silently staring angel, she grabbed onto the mental image of the taxi cab stand. It was mere steps away from this elevator on the first floor.

What if all the cabs were taken?

She had five dollars. No, seven dollars! It would be enough to get a few blocks down the road. Maybe she wouldn't mention to the driver how little money she had, and she could put some miles between herself and ... What was going on here?

She was running out on the church.

Her angel sent a pulse of emotion to her. What was she doing? His fate, his afterlife, was bound up with hers. She wasn't just going out on her own here.

But she was going out on her own. She was out of here. It was over, and it was on. She would tell the cab driver to take her to the nearest police station.

What if the driver was a church brother?

The elevator hummed as it moved downward. The light was harsh florescent. The floor was threadbare carpet, with a fleur-de-lis pattern and numerous mystery stains. The digital screen above the door went from 6 to 5. Her soft voice sounded in the confined space.

"... Believe Only ... Believe Only ... Believe Only ..."

She needed only to get away for a short while. She needed just a short time on her own, to work out what she was all about. Piece some of the logjam together in a more coherent way. This was not necessarily anything irreversible, she said to herself. And instantly her own voice said, "You are not going back."

She was shaking. The red numbers went from 3 to 2.

Gravity increased palpably. A faint chime sounded. The doors parted.

Blocking the doorway, a hotel bell-hop stood with a phone pressed to his ear. Two more stood on either side of him. He looked at her, and the most awkward and insincere smile she had ever seen on a face came to his.

"... Prindibin?" he asked.

She locked onto the white plastic tab on his collar, with the numerous, tiny, colorful insignia, looking like little hieroglyphics. The other bellmen had them, too.

He said, "Have you gotten yourself lost?"

A hotel security man, collar tab packed with ink, emerged from the rear.

She heard her voice say, "It was the strangest thing! The doors opened and I got in thinking the others would be right behind me, and ... the doors just closed! It started going down!"

Security Man said, "You didn't see that you were alone when the doors closed? You did not attempt to stop the doors closing?"

She said, with some belligerence, "I was looking at the floor. I had a lot on my mind." She then put some lung power into it, turning heads at the concierge desk, *"I am going to be a Channel of Passage!"*

She pushed past them, stepping into the lobby. "Where's the Ladies' Room around here!?"

Two bellmen escorted her across the lobby to the restrooms of this MOR-owned hotel, and would be standing outside waiting until she emerged again. Prindibin stepped in, felt the relative bliss of the door closing between her and them, and then looked to see if there was anyone else in here, or any outside window. It was no to both.

She entered a stall, locked the door, sat down and buried her face in her hands. She had become expert at not crying.

Within minutes the door to the restroom flew open, and first one then another, and then another woman entered, each asking, "Prindibin! Are you all right?"

"Are you okay, honey?"

"Prindibin, are you okay?"

O   O   O

Sixteen hundred miles away, a pungent biological odor of swamp water filled the air of a sumptuous apartment. It filled all of it. An elegant young woman sat alone at an oak desk in the center of the main room, burning three sticks of incense and playing an old arcade game on her laptop computer. There came a tentative tap on her door.

Her voice rang out, "What!?"

A timid, girlish voice came back, "It's just Delboax, ma'am. I – I am to bring you the household planner for the week. An event has been added."

When she got no reply, Delboax eased the door open slightly. On not being told to go away, she entered.

"It's just the household planner, ma'am," she said, placing a sheet of paper on the desk next to her, "The ... ahhh ... selection of the Channels of Passage is to be held Saturday. Oh, you're playin' Ms. Pac Man? I haven't seen that since ... oh, before I first got into the church."

No response.

Delboax said, "I'll fill your water pitcher for you, ma'am!" She snatched it off the desk and went bounding into the adjacent bathroom with it. When she returned, she said, "It looks like your bidet is dripping in the toilet again, ma'am. I thought we'd got that fixed for you."

A hollow voice said, "Thought so, huh? They did fix it. And now ... now ... it's dripping again."

"I can put in another report on it." Delboax mumbled, under her breath, "Would you like for me to do your nails for you, ma'am? I could do your nails right now."

"You did my nails not long ago, Delboax. I have done nothing to scuff them up. I might as well have been laying on a slab in a morgue since you last did my nails."

"Yes ma'am," said Delboax, "Well, if you don't need anything, I guess I should be getting on back."

"I guess so," said the woman at the computer, "And tell them I said not to send anyone else around to check up on me ... And to get that *goddamned bidet fixed!*"

With the departure of Delboax, she reached in a drawer and took out her box of cannabis and a package of dark chocolates. She then snatched up the paper from the desk. The "household planner" – of her own household.

She saw the weekend event, the list of visiting dignitaries, and the names for "Selection of Channels of Passage." Seeing the list of names, she reached out and minimized Ms. Pac Man.

She went online, and opened the Gardener's Helper message board. Under the category of Ferns, she clicked to enter a response in a thread titled "What's Up with my Drooping FERNS?"

Her silvery and jewel-studded bangle bracelets rolled on the desk as her perfectly shaped, cherry red and rhinestone-speckled fingernails expertly entered two long paragraphs of text on basic botany, a decoy should there be anyone around here who had the desire to read her internet posts. The third paragraph was the departure:

"I believe you are interested in a Prindibin. She will be at the GPS coordinates below on September 10th. Probably three days at least. They're going to make her a Channel of Passage. Big event! Here are the others that will attend ... "

Having been an administrative assistant at one time, she expertly typed out every name on the household planner at high speed. Then she lit up a smoke, and checked the clock. In ten minutes, she would go back in and delete the post.

Her hard, pointy, red fingernail came down and clicked "Send."

Three seconds later, in the hill country of North Carolina, a notification chime sounded on the computer of Charles Bienville.

Part Three

"Freedom from coercive ideology is both a human right and a fundamental civil liberty."

A. C. Grayling

L ate that afternoon, as he sat down for a lunch of re-heated Chinese food, Pleasant finally caught a semblance of a break. It came in the form of a phone call from Charlie.

"... There has been a development," he said, "You will need to drive out here. ASAP."

"You can't just tell me over the phone?!"

Matt made the two-hour drive to Santa's workshop.

When he turned onto the crumbling concrete driveway, the big man was sitting in a golf cart out front. His wife handed him a can of grape soda and gave a minutes-long whisper in his ear. Her face was joyless when she made a silent nod of greeting to Matt. Jin Kyong would talk to Blaine and Deidra. Rarely a word, and so far, never a smile for him.

Charlie stood up, can in one hand, cane in the other, "I was going to drive us in the cart. The engine noise is hard on their eavesdropping equipment. But I could use the walk."

He slung a satchel over his shoulder, from which a bebop jazz piece blared out. Matt looked off into the trees that ringed the property, "What, you think they have guys with parabolic microphones monitoring you?"

"Those mics cost fifty bucks at Radio Shack," Charles replied, "And the guys work for free. Do you know what the Church's annual budget is for harassing critics?"

They ambled slowly down the dirt road that led to the pond. A box turtle crossed in front of them. As Matt was starting to grow impatient, the old guy spoke.

"Some of her highest superiors have nominated Prindibin to audition with the regional honcho for the position of child-bearer for the cult. If she passes the physical examination, which is more religious than medical, Prindibin will become a Channel of Passage."

Matt scowled and walked along, trying to keep a slow enough pace that he didn't get ahead of him. He folded his arms and said, "So, that's what you couldn't tell me over the phone?"

"There is something else, actually. The event is coming up soon. Like, ten days from now. On September 10th. I have the coordinates of the location. It's closer than California, but still pretty far away, I'm afraid."

"Uh huh. Where?" Matt asked.

"Umm ... Louisiana?"

"Louisiana. Okay, and now I have something to ask you," Matt said, "How is it that you know all this? Hmm?"

Charles seemed set back a bit, and took a big pull of his grape soda. Before he could speak, Matt said, "And don't tell me it's from any extended network of former Adherents, because they wouldn't have that kind of knowledge. They're *former* Adherents."

"That's right. No, they wouldn't know," Charles said, and stopped walking.

Matt re-folded his arms.

Charles said, "I guess there's no time like the present to tell you ... It's like this, Matt ... I seem to have a mole inside Mountain of Radiance."

Matt examined his face for lying. At present he saw nervousness, but nothing else.

He said, "You're kidding me."

"No, uhh, no Matt, I'm not."

"May I ask why you let me spend all that money on private detectives if you have an inside man?"

Charlie replied, "A few different reasons. One was – need to know. You remember, from the Army? Need to know? You didn't need to know."

He went on to say that this informant was the most valuable thing he'd ever had in his counter-cult career. "For over a year, I have received reams of information on MOR from them, all of which has subsequently checked out. This, in an organization that does not leak." Charles said, "Whoever it is, they are either an extremely well-placed potential defector, or they have direct access to somebody who is. But there's a problem ...

"While this person has always given solid information, they are not reliable in terms of their availability. The information is always a bullseye. But I can send out my signal to them online for weeks sometimes and get no response. Other times, the mole contacts me unsolicited, with something they think I ought to know. That's what happened today.

Matt, I know exactly nothing about this person. Not a name, gender, age, race, location, how many of them there are ... nothing. They consist of messages online, which are deleted at the end of a brief window of time. I simply could not tell you about them until I had something actionable."

Charlie added, "It's not guaranteed she will be accepted for the 'great honor.' First she and some others go to a residence of their Shebbovotan. They have a ritual prior to final selections."

She was chosen during the 50th Anniversary thing, he said. The decision, once made, had triggered a report to Bienville from whomever his online benefactor was. It came with a time and a place, in GPS, for Prindibin. Audrey Crane.

He invited Matt to stay at a cabin tonight. The peace and quiet would be good for thinking, and drawing up plans. The time frame was horrifically short.

Over a blueberry pancake breakfast in the curtained conference room in his home, Charles reiterated that the site of the big event was a residential property of Emzharotav. Randolph Poleander. The event would include representatives and leaders of certain smaller cults, from contacts made at Trailblazer Stadium. These folks would be asked to enter into a full-blown grafting with MOR. The fertility rite would be part of the evening, partly to impress the visitors.

Matt had a sip of coffee and said he wanted to go, and try to slip into the place. He was never in Special Forces or anything, but he knew a little about covert operations from hanging out with such guys, and reading.

"Slip in?" Charles said, "I was thinking you could cross paths with her when she arrives to go out to the compound. See her at the airport. The actual residence is – way the hell out in a bayou. There's no road. They use a launch, like a ferry boat, to get out there. It leaves from a certain fish camp. *That* would be the place to try to meet her. That's the last public place."

Matt thought about it, and said, "While she is in transit, she's a moving target. When she is inside the place, she is stationary for a few days."

Bienville asked in disbelief if he was seriously contemplating going inside the compound, and reacted with a shouted opposition to the idea.

"But it's the first pin-pointed location I have ever had on her!" Matt exclaimed.

"Going into that property would be like going into a hostile foreign country," Charles said. This drew a bemused sidelong glance from Matt. The older fellow saw it and recalculated. He said, "The fact that Emzharotav is hosting all these 'visiting dignitaries' means it will be swarming with even more security than normal! You're proposing to walk into a police state."

"It turns out, that actually helps," Matt said, "I'm planning to go in disguised as an MOR 'Honors' officer."

Charles shook his head. Matt continued, "You have lots of photos of what their uniforms look like. They're not complicated. It's gray denim. Right? My mother has a sewing machine. We can make one. Audrey's sister, Yvonne, knows some of the jewelry crafters from her Dad's old business. They are going to make duplicates of the medals those guys wear."

As the reality of the plan began to gel in Bienville's mind, he vociferously opposed it, "Matt, you are proposing to trespass into Poleander's private home."

"Nowhere near as much as he has trespassed into mine," Matt said.

"Uh-huh, well, I hope you know what you're doing, my friend. I don't think you do. I'm not going to try to stop you, but I can only support this under protest. I wish now I never told you about it. I figured you would meet her at the airport, or the fish camp or something. Not inside the damned compound itself! You could be heading into the biggest disaster of your life." With emphasis he added, "People disappear in this cult."

Matt said, "Yeah, I know. My girlfriend did."

Charles insisted again how much safer it was to stick to public interactions, like the concerts.

Matt said he nearly had his head stoved in last time, even in a safe public place! He didn't want to seem disrespectful to the old guy, so he watched the tone of his voice.

He tried to show him the preparations he had put together so far, literally overnight. He said he was psyched to go for this. He will go in alone. He just wants some support waiting nearby, within two miles, when he comes out. They won't have to come in and get him, just be there to help him get away. Yes, he is talking about his sister and her boyfriend, and Reverend Moultrie. He had talked to them all, and they are rearranging their schedules to go.

"... Moultrie too?" the old man asked, "Moultrie is going?"

"Not any closer than two miles! Surely two miles can't be too close!" he exclaimed to the now thoroughly appalled Bienville.

Matt was calling in all markers. Time was too tight. He needed Charlie to shake the tree of his network of former Adherents and find out if anyone had ever been to this place, especially inside. A map of the layout *inside* would be invaluable. He was leaving in the morning to make a trip to the site itself to reconnoiter the exterior, and figure out how to proceed from there.

He said he was acquiring a drone for surveilling the isolated property, which GPS revealed is indeed deep inside a vast bayou. No towns were anywhere near it. He told Charles he was getting a drone kit with goggles to allow him to watch the view in real time, and also record it.

○   ○   ○

Less than a week later, Matt was reclining on a lawn chair in murderous humidity outside a motel a few miles from Chalmont's Fish Camp. A little chime in his pocket announced an incoming text: Deidra and Blaine had arrived, rented a car, and were waiting to pick up Reverend Moultrie at Lafayette Regional Airport.

220

That evening, as soon as they arrived, everyone piled into Matt's room to watch drone surveillance he had captured the day before.

He said he felt he had positioned the thing along the tree tops such that it would have been unlikely anyone spotted it. He pulled open a closet door, and there the gizmo sat.

"It is small, quiet, and hellishly expensive," he said, "And it will be for sale when I get home."

The four of them submerged into sober concentration as the aerial view of the secluded compound locked down the reality of what would soon be going down. The place sprawled for acres of conjoined structures, seemingly built at different times for different purposes. The way people come and go is by water, or helicopter, he said. They could see a helipad, and a prominent dock lined up with small boats and a mid-sized passenger ferry.

Moultrie inquired about the squat, round building at the edge of the water. Matt said, "Funny looking, isn't it? Like a World War II 'pillbox,' but bigger. It must be the oldest of them. Seems to be made from river stones and mortar. Probably used for smoking fish or tanning hides." It had an opening sticking out into the water that would accommodate small boats, but a cyclone fence went out into the swamp around it, sealing it off.

"Now, over here is your basic rifle range. Where these spiritual giants practice their marksmanship."

DeeDee asked, wouldn't they have motion sensors? Matt said it was a possibility, but look at all the vegetation and Spanish Moss all over the place. With all that blowing around, he didn't see much utility in a motion sensor. He had some concern about night vision, or thermal surveillance. That had been a concern early on, but he had better ideas now.

For one thing, there was this. He pointed out a dock on the back of the main building where crates and boxes were stacked up. It sure looked like a spot where supplies came in by boat. They chuckled at the tiny image of a guy in an apron, sitting on a barrel. A double door led right inside from the dock. Where the water went under that dock would be his entry and exit point, he said. Unless they run thermal imaging cameras under their docks, he felt he should be okay.

As it turned out, he told them, he had also caught a break and picked up some good information about the place from locals. He had chanced upon this rundown convenience store when he went out to fly the drone, and struck up a conversation with some teenagers who were hanging around. They told him how they liked to pester the guards at the compound. Matt had asked them what the creepy place was all about. Their replies give him encouragement that there were no thermal sensors.

Locals apparently had only contempt for the holy compound. The kids told him there were guards on patrol, but they were never aware of the boys being there. They could stand a few feet away in the woods drinking beers and watching the patrols go by, every twenty minutes, 'round the clock, every twenty minutes. They could stand there as long as they liked, watching these guys. Then they would blow their whistles or throw firecrackers, or whatever prank they were pulling that night, and run like hell through the woods. They never got caught.

His sister again spoke up, "One more time, once you get in under the dock, lose the wet suit, and walk into the place ... what exactly are you going to do, again?"

"I am going to locate Audrey. I will have on an MOR uniform, perfect to the last detail, with collar tabs and insignia that designates me as one high-ranking capo dei capi. I know enough of their jargon to bullshit my way through basic questioning. I'm going in late at night when hopefully she will be asleep. I have obtained a very rough schematic of the place, through a friend of a friend of Mr. Bienville. Fortunately, most of the compound is off limits to regular

Adherents, which narrows it down. Through a process of elimination, I have it down to where the communal berthing areas should be. If it's not there, I'll find it.

"From logical deduction based on where the Adherents' shower facilities are, I think I can get to it. If there's a guard I am going to bluff my way in by saying I have orders from on high to see one of the women in her group of three. I am not going to ask for Prindibin, but one of the others we know she is grouped with. That way, if things fall apart they won't know who I was really looking for."

DeeDee said, "And what if you get caught, and get in trouble with these fanatic people? Hmm?"

"... Guess I might end up with a black eye, huh? Maybe a broken nose. Think what I'll have to spend on a nose job." Seeing the look on her face, he grinned and added, "If they get too heavy with me I will tell them I have friends who know where I am, so unless they want a big public relations stink, they should just mellow out. Call the cops and charge me with trespassing. I'll have my disposable cell phone, and I'll make a big thing of calling in some code to the Reverend. Which would be your cue to head back to camp and call the State Police, Moultrie. And if you two don't hear from us in twelve hours, *you* go to the State Police."

Blaine said, "And, ahhh, when you do find Audrey, what then?"

"A lot will depend on the situation. If I have an uninterrupted moment, I will be able to say more. If I am being restrained by a platoon of goons, I will just shout out that I love her, and we all want her to come home. The ideal would be to find her asleep, wake her up and talk softly to her. I have a good idea what to say, but I'll go with my gut when the time comes."

Blaine looked to DeeDee, then to Moultrie, and then he said, "There is one other option. You could abort mission and come home with us. Keep looking for her in public venues if you want. But don't go into this place."

The Reverend said, "Let's go fishing in the morning. Get some sun. And then let's go home. Not too late for that."

Matthias smiled and said, "I appreciate your concern. All of you. I really do. But it is too late."

O   O   O

The following afternoon, Deidra and Blaine sat fishing on a stone hurricane wall, observing various odd people noisily boarding a colorful tour boat docked some distance away. When it hoisted anchor and moved forward, she hit a button on her phone and a bouncy pop tune sounded off in Matt's pocket.

"Okay," he said, "That's it. Let's go."

He and Moultrie set out in a flat bottom aluminum boat powered by a quiet motor, and rigged up with numerous hidden compartments duct-taped underneath. They followed the slow ferry carrying leaders of other cults to Poleander's place. The boat had music playing, and just enough festive lights that they could track it from a far distance.

Time passed and the bayou came to look like something from a documentary on dinosaurs. Ancient, gnarled mangrove trees were hung with Spanish Moss. The broad waters glistened in fading afternoon sunlight. Mosquitoes were whining everywhere, but as the guys had soaked themselves in Deet, it wasn't too bad.

He watched the GPS numbers changing in his hand. They dropped anchor by a cluster of mangrove stumps a couple of hundred feet from the shore, and two miles away from the compound, if drone and GPS were accurate.

Matt would swim keeping the bank to his left. They spotted another small craft in the far distance, which could have spotted them, they didn't know. So, Matt lay in the bottom of the boat and wriggled into the MOR paramilitary uniform that he and his mother stitched together in Fayetteville, complete with phony medals that a jeweler friend of the Crane family had fabricated. He struggled to pull on a wet suit over it.

Craig asked, "So, you're not worried about, you know – snakes? Or alligators?"

"No. They're more afraid of us than we are of them. They avoid people. I'm more concerned about the two-legged snakes."

Moultrie was to wait on the boat, all night if necessary, while Matt swam over. Disposable cell phone – check! Yes, Louisiana has coverage statewide. Three clicks means I am safe, or to answer yes. Two clicks answers no. With a handshake and a thank you, he slipped over the side.

His afternoon swim led him by locations he had seen from the drone. What a perfect illustration of eeriness this was. Shadowed, impenetrable forests all around, dripping in moss.

A rush of relief came with finally finding the property. First he spotted the old-timey "pillbox" building, embedded with stones, and then the more recent constructions. Treading water, he observed the utility dock, with crates stacked on one side. Visiting passengers would disembark at the nicer, painted dock that the drone showed as being farther up.

It was good to see two old women push open the double door and step out on the dock. Maybe it would remain unlocked when he got there. As he bobbed in the dark water, they stood and shared a cigarette for a few minutes.

The two-man patrol marched into sight, making their way along the fence. Hopefully the kids were right about the twenty-minute rotation.

He silently swam in, crawled out under the dock and stripped off the wet suit which he left behind in a garbage bag. Stoking up his confidence, and combing his hair, he emerged to slip in through the double doors, quietly passing a kitchen and dining area.

He had just enough jargon memorized to put on a good show for when, not if, he encountered someone. He was aware that cameras might be in use in here. They may have even spotted him by now. But he was looking good. Looking like a proper MOR Honors Hero, of which there had to be plenty walking around. He resolved to bluff his way as far as he could. If he gets caught, he'll deal with that when it happens. The goal was to find Audrey, and say at least one or two statements to her.

He heard a chorus singing. It was a rehearsal, as it would stop suddenly here and there. An amplified male voice spoke, reverbing so much he couldn't understand it. The floors in this part of the place were plywood, hollow underneath, and uncarpeted. Footsteps clomped along in the distance. It would give him a warning when people were coming.

Nearing an intersection of corridors, he was prepared when a group of three uniformed men strode around a corner and came toward him. He eye-contacted each one, and then looked away before passing them, offering a terse, "Believe Only." They kept going.

Matthias holed up in a kind of alcove, a closet with its door removed, figuring he might remain undetected here until everyone was settled in for the night. Listening to the mostly female singers, he thrilled to think that one of them must be Audrey.

Smelled bad in here, like bleachy mop water. Sure enough, there was the rolling bucket. Many sounds reached him. Like a blind man he tried to work out clues from them. A generator was running somewhere, but not close. A youthful male voice, bossy-sounding, would yap out an order at times. The singers seemed to be reaching a crescendo, sounding as if a show might be coming to a close. Several minutes later he heard the quick patter of many feet, not as heavy and hobnailed as what crossed the floor before.

Whispering young female voices reached him, quite a few, as a large group were walking the corridor that intersected near to where he stood. It was late enough that he deduced these were singers going down the hall to their barracks. He maintained his wait, radioing in at 20 past the hour the three clicks to Moultrie that said he was all right. Three came in return.

When he felt the time was right Matt made his way in the direction that the procession of women had gone. At the end of the corridor was a door with a gray-haired lady sitting, reading a book. At his approach, she nervously stood. He regarded her sternly for a several seconds, and said, "What is your seventh permanent order?"

She stammered out, "I will sacrifice myself unto my last breath for the Shebbevunseh if I am commanded, or I see the need." Matt viewed her with contempt and growled, "You have an Adherent by the name of Zintopell in here?"

"Zintopell?" the lady stammered, perplexed. She wasn't sure, and didn't know all their names. Matt ordered her to let him look, figuring there couldn't be many in the room.

There was no need to worry if any of the other women would look at him or challenge him. They were all snoring in their bunks. After examining about a third of the beds, he saw Audrey, also fast asleep. Her hair was now grown out into a little bob cut, like a jazz baby of the 1920s. Heartache grabbed him for a moment, but he was underway and working here. He told the matron to return to her post.

In the darkness, he shook her shoulder, and intoned, "Stand and come with me."

Near the door of the chamber, he stopped by the wall, and said to her, "It's okay. You're not in any trouble. Least of all from me." Shining a little LED light on the wall reflected a glow on one side of their faces. He said, "... Never from me."

She was agape, struck mute. Not that he could see her very well. He smiled in a hopefully disarming kind of way, "I don't know what they've told you about me, dear, but I bet it isn't good. Or true. You see, I still care ..." He didn't touch her, just spoke in a firm but gentle voice, "I will come back again as soon as I can, and try to help."

Was she about to start screaming? He had hoped to ask her to walk out with him. He shifted the light a little to see her. She looked entirely electrified, but also possibly panicky. He made a split-second decision to keep the pressure as low as possible on her.

He shifted the light onto his own face, from the side so as to avoid any horror movie style lighting from below. In as nice a voice as he could muster, he said, "Until then, I just wanted to say, all of your family and friends want you to come home. None of us blames you for what happened ... Okay, if Nurse Ratchet out in the hall asks why I was here, you say you were sleeping. You thought you had dreamed it. Tell 'em anything. For now, I guess you better go back to bed. Oh, wait, I don't want *you* to think it was a dream when you wake up. So ..."

He produced a ballpoint pen and quickly drew a heart on the palm of her hand.

Very steadily, she reached out with her other hand and closed it onto his, the one holding the mini-flashlight. She moved it to guide the beam down onto her palm, and viewed the tiny heart. Neither said a word as a half a minute went by.

She then heard her own voice speak, in a breathy monotone, "... I can't talk to you ..."

He remained standing there in silence, in the darkness, looking down at the spot of light.

He heard her say, "... Not right now."

"I know. All right," he said, "The last thing I want to do is get you in trouble. You call me. Anytime. We'll talk. I'm always there. You remember the number. Call any of us! Call your mother, honey. She worries about you."

She just stood there. He saw her head nod in a slow affirmation.

He said, "Call the Cattery! They're havin' litter box issues!" He smiled ear to ear, and was trying to engage a little laugh from her. But with his eyes adjusted to the dark, he saw no smile on her troubled face.

"We don't have phones of our own, Matt," she said, "So ... I can't. I mean, it's not easy."

Her face as he could see it looked both nervous and bereft. She was wide awake now, and seemed strained. Unsteady. He said only that they would figure something out. This time she had no response, and lapsed into uneasy silence.

"Audrey, be strong. We'll talk again. Soon." He reached out and lightly squeezed her shoulder, "... *I love you.*"

His mini-light clicked off; he whirled away and disappeared through the door.

Audrey's experience was internal chaos, like crazy music. It was three different jazz tracks playing at once in her head. There was a heavy sense of dread moving through her, but at the same time something on the order of – triumph. She carefully made her way back to her bunk in the dark, thinking that triumph was the word for how she felt, for sure. Remembering how much that word was thrown around by people in the church, she thought that none of them meant anything like what she was feeling now.

Sleep returned for her easily, but in only a few hours, before breakfast or even sunlight, Prindibin and two others were shaken awake by the matron and told to go with a burly male Adherent who stood nearby. Judging by his collar tab he would be fairly high-ranking. The only explanation she got was something vague about a requirement to be "checked by doctors." It was all underway before she had time to worry if it was something connected to Matt's visit.

The hefty, somber young man led them on a circuitous route through the compound. With her thumb she rubbed the ink heart off of her hand as she ambled along, lest he see it.

They arrived at a tiny room with two metal folding chairs, where the other women were told to wait. Prindibin then ended up in a smaller space much further back. It was big enough for an examination table. She beheld three whiskery, blank-faced little old men in white medical scrubs and aprons. The odor of clove cigarettes smashed into her sinuses.

They moved in closer to her, surrounding her. One put a light in her ear. He then gripped her chin and forced it down to look in her mouth. He said something in Ascendant vocabulary.

Prindibin's heart rate spiked as a claustrophobic panic took shape. The dirty-looking medical man clapped a calloused hand on her forehead and then on her cheek, as if checking for a fever. She looked from the dead eyes of one old man to the next, and finally to the young brother who had walked her over here. He was a void of humanity; a hulking humanoid devoid of soul.

Nothing was to be seen in any face; they might as well have been wearing clear plastic masks. She saw no point at all in trying to speak or communicate in any way with him or the three hoary grotesques standing around her. They shuffled in closer, mumbling.

A moment later her memory was interrupted. A blank was all there was. She found herself walking back the way she had come, just ahead of the heavy-set church brother. He wasn't happy with the pace she was keeping, and growled at her to move it. Body aches shot through her all over as she struggled along.

Whatever had happened it had taken her to the point of passing out, and now she had only fragmented memories from however much time it had been. She saw motionless images of the doctors, or whatever they were. She saw the brother, who now poked her in the square of her back and said, "Come on! I'm not going to carry you!"

She stopped, turned and slumped back on the plywood wall. Her attempt to speak to him came out in a babble; to her shock, she found she could not talk intelligibly. She stood, wide-eyed and slack-jawed.

He snarled, "Look, you passed the examination. Shake it off … Let's go!"

She was marched across the breadth of the compound and put on a kitchen detail. Still stunned, she fell into it with robotic movements. Chopping boiled eggs. Chopping celery. She struggled to remain on her feet, and leaned heavily against the steel table. Muscle aches went rampaging through her body.

After an undefined blur of time in the kitchen, she was pulled away by a new brother and told she was to be honored to perform a silver polishing detail at Poleander's private apartment.

Another foray across the property, and she emerged on an interior balcony overlooking an expansive private office. The swamp was visible through plate glass windows on the far side. Prindibin's attention was directed to a wall-sized display case of gleaming platters, plates, tureens and utensils, all of which seemed well polished already.

The brother pointed out a bottle of polish and rags, and said she was to do the full service for twenty diners, then report to scripture study in the Singing Bell rehearsal room. It was a light duty day, in celebration of the guest banquet that would be held that evening. Singing Bell would be performed before and during the dinner.

Emzharotav's display case of silver would be visible from the Mahogany conference table in the stylish, spacious room below. Past that, across the room, his imposing desk was partially visible to her in a step-down nook by the plate glass walls. A doorway to the right would probably lead to his personal chambers. Another door on the left would likely go back into the rest of the building.

After polishing a few etched-silver platters, being still so devastated from her encounter with the so-called doctors, Prindibin rested herself, curled up on the carpet. Soon she was dozing.

Only much later did she snap awake at the sound of voices from below. Peeking down through ornamental scrollwork openings in the balustrade barrier of the balcony, she saw Emzharotav, in a red golf shirt, seated at his desk. Though he was only partially visible to her, his voice was unmistakable. Honors soldiers stood nearby. Another gentleman was seated facing him, with his back to her. His long, shiny blonde hair was hanging down the back of the chair. How long had she been asleep!? The sunlight had shifted in the windows.

She thought of quietly resuming the polishing, but rejected it. If her minders came checking on her, she would pretend to be asleep. The punishment for that would not be so bad. She remained lying there, listening, as her Shebbovotan interviewed someone who was apparently the leader of a business they called Nutritionals Understood, or something.

Their chat had started out with excited comments from the lone, blonde visitor. This person was agog about whatever he saw hanging on a wall next to Poleander. Prindibin couldn't see it.

Poleander said, in effect, let's cut the crap and get down to business. One of the three Honors soldiers who attended him handed him a tablet. This visitor had been evaluated.

The Shebbovotan said, "You have a healthy footprint after five years. Your multi-level business is flush, and seems to be patterned after our own Golden Waves Inc., though you are denying any direct rip-off. The youth of your base is appealing. You are expanding in Florida and Texas. We like that. We stated that you should merge a religious push along with the, ah, nutritional science aspect of the package. And, of course, we can easily train you on that."

All in all, Nutritionals Understood Partnerships were declared to be a fine candidate for "friendship" with Mountain of Radiance. "You should know that there are levels of friendship with us. You don't wanna drop below the minimum!" Poleander said, laughing heartily.

The visitor was informed that he could expect an infusion of cash, exposure, and prestige. In return he would publicly adopt enough of the MOR teachings to be considered an Arm of Earnest Seamark. He was promised his independence, but friendship works both ways. He must maintain certain standards, and MOR sets them.

After what amounted to a ring-kissing ceremony, the nutrition guru was escorted out by MOR soldiers and, as Prindibin lay listening, another dubious personage was shown in.

The new entry was introduced by his assistant as the owner of a "major chain of martial arts studios." When the man himself actually spoke, it was with an abrupt demand for specifics. This guy wanted numbers. He gave the Shebbovotan attitude – and got it in return. There was no need for friendship. Doesn't have to be a bit of it. This cat was promptly dressed down and thrown out. If the visitor had hoped to make his presence felt, or come off looking strong, he had flopped badly. And out he went.

After the door banged shut, Prindibin heard Poleander addressing one of his soldiers, "Give me a couple minutes before you send in the next one, Emblagua."

And then, a woman's grating voice followed, "... He's going to need more time than that, Emblagua."

Prindibin raised her head to peer out of the lowest opening of the scrollwork, where she saw someone she first took to be a singer from the Bells. Her blonde hair was reminiscent of the wigs they wore. Then she decided it must be the woman's actual hair. She looked like what her sister, Della, would have called a "clothes horse," being radically over-dressed for the time of day. The woman jammed her hands onto her hips. Bangle bracelets rolled around her wrists.

Emzharotav could manifest a grating voice, too. He said, "Now, I believe I have had word sent to you that today has the busiest schedule I have had for some time, and I am not going to be able to ... chew the fat with you. You will be joining us for dinner, but ..."

"No. We're going to chew some fat right now, Randy," she said, as Prindibin's eyes popped.

The lady snarled, "That cheap-assed bidet you put in has started leaking again. I am sick of listening to it drip. And God knows I don't go anywhere anymore, so I get to listen to it a lot. And that brings me to the main item ... *When do I get to visit my friends?!*"

He raised his voice, "You have picked the busiest part of the busiest day of the ..."

But she was right on it, "You were stringing me along for a month because of the big fiftieth anniversary thing. Before that it was a speaking tour. Before that it was some big dealie's funeral. Do you know how long it has been since I have seen my friends?! And how long I have been hearing you promising that I will get to see them!? And how long you have been *keeping me cooped up?!*"

"You went with me to California for the convention and you have been with me at other events this year," Poleander said, in monotone, "It wouldn't look right for my wife to be seen bar-hopping with ... whatever those people are. I told you that you could visit them sometime, and when we can swing it, we will."

"Not sure how many states would consider me your wife, just based on your say-so."

"Okay," he muttered, "I have an important prospect waiting outside to talk to me. We will have all day tomorrow to get this settled."

Her voice took on a rasp, "Yeah, and let me tell you how it will *be* settled tomorrow. The first thing you are going to do is tell me which of the next two weekends I will have for a long weekend in Las Vegas with my friends. And I want suites at Bellagio, of the kind you can afford, and I want first class flights for *all six of my friends!*"

The words *my friends* she punctuated with a stamping of her foot. Prindibin stared at her, entranced, and watched her whip her index finger up to point at him, with its long, ruby red nail catching the light. The woman hissed, "And just bear in mind, I don't disappear as easy as maybe some others did."

An achingly long silence transpired, before Poleander said, "Now you sound full-on mental."

"Fine," she said, "Just so you remember, I won't disappear so easy, because I have real friends out there ... *Unlike you,* I have friends!"

She pivoted on her platform heel and stomped back through the doorway, slamming it behind her.

The three Honors soldiers in the room looked away in three different directions. Poleander took up his phone and punched out a couple of texts. Then he made a call to somebody, and mumbled to them for a minute or so.

He tossed the phone aside and barked at the soldiers, "Okay let's go! Get 'em in here!"

The next interviewee entered the room, out of how many more to come she couldn't guess. This one was a towering black man with a gleaming shaved head, wearing a dark green military dress uniform with epaulets. He spoke in a harsh, booming voice to a retinue of four shorter men in what sounded to be an African language. The words were so strange to her that Prindibin thought at first it must be Ascendant language, but the pacing of his speech flowed naturally, unlike the stilted delivery she always noticed in speakers of the MOR idiom.

He took his seat across from Emzharotav and was offered a cigar, to which he nodded. Poleander clipped the end and held up a lighter for him.

To a translator, Poleander said, "How did the Field Marshall enjoy Las Vegas?"

The big man nodded as his translator said, "Very much. Very different from our country."

Poleander said, "It is my great pleasure to say that the agreement as drawn up last month has passed examination by our Council of the Nine ..."

A rapid-fire translation into the foreign language spilled into the dehumidified air of the office. The Field Marshall, or whoever he was, puffed his stogie and nodded.

"... And it is ready for the handshake!" said Poleander, "We will have that observed, right after a little concert from our Singing Bells and a fine steak dinner! The first course of the banquet will be 5 pm sharp. Oh, I am also selecting the women for Channels of Passage this evening. You will want to see that."

The Guest of Honor had a question, spoken with military emphasis on every syllable, of whichever language this was. The translation came as, "Field Marshall says before we leave for New Orleans tomorrow ... we see weapons demonstrated."

"Absolutely! I thought that was understood. Yes, the rifle range is just here at water's edge. We will have demonstrations of the lighter pieces before dinner. For the heavier items we have a video presentation, but you can examine some actual ordinance in our hangar."

Once that was translated, the Field Marshall wanted to know something else, which translated out as, "You understand securing coast as well as interior is guaranteed by us only as long as ammunition is steady supplied. Any break in supply, all is off, and we go our own way."

Emzharotav replied, "Sir, you gain a foothold on the coast, with the space for ship berthing as we described, and you will have all the bullets, shells and rockets your guys could ever shoot." Joy welling up in his voice, he added, "You can name the country whatever you want, and you will be president for life. We will have a permanent presence there. As long as the sun shall shine. And you will always be supplied. For always."

This translation was less rushed, more imbued with a sense of satisfaction. Prindibin watched the bald head nodding.

The imposing man took to his feet and bellowed out several words in his language as his retinue broke into applause. Poleander did likewise, and said, "Dinner at 5 sharp!"

Moments after the last of the Africans departed, to Prindibin's horror, Matthias Pleasant was marched in to the hot seat. She could see the back of his head, his hair longer now, but still with the little top knot. She was only certain it was him when he spoke.

"... Yeah! Just wanted to have a look around," he said, "Nice place!"

Prindibin had a sensation she feared was a heart attack. Something jolted inside her chest. Along with that came another feeling that, bizarrely, seemed not to be from her. It was like a sensation from someone else, inside of her. Like a statement without words, a mental message was delivered, and it was – "Help him."

There was no message as to how.

Emzharotav conferred with the soldiers who hauled him in, and then abruptly told him he was a criminal trespasser. But not just any ordinary one, "This place is supposed to be hard to find. I am genuinely impressed that you found it, and I really mean that!"

Matt had gray uniformed troopers standing at his left and right, and one directly behind him as he sat facing this man. On the wall, next to where the plate glass began, was mounted a colossal black taxidermied alligator, so big it didn't look real.

Poleander asked him his name, and Matt replied, "Jasper Lamar Crabb."

"Okay, bullshitter. Why are you here?"

Matt shrugged and said he was doing research for a book.

"A book about what?!"

"Mind-control cults," said Matt.

As if to show his men he could come up with a flip quip of his own, the MOR boss said all he had to do was make an appointment. He then demanded to know where he got that uniform.

"I made it! With a sewing machine! Wasn't difficult ... I guess you'll be wanting to charge me with 'Stolen Valor' now, huh?"

He asked Matt where he got the medals for the uniform.

"Halloween Super-Store," said Matt.

At this the man's face seemed like it might turn the same shade of red as his golf shirt. It was if his mind was rending to conceive of anyone being this impertinent to him. Matt jabbed his thumb at the trooper behind him, and asked, "Isn't that where he got his?"

"One last time. And this is the last time ... How did you find this place?"

Matt said he knew that one of the other gurus was coming to a big meeting, due to the carelessness of communications within that outfit, and he simply threw together some clothes and followed him out. Poleander said he had to have help. Inside help. Matt said he just followed the others out.

He told Matt he couldn't get here without help. He rattled off a list of strange nicknames, one of which was Santa Claus. Then, Emzharotav said, "Yeah. I'm thinking it was Santa."

He plopped some 8X10 glossies on the desk. "Is this you?" The shots showed him at some of the MOR events he had visited.

"No," said Matt.

"Our matron said you were asking for somebody in particular last night ..." Poleander said, and Prindibin's breath stopped in her throat.

"You lookin' for somebody in particular?" he growled.

"Nope."

"The matron said you were asking for a Zintopell."

Prindibin silently mouthed the word.

"Wasn't me," said Matt.

"You're denying this is you in these pictures?"

"I am."

Poleander said with an odd sadness that it doesn't matter much.

His voice took on a crazy tone of almost submissive politeness, which made Matt's skin crawl. There was something about it that he took as a very bad sign. The MOR leader began talking, nicely, about his youth, growing up not far from here, and how humble his origins were. He said this current property was built alongside a much older place where they used to smoke fish and game. This place is one of his favorite homes, he said. It was as if they were hobnobbing at a garden party.

He mentioned the alligator-wrestling tourist attraction his father had on the highway. The one on the wall had been one of theirs. "That's a thirteen-footer! Thousand pounds he was." He had been in the show as a teen, but life really began when he got into preaching, he said.

The paralysis holding Prindibin was such that she feared losing control of her breathing and making a gasp, which only compounded the electric terror.

"You're a trespasser," said the man in the bright red shirt, "You are trespassing on my home, and on a house of worship."

"House of worship?" Matt exclaimed.

"Anywhere I live is a house of worship." Poleander said, "You will be turned over to the local law. They'll go over things with you, and they aren't cordial like me. Then, well, you'll get prosecuted."

A soldier rapped Matt on the shoulder, summoning him to stand up. Poleander said he was sorry he couldn't invite him to the banquet, but, "You'll be in my thoughts as I have my dinner."

The troopers escorted Matt to the door. Prindibin saw their feet heading her way and softly rolled over on the carpet to avoid being seen. The soft sound attracted a soldier's attention, and Matt's. The Shebbovotan didn't notice, and stood up, saying, "I think I will go along and see you out." He plucked a walking stick from an umbrella stand.

When the door closed behind them, Prindibin left the unpolished platters and hurriedly straightened the area up. She wracked her mind for a plan – and found none. For now, she hastened to rejoin her group.

As Matt walked down the hall with these men toward a steel fire door, Poleander mumbled, "When I said I would be thinking of you while I have my dinner, I really meant it." He twisted the handle of the cane with a click, pulled an ice pick, and slammed it into Matt's belly.

The first stab was the worst, as he was caught flat-footed. He was struggling for the other two. A soldier punched the back of his head so hard he saw stars. Another one opened the door, to darkness, and humid breeze from the bayou. They shoved him into a black void, down three steps, onto damp sand.

The door slammed, and he lay there, taking stock. Blood trickled at his abdomen. Potentially it was a fatal wound, he knew, depending on its depth, and whether it pierced the intestine. But he should have some time before he became useless. He applied pressure, and lay still, waiting for his eyes to adjust to the dimness.

After a minute he looked around, and deduced he was inside the old stone "pillbox" that he saw before. Knobs of river stones protruded from the walls, just like on the exterior. A body of water stretching before him gave off a swampy smell. Like a lagoon, it filled most of the interior. It had an opening on the far side big enough for small boats. Fading sunlight entered there.

He looked back at the door they had shoved him through, with light coming in at the bottom. No shadows of feet. Turning again to the interior of this place, he tried to take stock. At the top and center of the structure, about forty feet up, a glow of sunlight was leaking in through some sort of a partially obstructed opening.

He plucked his little six-bulb LED light from Velcro under the back of his collar. The joke soldiers of MOR's lightweight army had given him an inadequate frisking. Once they determined he wasn't packing a pistol they didn't seem concerned about anything else.

The flashlight was tiny but brilliant, and dispersed enough gloom to reveal a wooden slat wall about eight feet high. It formed a circle about sixty feet in diameter around the pool. Above the slats, curved walls of stone and mortar rose another thirty feet. Iron pipes spanned the interior in places, some with chains and hooks and vertical support poles going down into the water.

He allowed himself a minute to study the place. Rotten wooden rowboats hung on the wall, adding to the sense that this place dated back many decades.

It was then a voice whispered, "... Matthias." He whirled his light around to discover a crumpled shape slumped against the wall, a few feet over from the door. Reverend Moultrie. Moving closer revealed a horribly swollen black-eye and a bloody lip. He reached out and gripped him by the shoulder. The poor guy would be at home on a sofa right now if not for him.

"They came for me in motor boats not long ago," Craig said, "I'm beat up bad, Matt."

Matt said he had a little dribble of blood, too, but thought he had some fight left in him.

Craig said he had a heart-breaking confession to make. During interrogation he had let slip that there were others with them back at the Fish Camp. They had tricked and beaten him, into giving up the existence of DeeDee and Blaine. Not by name, but he gave their location.

Matt told him, "Don't waste energy fretting over it. I have a plan to get us out of here. I got us in and I'm getting us out."

The opening at water-level, wide open, seemed too easy. Moultrie said he didn't know why, but he didn't want to go through there. Matt nodded, and said he had seen it from the outside and it was fenced off. "That's not what I had in mind," he said, "Check this out ..."

He took in a deep breath, assembled his thoughts, and prepared to explain a plan. At that moment, they saw the water surface bow up with the entry of the first submerged alligator.

It clambered heavily out onto the sand. Glistening in the limited light, it was not much smaller than the one on Poleander's wall. Taking multiple steps, it got itself turned to point its blunt, shovel-shaped snout in their direction. Others moved in from behind to join it.

"Up," said Matthias, and they were up and jumping to grip the splintering top of the dry-rotted slat wall.

They held tight and pulled themselves up, with Matt's abdomen in agony as if from a molten spear. He said, "Pull up ... Now, slip off shoes and socks. Stick 'em in your back pockets. Need to be barefoot to climb these stones."

They commenced an excruciating climb up protruding stones, broken mortar, and other irregular surfaces on the curved wall. Alligators lunged up at them, slamming immense weight onto the wooden wall. Jaws clapped shut before the giants crashed back into the pool. They were astoundingly aggressive, unnaturally so, Matt thought.

He didn't focus on it for long. As was his nature for much of his life, he retained the capacity to keep his mind entirely on task, without getting preoccupied with despondency, fear, or shame at having gotten them into this.

"Hang on," he said, "We're higher than they can jump. And we *do* have a way out."

He put his flashlight in his teeth and saw rusty metal flanges in places on the wall. They looked to be part of the frame on which the building had been constructed, ages ago. Iron pipes crossed the space at higher levels. On the ceiling, a conduit for electrical wiring ran along to the open spot at the center. It was partially open, anyway. Some sort of metal housing on four legs stood over it.

Matt and Moultrie painstakingly inched their way higher, at times nearly losing it only due to the sound of frenzied alligators thrusting up and impacting back on the water. These were not the sedentary gators of the zoo. Matt thought to himself, "These things are drugged or starved, or something."

The two men went much slower than they had to, only caution mattered now. They rested frequently, whenever they came to anything that provided a good grip. Metal flanges. Stones. Pipes. Brackets where pipes used to be. Matt continued inspecting the scene with his light.

Suddenly came a scraping sound, and a gasp from Craig. A stone had come off in his hand when he put weight on it. First it thumped off of the back of an alligator, then splashed in.

"Test the stones before you trust them," Craig said.

He was trying to sound chipper, but his voice revealed he was not holding up very well. Matt told him to conserve his strength. "We're not out to set a speed record with this." But not a minute later the stone wall failed them again. Matt was pressing his foot down on a stone, and it was as if it disappeared.

He dropped, scraping along the rocky wall. Three feet, four feet, five feet, to the top of the wooden wall. With a mix of instinct and luck, he jammed the front of his bare feet into the gap between the slats and the stonework behind it. Bones in his arches may have been fractured, or maybe it was rotten wood cracking. He blocked out the shock and made an instantaneous grab of stones to keep from toppling backward. A sound of rushing water hit him, and a resounding clap, as jaws slammed shut somewhere underneath him. Air puffed against his Achilles heel.

When the reptile hit the lagoon it displaced water like a car going off a pier.

He first did nothing but hold on, silently. At the brink of passing out, he held fast, maintaining and maintaining, keeping respiration steady. The whimpering, weeping sound of his comrade a little higher up reached him. Matt couldn't speak for a moment, then as soon as he felt that possibly he could, he kept up appearances and spoke in a strong, calm voice.

"I'm okay. Let's just keep it going slow. We only have to make it up to that top pipe."

For the first time he heard anger in the other man's voice, "Then what?! That can't hold our weight!"

Matt loudly disagreed, and said it would have held weight far beyond the two of them, "These pipes had stuff hanging on them at one time. They aren't gas pipes or water pipes. They were supporting something."

Dark iron piping stretched across lower places, too, but the high one was the objective. It looked to run about four feet from the ceiling. Vertical iron supports reached down to it.

"That's not flimsy. When we get to it, we should be able to hold onto the cable conduit on the ceiling and sidestep out to the open place. Dead center. If we can get that metal piece off we can climb out. And I have a plan for that." He started climbing again.

Moultrie said it was too far. He was hurt. He can't do it.

With the fearful distraction of thrashing water beneath them, Matt said, "No, in fact, you can't do anything else. There is no other way out." He had to keep this guy's head together. He couldn't let him falter, "... You're going to die somewhere else. Did you know that? I'm thinkin' at home. Many years from now. Surrounded by family and friends."

Only silence from Moultrie. He couldn't see the man's expression, which made it tough.

Over torturous minutes, with no other choice, the two of them closed in on the pipe that was their objective. The route they were climbing was almost directly above the steel door where he had first been thrown into this place. Suddenly, it swung open beneath them.

An intense flashlight beam shot out, and swept across water roiling with agitated alligators. Whoever it was, they checked the sandy bank on all sides, and everywhere else, except for the wall directly above them. After a minute they clicked off the light, and closed the door.

A distant sound of singing filtered in. Involuntarily, they paused in the climb, and listened.

The Bell, totaling forty mostly female singers, warbled out "You've Got a Friend," as the Shebbovotan sat with his fashionable consort at his side, her bangle bracelets bouncing as she applauded. His guests, alternately blank-faced or leering, gorged themselves from the endless supply of local seafood, roast turkey and barbeque pork overflowing on the banquet table. The singers on the back side of the Bells faced a brick wall, but were expected to sing just as loud and clear as ever, to fill the chamber with song. Prindibin wished she was back there with them.

Emzharotav had been staring directly at her for minutes. The table was close enough that from where she stood she could make out his well-combed hair and all the contours of his face, shining in sweat in the humid room. Of all the people visible to him, his eyes were trained on her. It was no mistake. While all the other singers had big stagey smiles plastered across their faces, she just couldn't. She was likely the only one up there without a smile.

He would have had to notice the way Prindibin was focused right back at him, and with no smile. Gradually, it looked as though he was putting two and two together. His face revealed a sudden insight as he watched her. She could only guess that he was figuring out that it was Prindibin that the trespasser had come to see. Poleander would have access to the information that Zintopell was someone who used to serve with her, but not anymore. Only one person in this compound had ever had any connection to somebody called Zintopell.

She could not be certain he would know. But she was certain.

His face took on an open-mouthed grin as he stared at her, a veritable jack-o-lantern. He had made a decision. She knew what it was. Her time had come. She was to become a Channel of Passage, a mother of the church's new generation.

Their hands covered in rust from old pipes, Pleasant and Moultrie took another moment's rest as they stood on the high one that had been their goal. Craig braced himself on stones in the wall, and Matt stood gripping the conduit on the ceiling. The periodic splashing below them continued torturously on.

Matt said, "Always hold tight, but not so tight that you constrict blood flow."

After a little rest, he said, "When you feel ready, take hold of the conduit, and start stepping sideways. Follow me out to the opening." It was doable, though now the pain in his belly bordered on incapacitating. It was a coin toss as to whether he was going to make it. Blood loss, or something, was giving him definite light-headedness.

The black water, forty or fifty feet below, churned and slashed. Vertigo and tinnitus went rampaging through his head, as bad as in

Afghanistan. His interior fortress was closed, for the first time ever. But he could not dedicate any energy to thinking about that.

The two men did a sideways slide-step out to the spot in question.

Sunlight of the end of an overcast day streamed in on their faces when they got there, and it did offer a small sense of accomplishment, given all they had surmounted. But now, they beheld four metal legs caked in red rust, supporting an empty metal box. Probably at one time it had held a lamp, or a ventilation fan. Now it stood only as the face of death.

If they could remove it, they would have a chance of at least getting out on the roof. The opening was close enough, and wide enough that they could wriggle through diagonally. One man grasped one steel leg and one the other. It would not budge. The thing was caked in rust, but unmovable.

"Okay, now, listen carefully," Matt said with a sigh, "I am wearing a money belt. I'm going to try to unzip it with one hand. Hang on." He picked at the inside of the belt and soon pulled out a ring, attached to a thin steel cable.

"This is a wire saw. Diamond carbide. Stick your finger through the ring and hold tight."

When he saw it was secure in his hand, he draped the other end around one metal leg. The other ring he put on his finger. With an orderly count, the two ripped away with the tungsten carbide wire. Being a new blade on old metal, it made good progress.

"Go slow. Don't want to break the wire. Don't look at it! You'll get rust in your eyes ... Don't look down either!"

In short order they severed the first leg and started in on the second.

When that one was sawn through, they each gripped a leg and started pushing up. It required gaining momentum, but then the other two legs buckled without sawing. With enough clearance achieved, Moultrie went first, up and out. Carefully, he avoided getting sliced on the jagged metal. He then helped Matt out. Once on the roof, they bent the fixture back so that it didn't show it had been moved.

They rested as they waited out the passing of the patrol. Singers provided them with background music. Eventually the two-man helmeted unit sauntered by below.

Climbing down the stony outer wall was easier than going up, as it seemed to slope outward a little. On reaching the ground they stepped to the nearby chain-link fence. Willow boughs and Spanish Moss swayed in the breeze.

Moultrie took the wire saw and went to work ripping an L-shaped egress in the fence, while Matt focused on staying conscious and applying pressure to his belly wound. He blocked out thoughts of internal bleeding. It seemed to take more than twenty minutes, but the patrol never showed up. They climbed through the fence, and pushed it back to conceal the breach.

From there, a harrowing ramble through boggy woods began, keeping the bayou to their left. Matt found a tree branch that worked as a crutch.

Moultrie said when they came for him they were in two motor boats; he was bundled into one of them. They had searched the aluminum fishing boat, and shoved it off into mangroves. It may have wedged in. If it's still there, he might be able to wade out and pull it in. A burner phone was taped under the boat in a waterproof bag, along with all kinds of other stuff. One problem was that it would be roughly two miles from here.

Pacing was everything. He was more worried about himself than Craig, who was only bruised at his face and ribs. He couldn't exhaust whatever energy he had left by going too fast, and they couldn't go so slow that they ran out of time. They found a pace that

Matt felt was ideal, and stuck to it. But their feet sank into soft, muddy ground at times, and would make a low sucking sound when they extracted them, which was not always easy. Now he had to determine how much time and brainpower to devote to the concern of quicksand. He saw no option but pushing on. He had not fully informed his friend of the extent of his injury, and had no plan to.

Navigating had been easier when he swam in. He kept the land to his left. Where there were breaks in the marshy land, he just looked ahead to where it picked up again. Now, walking, it was different. Breaks in the land meant wading, and exposing his wound to the bacterial soup of swamp water.

It took well over an hour to cover the two miles. But finally came the glint of the moonlight on the aluminum boat.

Craig Moultrie had to overcome a now nearly incapacitating terror of alligators to dogpaddle out to it. Matt told him the gators at the compound were concentrated in a fenced enclosure, and had been manipulated in some way for maximum viciousness. The open bayou would have a much lower density of them, and right here, the probability of none at all. He also helped Craig overcome his fear by spelling out their binary choice of getting the boat or remaining right here. He gave him his crutch to pull the boat in, and use as a weapon if needed.

Once they had it and climbed in, and cranked the motor, they put a lot more than two miles between them and the compound. Matt reclined on the bottom. He would not have been walking much farther.

Moultrie used the GPS from another phone taped under the boat to retrace their course out. Matt used the burner phone to call his sis. Once she heard that he was "fine," and just needed "a ride out of here," she told him they had had a terrifying encounter with some "oddball phony cops" which she would tell him about when she saw him.

Matt gave her directions to a bridge he remembered from the ride out. He even remembered the name of the road that crossed it. He and Moultrie would be waiting there.

"Get my flashlight and tie it to the center of the front bumper," he told her, "I want to see in advance that it's you."

Upon finding the bridge, no small matter in the dark, they climbed up a weedy, viny slope to reach it. Sitting off to the side of the road in the weeds with the ticks and the snakes, the wait began. Craig expressed his worry that the cult soldiers might have discovered their escape, and were out searching for them.

"No," Matt said, "When those guys swept their flashlights over that pool, they would have presumed us dead. I'm sure of it ... The way I feel now, they may have presumed right."

His energies were at the lowest ebb he could ever remember, except possibly for those Army hospitals where he woke up. He was full of pain-killers then, so this was different.

In a weakening voice, he said, "We weren't supposed to be strong enough or smart enough to get out of that place, Craig. We were supposed to lie there, all bloody and beaten, until we disappeared into their garbage disposal ..."

He got a bit of a smile from the reverend when he added, "But it didn't work out for them."

He paced himself, not knowing how long he could stave off unconsciousness. Momentarily he was able to further brighten the mood of his friend, when he added, "I found Audrey, by the way ... Had a nice chat. Brief. But nice. I told her I loved her."

He said he would give up all the details when it was easier to talk.

It took a hellish forty minutes, but Blaine and DeeDee found the lightless bridge. Matt saw the little glow of the flashlight between the headlights, and said, "Okay, that's them. Wave them down." When the sedan pulled over, the two were rescued. As they settled into the back, Matt told them to find a town big enough for a hospital.

Up front the young couple talked over one another as they drove, giving their horrifying tale of the "law enforcement personnel," as they called themselves, who knocked at their motel room some hours ago. They claimed they were delivering a message, that "Matthew" needed to see them. They were to accompany them, to see this Matthew.

Blaine told them he would follow them in his car, in case Matthew needed a lift back.

"We actually considered going with them for about a half a second," DeeDee said, "But it threw us how they got your name wrong. Also, their whole demeanor smelled. Blaine drove, and as soon as he started the engine we decided to make a break for the Interstate.

"When Blaine took off in the other direction ... they gave chase! They were in a plain black sedan with no markings, but they had rigged a blue strobe light on their dash."

"It was right out of a movie, man. I kid you not," Blaine declared, "But Deidra saved us. Tell 'em what you did, hon."

When DeeDee didn't speak up quickly enough for him, he went right on, "She pulled out the laser pointer she uses to play with her cat, and held it out the window with a socket wrench to look like a gun with a laser site!"

After a few seconds of it wavering in the driver's face, the pursuit vehicle veered hard left into darkness without slowing. They lost sight of it, and had no idea if it went onto a side street, ravine, trees, or the bayou. Never saw them again! Craig and Matt were mostly silent.

"Worked," DeeDee said.

Arriving at what looked like a town, they put in a call for paramedics rather than trying to find a hospital. The story they gave was that two of their party had been attacked by robbers where they were fishing, miles away.

If necessary, Matt told his friends, they can produce some cash from his money belt. He had $500 in it.

In half an hour Matt was in an ambulance, finally allowing himself to uncoil. But he harbored an irrational fear that these guys were going to take him right back to Poleander's place.

They hooked him up to an IV, and he floated into a mist of sedation.

O   O   O

After returning from a gentle, low-impact exercise period in a warm swimming pool, freshly showered Prindibin reclined into the cleanest, most comfortable bed she had experienced since the inception of her new life. MOR hymns droned softly from a speaker. She was nicely bundled in at the church's maternity center outside of Brunswick, GA.

Compared to what had come before, it had been otherworldly since her arrival. She was actually getting some sleep. The food was better. Workload nonexistent. She had attendants checking in on her. She called them her ladies-in-waiting, and they were so sweet and friendly.

And they were going to force a pregnancy on her through artificial insemination in 25 days.

She remembered when they first announced it to her. She thought it might as well be full-on rape. It was rape. Or it would be, if it really happened. It all seemed so unreal. Lately she wondered if they were putting drugs in her food; she felt – floaty. Her intellect still worked, and in periods of careful thought, she reasoned out that she was in a prison. Comfy, clean, and relaxing, it was a place where she was utterly controlled, and would be doing nothing that was not permitted by whoever was running this place.

The knowledge of that, coupled with all the pampering, only served to strengthen the original self that had been buried within her all these months, but whose internal voice was lately becoming more and more militant, and increasingly frightening to Prindibin.

With hatred she recalled the three dirty-looking, whiskery old men. They had deemed her physically and scripturally capable of bearing sacred fruit. She had been transported here to begin the 33-day regimen that would lead up to a ceremonial conception with the sperm of a high lama of the church, possibly her own Shebbovotan, she didn't know. Whoever he was, he was top level. It might even be Earnest Seamark himself.

Whenever she contemplated the child that would soon be growing inside of her, she spontaneously fantasized – about escaping.

No realistic way out of here presented itself. Not now, or any time soon. But *after the baby was born,* she would be sent to live somewhere without all the high-security. She could take her baby and slip away, find a job somehow, and live free of Church of the Mountain of Radiance forever. She could visualize it, like a movie.

Drifting in and out of sleep, as so often she was, she had no sense of time. No one would talk to her about the time or the date, and there were no outside windows.

A staffer who cleaned rooms had befriended her to an extent, after Prindibin started sharing food with her. One day, in one of their brief conversations, the woman casually informed Prindibin of something her ladies-in-waiting had not mentioned. After the birthing, her baby would be taken from her, to be raised in an MOR compound for elite children.

It was a disclosure that electrified her dreams of taking the baby and breaking away.

O   O   O

Matt awoke with a start to the sight of a sterile white hospital room. An IV drip bag was needled into his arm. The odor of rubbing alcohol pervaded, and nearby sat an unshaven, haggard-looking Blaine Wheeler, gazing out a window. Nobody else was around.

"Glad you came around before I had to take off, Matt," he said, "Do you remember much of our talk yesterday? You seemed mostly coherent. You told me some stuff to get for you. Remember? You do remember that you're in a hospital in Lake Charles, Louisiana. Right?"

He did not remember, but as Blaine talked and produced items out of a small vinyl pouch, it started coming back to him. It only became disturbing when he heard that he had been here for three days.

"So, this is the pre-paid phone, and I keyed in the numbers you wanted. Terrence Hyer, FBI agent in Dallas, Texas. Also we have FBI field office, New Orleans. The Weekly Speaker newspaper of Atlanta, Georgia, Editorial Office ... You never told me why you wanted that, or the FBI for that matter. Then I entered in all your contacts from back home, and at the bottom is the number for adding minutes. Here's a notebook and pens. Road atlas. The protein bars you like. And here's a fresh wallet with what's left of the five hundred bucks in your money belt that I didn't spend on this stuff. The nurses are holding your old wallet, with your ID and health insurance card."

"Thanks, Blaine. Where is everybody?"

"Gone home, bud. I put Dee on a plane this morning. She really wanted to be here, but she has classes she can't skip anymore. Moultrie flew out two days ago, right after they patched him up. They're going to call you."

"What's the verdict on my, you know ... intestinal fortitude?"

Blaine laughed, "Well, you have guts, Mattie. There are a few little holes down there now. But they told me that between the heavyweight fabric of the uniform, and the density of your abdominal muscles, it reduced the penetration of the sword." He always had such an intellectual sound. Even now, when he looked half asleep. "The placement of the deepest wound was fortuitous," he said, "The bowel wasn't pierced. You probably know that. You wouldn't be talking if it had been."

The doctor would be around to go over his antibiotic regimen, he said. All in all, he had been lucky. They were able to get ahead of infection. He was going to recover. And he had some pain pills that were going to redefine Cloud Nine.

"Pain meds will be kept to bare minimum," Matt said, "I have to hold onto whatever mental edge I have left. And the recovering needs to be in days, not weeks. Anyway, the phone is what I need right now. So, thanks again, Blaine. Tell everyone when I get home and get my head back to normal, I will be thanking them properly."

Blaine said, "Just do like the doctors tell you. All right? You've got internal stitches! Don't bust them!"

When Blaine left, Matt began assembling his memories of Poleander's compound on paper – a nice checklist. Then he got on the phone to an old pal from the military police, Terrence Hyer, now of the FBI.

After the shortest of greetings he came to the point. He reminded Hyer about their last conversation when he said that he might have something important coming up. It was far worse than he ever thought, he said, and began unloading on him.

"... Terry, what *aren't* they doing? They're murdering people out there! ... Homicide. Hell yes. And I can take you to a pond that will have human remains. Oh yeah. And they're running weapons by the ton. Internationally. They're holding people against their will ... False imprisonment? Yes sir ... They have drug labs going. They are into financial frauds that would crack your molars! I have a colleague that was out there with me a few days ago who can back me up on all this, and we have former members of this … organization. They are willing to talk to you, too."

He hadn't exactly seen any drug labs, and the gun running was based on conversations he overheard from certain Honors Heroes shortly before they found him hiding in the alcove. But all the rest of it was real, beyond doubt. Anyway, he had to get this guy's attention.

"What we need is a raid, Terry! And not next year! It's all sitting right there waiting on you, but *for how long* I can't promise. The GPS coordinates are in my pocket. I have been inside this place. I know the lay out. I can show you right where to go."

Agent Hyer said only that he would talk to his people about it. He seemed interested, from what Matt could glean from his voice. The Army connection helped. They were going to talk again tomorrow. Terry might fly over to Lake Charles himself, he said, which Matt found to be the most encouraging.

Next he was talking on the phone with a journalist he had found online in the early days of his search for Audrey. This lady was doing old school investigative journalism with a weekly paper that wanted to make a name in the field. His message for her was basically – stand by. Keep the presses warm. He was going to have something for her, soon.

She said she was willing to give him an interview, and whatever space the story deserved.

Twenty days later Matt was walking into the FBI field office in New Orleans, as it turned out, only to tag along on an operation that he now learned was imminent. He had set it in motion, with his series of phone calls and personal meetings with agents, first in his hospital room and later a hotel. He had the corroborating testimonies of several former Adherents, by way of Charles

Bienville. It had all been just enough for them to put the compound under surveillance.

In short order the Bureau had seen enough to determine they would raid the place. Pleasant was allowed in the vicinity only because he had been on the inside once. He could come along, but had to stay well back, out from under foot, "in the rear with the gear." His part would come afterwards, walking them through the property that he said he knew so well.

He was at the far periphery, with the last to deploy, when, in a thunderclap of helicopters and swamp boats, the FBI hit Poleander's bayou compound at dawn. It came off as a textbook operation, and was over almost as soon as they landed. No shots fired.

Some stuff that Matt had made up to get them interested turned out actually to be there. Drug labs were found in a single-wide trailer, which he had not known about. As he suspected, the lagoon under the stony "pillbox" produced human bones at first dredging.

Within forty-eight hours The Weekly Speaker newspaper was out with a front page that screamed, "House of Horrors on the Bayou. Part One of a Three-Part Speaker Series." Photos of Randolph Poleander, Matthias Pleasant, and Earnest Seamark surrounded a dark, creepy image of the compound as seen through Spanish Moss and Mangrove trees.

The article posed chewy questions, like why are there members of Congress running interference for this outrageous organization, and how come an outfit like this goes tax free? The content of the series was instantly mirrored nationally, and then internationally.

In most respects the raid was a stupendous success, but as far as Matt was concerned it could have been better.

Audrey wasn't there. Neither was Poleander. Still, it was one roundhouse kick to the teeth for the Church o' the Mountain. The public relations debacle for them was hideous enough to probably offset the entire 50th anniversary party. That aspect of it may have been worse for the cult than the celestial mountain of indictments coming down on them.

Matt even recovered the "box of rocks." He had provided the agents with a photograph of a Cherrywood gift box embossed, "Crane's Jewelers." They spotted it sitting on a shelf in a storage room full of loot.

For all the good that came out of it, the FBI raid may have been the last hurrah. He was low on money, and didn't want to go back to Della Crane for more. His compatriots could not keep helping him. The downfall of Poleander seemed to have eliminated his mole inside MOR. After the media storm dissipated, and the legal system began its interminable plodding, he saw that while he had struck a blow, Audrey may now be truly lost to him forever. For the first time, he had the sense that his best efforts had failed. In regards to recovering her, or even finding her again, no path forward presented itself.

He spoke to Bienville by phone, dropping unmistakable indications that he had finally seen the end of the road. Charlie said that he would keep antennae out for any further news of her. That much could be maintained indefinitely, he said.

Charlie then floated an off-the-wall idea. At some point, he said, he would have to retire. Someone needed to take up his work; someone with youth and energy.

"It would enable you to keep your hand in. You would have all of my resources," he said.

Matt found it to be the last thing he ever expected to be thinking about. He demurred. And then he declined.

O   O   O

A kind of pall seemed to fall across the maternity center around that time. After almost a month of special diets and exercise, just as she was gearing up in her mind for the upcoming reality of the impregnation, Prindibin suddenly no longer had access to her attendants. The ladies-in-waiting simply stopped showing up one morning. The other mother-to-be who shared her room was taken away. The woman, and her entire rolling bed were rolled away.

An oppressive silence filled the space; it turned out the women across the hall had been relocated as well. The MOR hymns had ceased their 24-hour play on the sound system, replaced with – nothing.

So few people ever walked by, and no one ever left the hallway to enter her room. There had been no dinner service the night before and breakfast had not materialized this morning. Her water jug was nearly empty! Pressing the button for a nurse produced nobody.

Nervousness turned into dread when her confidant, the cleaning lady, made a harried appearance and pretended to tidy the place up. She delivered the tip-off, "Your Shebbovotan was purged Wednesday night ... You are in big trouble."

She departed without another statement. It marked the end of Prindibin's sleeping.

The next morning at dawn, booted footfalls reverberated in the passageway. As they grew louder with their approach, she lay there in a sweat.

Three hulks in gray entered the room, glanced at her, and looked away quickly as if she were a taboo sight. They were packed in muscle, like Olympic weight-lifters. One of them barked out a single syllable, "Up!"

They wore gray uniforms of dense, canvas-like material. She was in a cotton nightgown, and nothing else. They pointed the direction for her to go, still seemingly afraid to look at her. The procession began down long hallways, with walls painted in different drab colors halfway up.

Arriving at a doorway, the soldiers pointed, and she stepped into darkness inside. When the door closed behind her it became completely lightless. She shivered, though it was quite warm.

A booming voice, possibly female, struck her from the front.

"Blood sucker!"

Someone was sitting in the dark, not far ahead of her. She gasped, and whimpered in thoroughgoing terror.

Another voice, all male, followed, "Your master is lost to you ... The hand of your puppeteer has been broken ..."

Prindibin immediately spoke, "I - I am so glad to hear it! You have rescued me from him!"

Conversation was not what they had in mind. A new voice roared out, "You are part of him! You begged to serve him!"

Warm lines of tears moved on her cheeks. They were going to kill her. She would not see sunlight again. No other possibility came to mind.

The voice of yet another person sounded. How many were sitting there? This one was calmer, less fevered, but no less threatening.

"Don't stand there and lie. We see your mind. You would destroy the Beneficence, and his entire church and mission."

She couldn't think of anything to say, and stood sobbing as quietly as she could.

After a short pause, the last voice to speak continued on, "You are dead to the church now. We give you two choices. Go on to the Off Mountain, or live out what's left of your days in labor on our ship."

When she did not immediately speak, he screamed, "Decide!"

Prindibin softly said, "I will work for you."

"Yes you will," he said.

Her jumbled mind tried to process all this as the door flew open behind her and the soldiers ordered her out with hand gestures.

Though emotionally cored to near-emptiness, she held her head up as she boarded a grimy white van, alone. With only the silent driver, she set out on a 200-mile ride down the coast.

An isolated pier somewhere in Northeast Florida saw her dumped onto a rusty transport boat, to be hauled out to the MOR vessel, Mountain of the Water. She learned it was undergoing final preparation for a voyage to ferry new recruits on missions to Mexico.

The boat carried her to the ship, where she was made to climb a rope ladder up its pitching, tossing side.

No sooner than she stood on the deck, before she was even shown to a berthing space, she was placed on laundry detail. In that first hour of folding steaming hot shirts, she had the pulverizing realization that she had become the veritable twin of the scary, shell-shocked woman she had observed during her voyage to Brazil.

No future existed now at all; she endured the ship day by day. She found herself at the crumbling edge of leaping overboard, more than once. Food they gave her was sometimes rancid. Once she fended off a sexual assault from a sniveling teenager, onto whose face she landed a full force slap. He screeched, "You can't raise your hand to a man!"

One morning while changing linens in the berthing quarters, she saw that numerous bunks were unused. These were intended to hold new Adherents, she knew. Boldly, she searched out the officer in charge of recruiting, and wheedled him to allow her to try her hand at it when they got into port. She was great at it, she said. He could take full credit for all the newbies she brought in, she just wanted to get off the ship and work crowds. She talked the jargon to the limit, and the officer shrugged and agreed to let her try.

She lived for escape now. Setting foot off the ship, she churned with the impulse to sprint. But they never let her get very far from the gangplank, and watched her every move. So, for now, she chatted up tourists on the pier, and actually landed a turn-over that first day.

Weeks passed in this vein. Then, when the ship returned to the States and was docked at Savannah, GA, she was able to bend the ear of a shore-based recruiting officer. She gave him an exaggerated version of her prowess as a recruiter, a big load of MOR slang, and essentially begged him to take her on his state-side recruiting team.

He looked her over, seemed to be thinking it over, and ultimately stated that he was interested, given the ineptitude of his current recruiters. But he was clear about one thing: she was a zero in the church now. Less than nobody. As such, she would have to work exactly when and where he sent her. She would have to out-produce everybody else, too, because it was just as easy for him to send her right back to a ship.

She entered 16-hour days of recruiting, looking always for that opportunity to bolt, even as the Prindibin side of her remained terrified of quantum damnation.

Internal division was destroying her, but increasingly, the side that wanted out was winning.

O   O   O

Matthias Pleasant was concluding a first date with a woman he had met on an online dating site. It hadn't gone well.

She told him to drop her off at a cab stand. He said goodnight and she said goodbye. It was the third flame-out in a row from the dating site. None of them had looked much like their photographs, but then they never stood a chance against the ghost that was competing against them in his mind. How many months since Audrey went away?

Being a freelance security consultant had sounded like a good move for a guy with his background. It might have been, had he been able to find some accounts who weren't phonies or psych cases. Now here he sat in his fancy custom van, seriously considering a return to the Army. They would take him back as soon as he walked in. The problem was, he wasn't twenty anymore, and his attitude was in worse shape than his body.

At his Farewell party at Fort Bragg, a buddy had given him the business card of a director of security at a small chain of casinos. They were always hiring, and might have something for him. He figured the guy on the card wasn't looking for a customer service rep, but more like a thug in a business suit. Making the call proved that Matthias Pleasant was right, yet again.

The casino director listened to him describe his military background, and said he had a major position for him. Associate Director of Security. For which casino? For the whole chain! He would travel around kicking butts of the security staffs at their small, highway casinos. "Trouble shooting." This guy's voice reminded him of an MOR boss.

He agreed to fly out the next morning for an interview in Tunica, Mississippi.

Sitting in the airport at sunrise, waiting for the call to board the flight, Matt's cell phone went off. He was going to let it go to voice mail, as it was not a number he recognized. But then he noticed the Fayetteville area code.

"Hello?"

"Coach Pleasant? It's De Juan Kendricks. From the Boys and Girls Club."

"De Juan? ... Well, yeah! Good to hear from ya, bud. Wow, how did you get my phone number?"

"It's on the 'Missing' posters you gave us to pass around, Coach Pleasant."

The kid had passed the flier to his relatives, and an uncle working at Atlanta Hartsfield Jackson Airport had spotted Audrey working at a Mountain of Radiance booth in a "First Amendment Zone" near the MARTA station.

"She was there yesterday, anyway," the teen-ager said, "He says it's the face on the poster ... One hundred percent."

Even though the words were carved forever into Matt's gray matter, he ripped a pen out of his jacket and wrote on a magazine – FIRST AMENDMENT ZONE BY MARTA STATION ATLANTA AIRPORT.

"I won't forget this, De Juan," he said.

Change of flight plans. The casino job was abandoned.

O   O   O

Books, pamphlets, calendars, photo magazines, and DVDs sprawled across a table top. All had mystical, unfathomable illustrations and slogans. All were upside down.

At least to Prindibin they were upside down, as she stood behind the table. She was at the rawest, most ragged brink of running away. Her mind teemed with little else but images of bolting from this table of religious booklets, and the surly young man who worked it with her.

Whenever a cop passed by on his rounds she perked up, thinking to approach him. But something like paranoia always stopped her. She could imagine the cop turning her over to her handlers, saying the police can't get involved in matters of the free practice of religion.

She could just walk away. Tell Junior she was going to the bathroom and keep going. But others from the church would show up around here, always when least expected. The two of them were not alone here. It happened just often enough that she would procrastinate about the walking away. And anyway, where would she walk to?

She hadn't a penny, or even an ID. The clothes on her back – that was it. Still, her breaking point was not so much at hand as it was at her throat. This was the time. She could throw herself on the floor, faking a heart attack or a seizure. She could start screaming, as if in a psychiatric crack-up.

Still she vacillated. Even now, after all she had endured, she felt at some level that breaking away would mean breaking the hearts of uncountable angels, arch-angels, ascended light entities, interdimensional space brothers ...

The Council of the Nine.

The Shebbevunseh.

The end of the shift was coming up. She would make the break tomorrow morning, for sure. But minutes later, as she stared down at the table, she heard a glib, cocky voice that instantly resonated with her. She looked up to see the profile of Matt Pleasant, putting on a performance for the MOR guy. It didn't appear to be real to her, and she looked away again.

Standing there with his arms folded, he grinned sweetly at the twerp, as if he had not noticed her at all. He said, "A hardback of Ummyashuntopudda! Just the thing for my comparative religion class."

He tucked it under his arm, and said that he really wanted to talk religion to the lady, "You see, we had been talking earlier." The spindly dude looked at her, looked back at him, and said, "Well, I am afraid she has already had her lunch break."

Matthias said, "You know, I'm thinking she might still be hungry! I was going to buy her a cup of coffee and a donut and talk some Scripture!" He took up another expensive-looking book and shot the guy a wink. He paid cash for the volumes. Only then did he make eye contact.

He extended his elbow to her, and smiled.

She paused.

She looked at the splashy sprawl of books and magazines on the table. Upside down. Momentarily, she raised a hand, and rested it on his arm, just like she used to. They strolled toward the food court.

A few steps away, Matt said, "That wasn't a total lie. We were talking earlier."

She started stammering, taking quick looks at him and looking away. Her breathing seemed off. They straggled along past the donut shop, and presently she blurted out, "Believe Only ..."

He thought to himself, don't speak in monotone. Keep it friendly, and vary the tone. He said, "You know, when I went back to Blue Bayou, with the FBI, we found something that belongs to you. The box of rocks, you called it." A change in pressure came over her hand on his arm.

He said, "I gave the agents a photo of a Crane's Jewelry box before they went in. Said it was stolen property. Belonging to you. They're holding it. All you have to do is put in a claim on it and they'll turn it over to ya."

He could just barely perceive a reaction to that. She had heard it. She batted her eyes, and registered it. But soon she was looking around, looking back behind her, to the First Amendment Booth. She spoke in a clear, firm voice, "Believe Only."

At some level she knew this could well be an intergalactic elemental, only appearing in the form of Matthias Pleasant. It could be a test that she was in the process of failing. She kept walking, focused straight ahead, not giving him a glance. She wouldn't be able to fool ascended beings, but if anyone from the church confronted her, she told herself she would claim that he had forced her to go at gunpoint. Even so, she doubted they would accept that excuse.

In a congestion of people rolling their suitcases, wheelchairs, baby strollers, and trash gurneys, they pressed on toward Ground Transportation.

She began again, "Believe ..."

"You can believe in me, Audrey," Matt said, "I'm on your side."

This time she held eye contact with him. He saw terror. He saw dissociation. She was breathing erratically.

A harsh, sharp voice broke out behind them, "... HEY!!!"

They looked back to see the MOR flunky from the table moving through the crowd. Matt stopped, turned to face him, and made a slow back-and-forth turning of the head. The kid stopped, whipped out a cell phone and desperately punched on it with his fingertip.

Matt gently took her hand and turned them both to face an upcoming glass door with sunlight streaming in. He leaned close, and said, "It's such a beautiful day outside. Hey, you know, your sisters have been asking about you. Both of them. They wanna chit chat with ya!"

Audrey was saying nothing. Her mind throbbed with imagery of monstrous heavy-jawed leviathans devouring the damned at the black morass below the eternal mountain.

Off Mountain.

She was beaded in sweat, breathing in short gasps. Stepping through the glass doors, a wave of fresh air washed over the two of them.

Matt called to a man about to board a taxi. Would he would mind if they took it? Medical emergency! The fellow was irritated until Matt pushed a twenty-dollar bill in his shirt pocket.

Audrey climbed into the cab of her own volition. She was quiet, sweaty, and looking around furtively. Her thoughts – a jumbled jam. Mournful, whimpering whining from her guardian angel played through her mind.

The voice of the driver asked more than once where they were headed. Matt was as silent as she was, and fully heartbroken by how strung-out she seemed. Tears welled in his eyes. When they looked to one another for more than a few seconds, the tears rolled.

Several minutes later, well outside of the airport, the cab pulled over on rough pavement and the driver turned around to face them. His face was outrageous, with wild eyes behind thick horn-rim glasses, and a bulbous, broken nose. His hair was frizzed out, like a character from an old underground comic book. Grinning splendidly, he politely asked them a monumental question.

"... Folks ... Where are ya goin'?"

O   O   O

As it worked out, the real question was not so much where, as when? How long was it going to take to uproot an invasive pest vegetation, the vines of which ran throughout her mind? How long was healing to take in this case? She would never recover completely, or be without scars. How long until this individual came back, to the fullest extent she was going to?

On a gray, rainless day at the passing of ten months, a pair of vehicles pulled over where a sidewalk ran up to sheltered picnic tables in Mazarick Park. Matthias and Audrey emerged from the backseat of a gleaming rented Lincoln, driven by Blaine with Deidra at his side.

Her sisters, Della and Yvonne, disembarked from a van with a wheelchair lift, which lowered Ms. Alyson Crane in her wheelchair to the sidewalk.

Up the slope, the Reverend Craig Moultrie leaned against one of the poles that held a roof over the tables. His foot was propped up against it, his arms crossed before him. His wife leaned against him, and their rambunctious kids were all over the place.

On the walkway, Charles Bienville, in a dapper blue business suit, sat in a wheelchair. Jin Kyong held it from behind, dressed in a springtime outfit. Her face was illuminated with a smile that was broad, and radiant. All but angelic.

One of Charlie's trouser cuffs was pinned up where a foot used to be.

The sugar.

Audrey and Matt walked up to him with a purposeful gait. She was wearing her two-galaxy necklace, and smiling brilliantly, which Matt could see reflected in the elderly man's expression.

She reached out for the handshake.

"I'm Audrey Crane."

THE END

Recommended Authors – and Action.

If you found *The Contraption* a compelling read, I hope you will explore further into what I call an orphan human rights issue. Abusive cults. It is a paradox of a subject: we find it fascinating, yet we don't want to think about it. Some see it as a problem that came and went in the 1970s. Unfortunately, nobody told the cults. They are bigger and more destructive than ever.

Keep up with the latest developments by taking out a membership with ICSA, the International Cultic Studies Association. www.icsahome.com. If you or a loved one are dealing with cult exploitation, ICSA maintains a list of therapists on the website that have experience with it. But even your local mental health clinic is better than struggling along in isolation.

Another organization worthy of your support is Dr. Steven Hassan's Freedom of Mind Resource Center. www.freedomofmind.com. The podcast and Youtube channel are outstanding.

Those are two of the bigger organizations, but people worldwide are working on this. My novel is a cautionary tale on the realities of what can happen out there. I don't call myself an expert, though I have long studied the depredations of cults and the memoirs of survivors.

Tell your friends about *The Contraption*, and please consider leaving a review online.

A portion of the proceeds from the first edition will be donated to ICSA. Keep up with my other literary journeys at https://BartonAllenStewart.storiad.com.

For non-fiction on the subject, consider these titles –

Any of the works of **Dr. Steven Hassan**: Combating Cult Mind Control, Freedom of Mind, Releasing the Bonds, The Cult of Trump

> **Robert J. Lifton**: Thought Reform and the Psychology of Totalism
>
> **Alexandra Stein**: Terror, Love and Brainwashing
>
> **Janja Lalich, PhD**: Bounded Choice: True Believers and Charismatic Cults
>
> **Frank Shaeffer**: Crazy For God: How I Grew Up as One of the Elect, Helped Found the Religious Right, and Lived to Take All (or Almost All) of It Back
>
> **Debby Schriver**: Whispering in the Daylight
>
> **Esther Ruth Friedman**: The Gentle Souls Revolution
>
> **Rev. Neil Damgaard**: Wounded Faith

And check out **Joe Szimhart** on Youtube - @josephszimhart9431, and at www.jszimhart.com

> Thank you for your time!
> *Barton A Stewart*

Made in the USA
Middletown, DE
06 July 2024

56909032R00157